TIME AND CHANCE

TIME AND CHANCE

JEFF MARIOTTE
and
SCOTT CIENCIN

ILLUSTRATIONS BY JEFF MOY

WILDSTORM PRODUCTIONS

BP BOOKS

ACE BOOKS

If you purchased this book without a cover, you should be aware that this book is stolen property. It was reported as "unsold and destroyed" to the publisher, and neither the author nor the publisher has received any payment for this "stripped book."

GEN[13]: TIME AND CHANCE

An Ace Book
A BP Books, Inc. Book

Special thanks to Ginjer Buchanan, John Morgan, and Aaron Watanabe

PRINTING HISTORY
Ace paperback edition / June 2001

Copyright © 2000
WildStorm Productions, an imprint of DC Comics.
All rights reserved. GEN[13] and
all related characters are trademarks of DC Comics.
Edited by Dwight Jon Zimmerman
Cover design by Dean Motter
Interior design by MM Design 2000, Inc.
This book, or parts thereof, may not be reproduced in
any form without permission.
For information, address: BP Books, Inc.
24 West 25th Street, New York, New York 10010

The Penguin Putnam Inc. World Wide Web site address is
www.penguinputnam.com

Check out the Ace Science Fiction & Fantasy newsletter,
and much more, at Club PPI!

Check out the BP Books Web site at
www.ibooksinc.com

ISBN 0-441-00856-9

PRINTED IN THE UNITED STATES OF AMERICA

10 9 8 7 6 5 4 3 2 1

This book is for some heroes of mine—the people who keep me safe and warm so I can write this stuff: Maryelizabeth, Nancy, Holly, David and Belle.
—Jeff Mariotte

To my beloved wife Denise, whose spirit burns brighter every day, and whose love never fails to inspire me.
—Scott Ciencin

PROLOGUE

The building seemed to have been carved from the side of the mountain itself, or to have grown organically from the granite and ice surrounding it.

But the term "building," Frank Parkhurst thought, barely described Schloss Reitberger. "Fortress" was more accurate.

Frank scoped it out through powerful binoculars from the patio of the Hotel Rheingarten, two miles away. The day was crisp and clear as only Alpine days can be, and two miles, in this air, was like nothing. The sun beat down on his parka and felt warm on his cheeks and forehead, but he knew the temperature hovered somewhere around freezing.

This exercise was for his own amusement, primarily—he'd seen the satellite photos and the building plans and the schematics showing electrical, plumbing, and ventilation systems. The stone walls, he knew, were three feet thick. Fifteen feet tall. Topped with coils of barbed wire, interwoven with strands of electrified wire, and inlaid with ground glass. Guard towers at the corners of the rectangular compound were staffed 24/7, and the guards were equipped with machine guns, grenade launchers, and searchlights.

Inside the walls, another thirty soldiers lived. When they weren't on guard duty, they were drilling, honing armed and unarmed combat skills, catching up on the latest high-tech weaponry, or resting for their shifts in the towers.

The ground below the walls was peppered with hidden land mines. The road—the only real approach to the compound, since it backed up to the mountain—was watched at all times, by guards and cameras.

Herr Reitberger was a very cautious man. It would take an army to break into this place.

Frank had a squad of ten.

He smiled, capped the binoculars.

Cake walk.

He went inside.

They made their move at sunrise.

The compound's west side faced into the mountain. As soon as the sun broke over the mountains to the east, across the valley, its rays would shine into the eyes of guards in the tower. They wouldn't be blinded, Wager had assured Frank. But they'd be inconvenienced. They'd be unlikely, at that moment, to be looking toward the east, or anywhere outside of the shelter of their own towers.

It wasn't much of an edge, but you took every edge you could get, was how Frank looked at it.

The moment the sun's first golden-red rays struck the walls of the Schloss, a truck swung into view around the last bend before the straight stretch of road that led to the compound's gate. It was a furniture delivery van, hired by Frank a week before to make an attempt to deliver three couches to Klaus Reitberger at exactly this time.

The delivery attempt would, of course, be unsuccessful. The driver and his assistant would grumble and curse, but Reitberger's men would check their boss's receiving list and, not finding any record of furniture delivery, would send them on their way.

If they lived that long.

Frank wanted the truck there as a distraction, another edge. He didn't care if the driver actually got to explain

3

to the gate guards what they were bringing up. He planned to be in action by then.

He wouldn't be coming from the east, up the road.

He would be coming from the sky.

The truck's appearance was the agreed-upon cue. On the snowy slope above Schloss Reitberger, seven men and three women saw it and flicked the switches that ignited the powerful engines in their flight packs.

"Under way," Frank said softly, as if to himself.

"I see," Wager's voice said in his ear. Wager sounded confident and assured, as usual.

Each soldier's helmet contained a microscopic camera. The signals were beamed via satellite to Wager's headquarters in New York City. Wager would, Frank was sure, be sitting in an expensive chair before a bank of monitors, a tall glass of cranberry juice over ice close at hand. He would watch the entire operation, making whatever comments he deemed necessary.

That was fine with Frank. The man paid the bills. And he was as smart as they came.

Ten flight packs, set on whisper mode, punched the snow and kicked up a dense cloud. Within seconds, from inside the cloud, the airborne squad floated into the air.

Each soldier knew the route. It wasn't complicated: passing over the outcropping they started on would put them directly above Schloss Reitberger, about two hundred yards below them. They'd need to drop fast—even on whisper mode, the flight packs weren't utterly silent. But they were as quiet as International Operations technicians could make them.

Wager had assured Frank that at this time of the morning, with the sun rising and the truck hauling up the carefully watched road, the chances of anyone looking straight up into the sky were point zero seven percent. Not impossible, but slim.

Good odds, anyway. And Wager had gotten where he was by playing the odds. Playing, and winning.

As many times as he'd used the flight packs, in practice, Frank had never quite become accustomed to the sensation. He was flying. Head up, feet down, as if standing, but the ground was a couple of dozen feet below. He was in the air, untethered to the ground, with only a slight thrumming sensation and a smell like burning diesel and a shushing sound like tires on wet pavement to remind him of what was holding him up.

"Precipice," Frank said. They approached the edge. As soon as they passed over, the compound would be in sight, and then the real danger would begin.

Twenty feet ahead, the world seemed to end.

The snowfield came to an abrupt halt, and there was a sheer drop-off, the cliff into which Schloss Reitberger was built. Frank had gone over this hundreds of times in his head, on paper, and in drills. But as the real edge loomed, he felt a moment's hesitation. Being twenty feet off the ground was one thing. In less than a second, he'd be hundreds of feet up.

Enemies with guns below.

"Don't worry, the packs will work fine," Wager's voice said.

Frank was sure he hadn't said anything, but in this situation, it was entirely probable that anyone would be a little nervous. Wager would, of course, know that.

Then he was past the snow. A moment of vertigo as the cliff's face fell away beneath his feet, and then he was looking at the others, all in line with him, all feeling the same thing. He looked down.

The Schloss looked just like the satellite photos had shown.

He pointed down. The others nodded and adjusted their directional controls, their speed controls.

They dropped like stones.

Ten seconds into the descent, Frank aimed his automatic rifle down toward the Schloss. The others followed suit.

Fifteen seconds in, they were spotted.

Seventeen seconds in, they were even with the guard towers.

But they had the edge. They knew they were dropping down from nowhere. They knew there would be hostile guards to meet them.

The guards, however, were taken completely by surprise.

Frank's squad opened fire, and the tower guards were dead before an alarm could even be raised.

The gate guards were slow in turning away from the unknown delivery truck. Frank targeted them, squeezed the trigger. His gun spat tracer rounds even as his knees buckled.

"I'm down," he said.

"One of them's still alive!" Wager's voice said urgently.

Frank and two of the others fired as one. The guard who had been struggling to turn over jerked twice and fell into a corner.

Wager could see the action from more angles than any one soldier on site. And he would have known there was a certain probability of at least one guard being wounded but not immediately killed. He would know what that probability was, and he would know the best course of action to take to circumvent it.

Sometimes, Frank thought, *it's almost boring to work for the guy who's always right.*

"Watch the barracks!" Wager's voice said.

Frank and the others turned to the barracks. As the doors flew open, their guns were already firing. The guards trying to spill outside were stopped in their tracks by the hail of bullets.

"He's in the main house," Wager's voice said. "Go."

This was, so far, all according to plan. Frank motioned to three of his squad, two men and a woman. The others remained in defensive positions, weapons trained on the barracks in case the soldiers inside made another dash.

Frank and his three went to the main house, a palatial

residence with turrets and oversized doorways and balconies on which the owner could take the air on warm summer days. This was October, though; summer had been over here for a couple of months. The balconies were iced over, and snow caked the sloped roofs of the turrets.

The front door was locked. Behind it, there would be more armed guards.

Frank unlocked it with a healthy amount of C-4.

He and the other three took positions at angles from the doorway. As soon as the charge blew the door to slivers, they fired through the doorway at every angle.

When they ran up the steps and into the house, the marble entryway was smoky and there was no one left inside who was still breathing.

"We're in," Frank said.

"He's got a safe room somewhere," Wager said. "They moved him there as soon as the first shots were fired, along with some guards."

Frank knew Wager was right. That's what he'd have done, if he were running security for a guy like Reitberger. You had a hardened room, with reinforced walls and door, somewhere in the interior. You had people inside it and out, and they defended it no matter what, because their job was to make sure that no harm came to the one who paid their salaries.

"Up or down?" Frank asked.

"We think he sleeps upstairs, and they'd probably want it close to that because any attack would be more likely to come at night," Wager replied. "But down would be closer to an escape route—I expect, a tunnel dug into the mountain, probably coming out near the road somewhere away from the Schloss. They'll have cars there."

"Which is it?"

There was one thing they hadn't been able to determine from the photos and blueprints—which room had been hardened.

Moments ticked away.

"Boss . . ."

"Down," Wager said at last. "Eighty-seven percent probability. If you're going to move from up to down, you're going to want to do it before the house is breached, not after. There's no escape from upstairs. Got to be down."

"Down!" Frank shouted, even though everyone had an earpiece. Everyone could hear Wager's words.

They moved through the smoke and found the staircase that led downstairs. Frank stopped at the top of the stairs, tossed three flash-bang grenades down, one after the other.

They boomed, echoed in the stairwell. Anyone down there would be blinded and deafened.

As he started down the stairs, he heard gunfire from outside.

"The guards in the barracks taking another stab at it," Wager said. "Your people will be fine."

Frank led the way, crouched over, his weapon held at knee level. The bottom of the staircase was empty, but there was a door at the end of a short hallway. It looked like steel. Inside the door were two slots, big enough for gun barrels.

"There they are," he said.

"Blow it," Wager ordered.

Frank gestured to Zell, who carried a grenade launcher instead of an automatic weapon. He hadn't had a chance to fire since they landed.

"Take it out," Frank said.

Zell nodded once. The others pressed themselves into the staircase, eyes clenched tight, hands over their ears. Zell swung his weapon into the hallway and squeezed the trigger.

Guns barked from behind the door, bullets spanging down the hallway.

Zell whipped his launcher and arms back around the corner, curling himself into a ball on the floor.

The explosion shook the building. Smoke billowed from the hallway. In spite of ear plugs, Frank's ears rang.

The gunfire from the door had stopped, though. When

he looked around the corner, the door was down. A couple of people moved around through the smoke, beyond the doorway. Frank fired on them, tracers whooshing through the smoke. He heard screams.

When there was no more movement from beyond the doorway, Frank led his team in.

Klaus Reitberger and two guards were still alive inside. Reitberger sat in a big padded chair, legs curled up under himself, his hands under his knees. The guards stood on either side of him.

Reitberger was terrified. He was not a soldier. He was a rich man who dabbled in dangerous trades—an arms dealer, an extortionist, a smuggler, a thief. But he was soft, pudgy, with long silver hair and small-lensed glasses and a round stomach that quivered under silk pajamas.

His guards held automatic weapons, but they didn't look as if they were inclined to use them. Frank made a downward motion with one hand, and they both put their weapons on the ground.

Reitberger looked at them, head swiveling from one to the other. The expression on his face was pure terror. His jaw was slack, mouth hanging open. A trace of spittle glistened at one corner.

His voice caught when he tried to speak.

"Wh—what do you want?" he demanded.

"He's speaking English," Wager said. "That means he knows you're there for me."

"You know what we want," Frank said. "Wager sends his regards."

"I—" Reitberger started. "I can't. Tell Herr Wager that I don't have it anymore. I offered to sell it to him first, but when he turned down my offer, I found another buyer."

"You tell him," Frank suggested.

The man didn't realize he already had.

"No, I—I don't want to talk to him again. He frightens me."

"You look pretty scared right now, pal," Frank said. "And Wager isn't even in the room."

"He's lying," Wager's voice said. "If he'd sold, I'd have heard about it. Sixty-eight percent chance the stuff is right there in the room."

"You're lying," Frank said. He made a show of inspecting the room's furniture—several chairs, a table, a television, some cabinetry, a small refrigerator. You could spend a few hours in here without much trouble. Another doorway opened into a bathroom. "And I don't have all day. You can hand it over, or I can kill you and look for it. I'm sure I won't have to look far."

"I offered it to Herr Wager at a fair price. He wouldn't pay it. What right has he ..."

"The price was ridiculous," Wager said. "An insult."

"The price was ridiculous," Frank repeated. You don't insult Wager. He's no fool."

"I never said he was," Reitberger protested. Behind his thick lenses, tears welled in his eyes.

"You treated him as if he were," Frank said.

"Reitberger isn't brave," Wager said in Frank's ear. "Threaten him—ninety percent chance he'll turn it over."

Frank advanced on Reitberger. The man quivered as he approached, but didn't move away. Bolder than Wager believed? Frank gripped a handful of Reitberger's silver hair and yanked his head back, so he was looking up into Frank's narrow eyes. The man's breath smelled of garlic. Frank shoved the muzzle of his gun against Reitberger's jaw, hard enough to break the skin. Reitberger let out a whimper.

"Now you give him the serum for free," Frank said, "and you live another day. Or you make it hard for me and you die right now. Your call, Herr Reitberger. What's it going to be?"

"Okay, fine," Reitberger said. "He can have it." Frank released him and he crossed to the refrigerator, tugged open the door. Frank tracked his every step with the automatic.

Inside the refrigerator there was milk, beer, cold cuts, bread, cheese, fruit. There was also a stainless steel rack, and inside the rack were four glass vials containing an odd, greenish liquid. It looked like dishwashing soap to Frank. But instead of having the sparkling shine of soap, it was dull, cloudy.

Reitberger handed the rack to Frank. Frank held it up before him. Seemed like an awful lot of trouble and expense, not to mention death, for this stuff.

"That's it, huh?" he asked.

"Yes," Reitberger assured him. "That's all there is. Be very careful with it."

But Frank hadn't been addressing Reitberger. "That's it," Wager echoed. "Well done. Tell him thank you, for me."

"Very well," Frank said. "Pleasure doing business, and all that. We'll just be on our way now."

"Finish it," Wager said.

Frank nodded, and at the prearranged signal, the other three soldiers opened fire. The two guards and Herr Klaus Reitberger performed a grisly dance as the bullets ripped into them.

An ocean away, in New York City, Wager smiled. He could barely restrain from rubbing his hands together in glee.

"That's the stuff you've been after?" Suzanne Sawyer asked.

"That's it exactly," Wager said. He studied Suzanne—tall and muscular, with her close-cropped platinum hair, powerful body, and a fighter's stance. He tried to keep her close by at all times, to watch his back, to protect him against any threat that might arise. In his entire organization, she was the person he trusted most, and the one with whom he was happiest to share this moment of triumph. He knew she'd understand. She had been at his side through the months of struggle to reach this point, and she would be there through the time of triumph that followed.

Unless, of course, she ever betrayed him in any way, at which point he'd have to kill her.

"So what's next?" she asked. "You take the stuff?"

"I will," Wager said. He lifted his glass of cranberry juice, swirled it, making the ice cubes clink in the glass and releasing the fruity aroma. "But not right away. I need to know more about it, and I need to understand exactly how it will react with my particular body chemistry. I need to run a few tests." He took a drink, and used a remote to turn off the bank of television monitors, which were currently displaying his squad's violent departure from *Schloss Reitberger*.

"I need," he said, "a test subject. And I know just where to look for one..."

CHAPTER 1

A frigid wind blew in off the Hudson, whistling through Manhattan's concrete canyons and making people pull their coats tighter, shove hands into their pockets or over their ears, and complain bitterly through clenched teeth that yes, the weather had finally changed, and it looked like the winter would be a hard one after all.

At the Lower East Side's Mary McCardle Shelter, each new gust puffed open the double steel and glass doors, causing the string of bells that hung from one of the pull bars to tinkle. Each time, Sarah Rainmaker looked up to see if someone new was coming in. And each time there was a newcomer, he or she was met by a blast of hot air. The shelter's furnace was on the fritz—it was either on or off, but the thermostat had broken and there was no controlling the temperature. It was too cold outside to leave it off, so the most arctic night of the year outside had become a steam bath inside.

It would be fixed when there was money to fix it. No telling when that might be.

The shelter, Sarah knew, had been named for Mary McCardle, a woman whose attempt to persuade the city's government to finance shelters for the poor and needy had been a dismal failure. Rather than giving up, though, Mary—a widowed mother who had fought her own way up from poverty through hard work and frugal living—had put on her one decent dress and gone knocking on the doors of business leaders and corporate fat cats, without appointments or introductions, admonishing each in turn to give to those who had nothing.

Within a month, she'd built the shelter.

This had been in 1930, the height of the Great Depression. The center had been in continuous use since then, even though Mrs. McCardle had died in 1949. It wasn't until after her death that her name had been added to the operation.

Sarah considered Mary McCardle a hero. She was proud to help carry on the tradition, in whatever limited way her schedule allowed. She worked three nights a week, on a volunteer basis—there were only two paid staffers. Most nights, like this one, she dished up warm food for the homeless who wandered in off the streets, or who came regularly for their one daily square. To others, she served as a counselor, mostly for the young teens or the women trying to escape from abusive relationships.

Tonight, the evening's chill seemed to be sending people inside in droves. The available beds were long since taken. They'd serve as many hot meals as they could, but some people would be sent back into the streets after they'd eaten, to look for some other place to escape the night.

Sarah Rainmaker wished she could do more.

She was a superhero, but sometimes she felt completely powerless.

This was one of those times.

Bobby Lane had taken to coming down to the shelter with Sarah once in a while. Helping people was cool—that's kind of what Gen[13] had turned out to be about, once it stopped just being about running from the government's agents and having fun goofing on their new-found super powers. Plus, it was a chance to spend quality time with Sarah. Okay, not exactly the kind of quality time that involved lots of close physical contact, or anything. But Bobby knew that if he was going to get there with Sarah, the emotional and spiritual contact had to be in place first.

And doing this stuff, feeding chow to old folks and the homeless and all, was way spiritual as far as she was concerned.

And they got to ride down on the subway together from their hotel suite uptown.

Plenty of face time.

The joint was really busy tonight. Bobby had been hoping for a slow evening, maybe leaving early, talking Sarah into a movie on the way home. But instead, the door kept opening and people kept filing in, looking for food. Bobby was on kitchen duty, and it was apparent that the demand for dinner was going to outstrip the supply very soon.

Unless he could help somehow.

Bobby was cooking with another volunteer, José Arango. They had a kettle of soup going, but it had just been emptied and a fresh pot started. There were chicken legs over a grill, but again, a fresh supply had just come out of the freezer to replenish a batch that had run out. Vegetables boiled in a big cast iron pot, and rolls baked in one of the ovens.

None of it was going to be ready in time. There were people out in the main hall waiting for their food already. By the time this food was cooked, there would be a new batch of folks, and the kitchen would get even more backed up. You could only cook as fast as you could cook, but on the other hand, there were a lot of mouths to feed, and Sarah had told Bobby that people would be looking for beds tonight. The sooner they got fed and got out, the better their chances would be.

"José," Bobby said. "Go out front and see how the chicken's doing."

"Man, they're already out," José said. "Sarah told you that."

"I thought she said they were low," Bobby argued. "Just check, okay?"

"I ain't got time to check that," José replied. "I'm tryin' to get this stuff cooked up."

TIME AND CHANCE

"I'll watch it," Bobby offered. "Just do it."

José grumbled, wiped his hands on his apron, and pushed through the swinging, windowed door to the vault-ceilinged dining hall, where Sarah and other volunteers stood behind long folding tables, dishing out food from the candle-lit hot plates.

As soon as he was gone, Bobby went to work.

His Gen[13] code name was Burnout, and his power was absolute command over heat. He could fly by creating a super-heated field around himself, causing the molecules within the field to become lighter than air. He could generate terribly destructive plasma bursts. But he could also more finely control the power, though.

Which is what he did now.

He placed his hands on the sides of the big iron soup kettle, and willed them to warm just enough to quickly cook the soup. That done, he held them over the chicken legs and created a small flame that rapidly roasted them to perfection. Then he opened the oven, and held his hands inside it, baking the rolls just right. A short blast from a fingertip got the vegetables boiling rapidly.

The swinging doors flew open and José returned. "Like I said, man. They're out up there."

"Figures," Bobby said with a shrug. He stroked his blond goatee, as if trying to figure out some great mystery. "Well, dish up some of this and I'll get some more going."

"It's done already?" José asked, a note of incredulity in his voice.

"Yeah."

José rubbed his eyes. "I guess I need to get more sleep or something," he said. "I'm gettin' all confused around here."

"Working too hard," Bobby agreed, ladling soup into chipped white china bowls. "Happens."

Sarah served up the soup and the chicken legs and the boiled vegetables as quickly as it was brought out from the kitchen. On each plate she set a roll and a pat of butter on a small paper square. It was a reasonable meal, more healthy than most what these people would eat during the day, she knew.

But each one who came up to her with his or her tray made some kind of comment about the temperature inside the building. It was hot, she knew. She had taken off her coat and sweater and was working in a tee-shirt and jeans, and she was sweating, especially the back of her neck underneath its blanket of straight, ink-black hair. Those coming in from the outside, sometimes bundled in all the clothes they owned, couldn't as easily peel away layers. It had to be ninety in the shelter now, and still climbing.

Sarah wished, not for the first time, that she was back home on the reservation in Arizona. People were poor there too. But it was a different kind of poverty, it seemed to her. Sure, there were problems. The schools weren't great. Many of the men had given up hope. Alcoholism existed there, just as it did here in New York City.

But most of the poor people back home were working poor. They had extended families whose homes they lived in. They might not have had jobs the way that city dwellers thought of them, but they farmed, or gathered fruit, or made jewelry or clothing or art objects.

In New York City, the poor seemed to exist all day on the streets doing nothing except begging. It wasn't their fault, she knew. It was just the way of the city. There were too many people in the city, too much glass and steel and cement. There was no place that you could go and not see the work of man.

She missed the sprawling desert, where you could walk for a day and never see a single man-made object. Where the temperature was determined by the sun and the season and the clouds and the wind.

In the city, you had to go in search of nature. At home, nature was everywhere. It came to you. And people, even poor ones, felt more at peace.

"It's so hot," a woman said to Sarah as she set a bowl of soup onto the woman's tray. The woman had been in a couple of times before, but Sarah didn't know her name yet. She was in her mid-fifties, Sarah guessed, although sometimes the street aged them prematurely. She wore three coats, each buttoned over another, each a different size and style and color. From beneath them, dark pants, like a man's work pants, peeked out. Her shoes were worn and scraped, with a hole in one toe through which Sarah could see a filthy white sock.

"Yes, I know," Sarah said. "I'm sorry. We'll turn the heat off in a bit, and let it cool down some."

Which they'd been talking about doing for hours, but Jennifer, the paid manager on duty, was afraid that if they shut the furnace down the temperature would drop too quickly or climb too slowly, and those who came in from outside would find no relief from the cold.

"Can't something be done now?" the woman pressed on. "It's very hot, you know."

"I understand, ma'am," Sarah said. She was beginning to worry that this woman would turn into one of the occasional problem cases, people who made unreasonable demands of the volunteers, preying on the guilt they felt for having more than their clientele.

But then, the woman took her tray to a table, and guilt of a different nature struck Sarah. The woman was uncomfortable, and was expressing it. That was all. Sarah had jumped to a conclusion about her—possibly because the oppressive heat was making even her a little cranky.

And the fact was, something could be done about it. The solution just hadn't occurred to her before.

Sarah's Gen-Active power was control over weather. She could sometimes affect the weather on a large scale, although that had turned into a problem in the past and she had resolved to be more cautious. But affecting it on a smaller level, she was good at.

She had been so focused on the problem that she had forgotten to look for a solution. The whole story of homeless shelters, in a nutshell. The problem was that people had no jobs, no hope, no opportunity. The symptom was that they lived in the streets and went hungry. The shelter treated only the symptom.

Much like Gen¹³, Sarah thought. *We can fight super-villains all day long, but never attack the real problems, the greed and evil and fear that drive people to commit crimes.*

Maybe she couldn't do anything about that by herself. Maybe she shouldn't even try—wasn't it possible that the best place for her was right here at Mary McCardle, doing what she could on an individual, human basis?

But for now, the problem she faced was one of temperature. And that was within her ability to do something about.

When no one was looking her way, she wagged her hands in the air. Stirring up a breeze.

The air in the room began to circulate more quickly. Sarah created a cold spot, twenty-five feet up near the high ceiling, and sent her breeze rushing past it before spreading throughout the shelter.

Within five minutes, the temperature had dropped three degrees.

She kept it going. Every now and then she let the breeze waft through the main room so powerfully that people could feel it. They'd just assume it was a gust coming in from outside, she figured.

Within fifteen minutes, the temperature inside was a much more livable eighty. When it dropped to seventy-five, she drew back the wind, maintained it there.

The level of conversation in the loud room increased, as people noticed the change in temperature. There were more smiles in evidence. People even began to compliment the cooking.

Jennifer, the paid manager on duty, came to the serving table, a big smile on her broad face, eyes twinkling behind her thick glasses.

"Maybe we don't need to get the furnace fixed after all," she said. "Seems to be working fine now."

"I'd get it checked anyway," Sarah suggested. "Just in

case. You never know with stuff like that."

"I guess you're right, Sarah," Jennifer said. "But it sure feels better in here now."

"That it does," Sarah agreed.

Where is he?

As the shelter filled up, Bobby found himself looking for a familiar face and not seeing it. He had begun having conversations with a man he knew only as "Mr. Joe." Names didn't mean much in a place like this, and many of the "clients," as they were called, were not interested in revealing theirs. They were leaving things behind—failure, tragedy, loss, wasted lives. Names only reinforced who they were, who they had been.

Mr. Joe was one of the quiet ones, at first. A mumbled "thanks" here when you put dinner in front of him, maybe an "excuse me" there if you crossed paths in the narrow corridor that led to the rest rooms and then beyond them to the barracks-style sleeping area. But during slow times, he'd started talking to Bobby, hesitantly at first, just a few words, and then more and more as time went on.

And, Bobby thought, *he turned out to be a pretty interesting guy.*

He didn't talk about himself, so much. Like others here, his own recent history was not where he wanted to dwell. But he talked about places he'd been, things he'd seen—the collapse of the Berlin Wall, the temples at Angkor Wat, the parade of tall ships in Boston Harbor, sitting on the banks of the River Seine at sunrise, drinking strong French coffee with philosophers and writers. Being arrested in El Salvador and escaping in the dead of night with three nuns.

Maybe his stories were true, and maybe not. That wasn't what mattered.

Bobby figured he'd be around for sure on this cold night, and was surprised not to have seen him yet. Bobby's father, Jack Lynch, had been a kind of mentor for Gen[13], but had decided that he was directing the group too closely and, with the move to New York, had taken kind of a back seat role. That left him time to do social things with Bobby once in a while, but meant that on a daily basis, Bobby saw much less of the man than he had before. Mr. Joe had, Bobby thought, been filling some of that role—telling Bobby the kinds of tales a father should tell a son, but that Bobby had grown up without hearing. He also seemed remarkably intuitive and insightful as far as Bobby was concerned—able to recognize Bobby's moods and know when he should talk, or listen, and just what to say when Bobby had a problem.

Finally, when Jennifer passed through the kitchen, Bobby stopped her. "Have you seen Mr. Joe tonight, Jennifer?"

She thought for a moment, shook her head. "No sign. Maybe he's spending time with his family."

Bobby was stunned. "He has a family?"

Jennifer leaned against a stainless steel countertop, crossed her arms. She seemed to know the lowdown on all the clients here, and never minded sharing their stories.

"He's got a wife and two kids, a teenage girl and a younger boy. They live with relatives, somewhere way uptown."

"Why doesn't he live with them?"

"That's hard to say. Apparently he used to have a good job. They had a nice apartment, a car, a housekeeper, the whole bit. But he fell apart, somehow, lost the job, their home. When they hit the streets he felt useless, like he was a total failure. The impression I get now is that he feels like his family is better off without him, and until he gets back on his feet he's having very little contact with them."

"That bites," Bobby observed. "Big time."

"Totally," Jennifer agreed. "Personally, I disagree with him—when times are tough, that's when it's most important for families to stick together and support each other. But he's too embarrassed, or something, to be around them."

TIME AND CHANCE

"Then why would he be there tonight?"

"I'm only guessing that he might be," Jennifer said. "Maybe it's cold enough to help him overcome his humiliation."

"Hope you're right. Maybe if he spends some time with them he'll realize it's for the best. A father should be with his kids." Realizing, even as he said it, just how little of his life Bobby's father had actually spent with him.

"If I see him come in," Jennifer said, "I'll let you know." She headed for the double doors to resume doing whatever it was she was paid for.

"Thanks," Bobby told her retreating form. *Not that I'll have any time tonight to talk to him, busy as it is.* Anyway, his shift was over in another twenty minutes, he realized, and he had promised to go to a political rally with Sarah, something about global warming or dolphin-free tuna or the rights of political prisoners . . . he really couldn't remember which one it was tonight.

But he was hoping that by the end of it, Sarah would be all charged up with no other outlet.

"Dude!"

The double doors swung open and a short, broad-shouldered, muscular Asian-American guy with straight brown hair and a huge smile entered the kitchen. Percival Edmund Chang, better known as Grunge.

"Grunge! What are you doing here?"

"Score of the century, Bobby," Grunge said. He held two stiff pieces of cardboard up in one hand. "Backstage passes, dude," he said. The pride was evident in his voice and the gleam in his eyes.

"To what?"

"Gargantuan Sweetbread is playing tonight at that little club on 29th. The Trench."

"No way! That place is like the size of my closet!"

"Way," Grunge said. "Totally unannounced and unscheduled. I got these through that guy I met who works at the radio station—did him a little favor with his landlord, and he made a couple of calls, got me the passes. This is the musical event of the year, dude. What time you get off?"

"I'm off in fifteen minutes, Grunge," Bobby said, already feeling the energy. A band that big, in an intimate little club—and backstage, mingling with the band members and the women . . . the women.

Sarah.

"Wait," he said. "I can't."

"What do you mean, 'can't?' Take that word out of your vocabulary, Bob-man. You must."

"I sort of promised Sarah I'd go to this rally."

"Dude, no matter what problem the world has tonight, it'll still be spinnin' tomorrow. But Gargantuan Sweetbread is gonna be playin' stadiums on their next tour. You'll never have a chance like this again."

"Sorry, Grunge. I just don't see . . ."

Sarah watched through the window in the kitchen door.

She'd seen Grunge come in, which was basically unheard of. "Poor people freak me out," he'd said when Sarah and Bobby had told the team they were planning to volunteer. She had tried to intercept him, but she had a line of people waiting to be served. He'd found his way to the kitchen by himself, though, and she had caught the tail end of the conversation.

Enough to get the gist.

She pushed through the doors.

"Hello, Grunge," she said.

He spun, obviously startled, but he recovered quickly and flashed her a wide grin. " 'Sup, Sarah?" he asked.

"What brings you down to the impoverished end of town?" she said by way of reply.

"Just lookin' for the Bobster," Grunge said.

"I heard."

Bobby looked at her, all puppy dog eyes. "I was just telling Grunge I couldn't go to the concert with him. What about Caitlin, Grunge? Did you ask her?" Bobby asked,

TIME AND CHANCE

naming their redheaded team leader. Grunge had had the hots for Caitlin Fairchild since they'd met, Bobby knew, so if she was available to go out tonight, he would certainly have asked her first. "Or Roxy?" Also known as Freefall, and the fifth member of Gen[13], Roxy Spaulding's crush on Grunge was at least the equal to his lust for Caitlin.

"Kat's been at some museum all day, and Roxy's going to be there, but not with me. She met the drummer of that band, remember, and she's supposed to meet him there."

"That's right," Bobby said.

"So it's gotta be you."

"Grunge, I . . ."

Sarah looked at Bobby, doing his best to turn down tickets to a show he'd really love to see. *He doesn't care about the rally,* she thought. *Not really.* His interest in political causes was a subcategory of his interest in her, that was all. And she wasn't in a position to offer herself to anyone, especially any boy, right now.

"Just go, Bobby," she said.

"What?"

"Go. I'll be okay."

"You sure, Sarah?" he asked. But a smile was already beginning to play around the corners of his mouth and eyes. She had made the right decision. *Sad,* she thought. *But that's just the way he is.*

"Go to the concert," she said. "There'll be other rallies."

"Well . . . okay, Grunge," he said, snatching one of the passes from his friend's grip. "I'm there."

Ten minutes later they had their coats and gloves on and were pushing their way out into the chill wind. Bobby nearly bumped into a ragged, bundled up figure, then leaped back as he saw who it was.

"Mr. Joe!"

The homeless man looked up. He smiled, revealing teeth that had once been perfect and now had gone yellow and bad. His face had scars, many recent, but his eyes were sharp and alert.

"Bobby, old son. You have the look of someone who's getting up to something. Or am I wrong?"

Bobby grinned and looked away. "Just headin' out for a while. Havin' some fun."

Mr. Joe placed his hand on Bobby's shoulder. "Good. *Good.*" He nodded at Sarah. "The two of you work so hard, you deserve all the happiness you can get. If there's anything I've learned, it's that. Take your joy where and when you can. Do that and your life'll be worth living."

Grunge looked over. "Hey, Mr. Joe. Heard all about you."

Mr. Joe raised an eyebrow. "You watch out for this one, Bobby old son. He's got the devil in him." Then his smile broadened. "Maybe he can teach you a thing or two."

Bobby held the door open as Mr. Joe entered the shelter. He felt better—a whole lot better—knowing his friend was all right. And Sarah looked at him just a little differently too, some of the hardness gone from her elegant features.

They hailed two cabs, since they were heading separate directions. Sarah got into the first, and Grunge and Bobby waited while a strikingly tall, silver-haired woman climbed out of the other, and then they piled, laughing and shoving, into its back seat.

The tall woman scanned up and down the block once with a practiced eye and then went into the Mary McCardle Shelter. She took in the scene inside at once, and went straight to the serving table. She was dressed in all black, a cloth coat over a turtleneck sweater, black slacks, and boots. As she crossed the dining room she peeled off black leather gloves and stuffed them in her coat pockets.

"Hello," she said to the man serving dinners. "Who do I speak with to see about volunteering?"

"Just a sec," the man said. "I'll get Jennifer for you."

He left the table and disappeared down a narrow hallway. As soon as he was gone, Suzanne Sawyer turned and surveyed the people eating their free meals, including one who had just wandered in and held himself just a little higher and stronger than the others. A man who somehow reminded her just a little of her employer. She listened carefully and heard another of the homeless call him "Mr. Joe."

Interesting.

Wager said this would be a good place to start looking, she thought. *And one thing about Wager-you can usually count on him to be right.*

Interesting, indeed.

Caitlin Fairchild walked slowly and carefully across a spacious but crowded wing of the Metropolitan Museum of Art. She didn't pay any attention to the paintings mounted on the wall. They weren't what was really on display this evening.

She was.

And she hated it.

Turning her head slightly, she felt her beautiful, rich, long red hair cascade over her tight shoulders. Her white silk blouse and jacket whispered slightly as she pressed her arms to her sides and placed her hands on her purse, somehow attempting to draw herself up into a thinner, less tempting target for those in the crowd who knew exactly what personal space was all about—and were intent on violating *hers* at every possible opportunity.

I shouldn't have come here, she thought. *I should have known better . . .*

The muscles of her impossibly long legs, revealed by her short white silk skirt, tensed with every step. Her statuesque body, all six-foot-two of it, was coiled and ready to spring.

She was at war.

Her enemy was a shadow. A whisper.

A look.

It had a million staring eyes and half as many bodies. A single impulse powered its every act:

Want.

Mindless, animal desire.

And it was all around her. She could feel it. So many young, attractive men and women all squeezed into this place, caring nothing at all about the exhibits, only looking for one thing—and looking at her as if she were the most exquisitely crafted *piece* in the entire museum.

She had come for the art.

Dammit.

Just find the exit, Kat. Try and relax and stay focused on finding the way out. You can do this.

Scanning above the heads of the rich and sexually aroused, she found the sign and made her way toward it, drawing more stares.

She had dressed conservatively, for heaven's sake. Her outfit tonight was *nothing* like the skin-tight number she wore into battle—and that was a pretty necessary evil. She had learned from experience that evening gowns and casual wear ripped to shreds when you were hurling cars at techno-enhanced super-soldiers and taking hits from plasma rifles.

Resisting the temptation to use her enhanced strength to clear a quicker path through the suits and gowns and staring, *staring* eyes, Caitlin wondered why this had to happen every time she went somewhere?

Her anger and frustration building, she forced herself to stop, close her eyes, and take a nice deep breath. It was the only way she could keep herself from lashing out.

She had almost found her calm center when a voice intruded.

"Excuse me."

Caitlin stiffened, waiting for the inevitable pick-up line. When it didn't come on cue, she opened her eyes and studied the man before her.

Mid- to late twenties. Expensive three-piece suit with some real muscle beneath it. A Rolex. Short cropped black hair. Sculpted features. A warm smile. An earnest expression. Almost innocent looking.

She was certain he would seem absolutely sweet at first. They *all* started like that. At least the ones who didn't come right out and ask if she wanted to—

"I mean, excuse me, can I get by?" the man asked.

Caitlin looked around and saw that *she* was blocking the exit. She stepped back.

"Thanks!"

The man came nowhere near her as he went by. He didn't even look back. Instead, he walked into the next wing, which was considerably calmer, and kissed a pretty but plump woman with two children in a stroller.

He even called her "sweetie." And he wore a wedding ring.

Caitlin felt like an idiot. Not every good-looking man—or woman for that matter—was staring at her with *that thought* in their mind. As a matter of fact, if she had been in her old body, short, scrawny, plain, bespectacled and *flat*, and someone who looked the way she did now walked past, she would have found it hard to keep herself from taking a second look. And she knew exactly what she would have thought:

Another one of the pretty people. Probably thinks she's better than everybody else. I bet she's just loving the attention, the looks.

Probably had a boob job, too. No one looks like that naturally.

In fact, even she didn't look like this naturally. She'd been experimented on. *Changed.*

What had she been thinking?

Get thee to some Paxil, girl, she chided herself.

She stepped out of the crowded wing, feeling better than she had a moment before. Stopping to look at a collection of Cindy Sherman photographs, she became lost in the artist's work. Something about the stark black and white contrasts and the fascinating manner in which the photographer had used herself as a model to represent various female archetypes brought order to the chaos she'd allowed to engulf her. Using costumes, makeup, wigs, and inventive sets, Sherman had cast herself as a vamp, a housewife, a schoolgirl, and more—all from imaginary 1950s B movies.

It's all about how you see yourself, not how others see you, she thought.

The tension drained out of her. Glancing over at the married man with the two kids, she felt embarrassment take its place.

The problem isn't with these people. It's with me. Always has been...

"When I look at this, I think of connectionism."

Startled, Caitlin looked sharply to her left. She expected to find the man who had spoken staring at her. Instead, he seemed lost in the collection, almost unaware of her.

He was a redhead, like her. In his early thirties. Her height. A good looking guy in a sweater and jeans. David Caruso-looking. A little thin. Nowhere near the chiseled Greek God types who were always after her.

"Connectionism," she said.

He nodded. "It's a kind of one-sided school of thought within philosophy and computational psychology. It talks about parallel processing and neural networks—the interconnectedness of it all—to explain human thought and behavior. Popular in the '50s and again in the '80s. I think right around when these works were done."

"Okay," Caitlin said. She folder her arms over her generous breasts. "And what exactly does this have to do with Cindy Sherman's Untitled Film Series?"

"Sherman's work touches on feminist theories of representation and body politics just as connectionism plays to chaos theories of the mind," he said. "Parallels have been drawn between the strange attractors in the neural nets to Jungian archetypes. This work strikes me as Jungian, so—"

"Strange attractors, hmmm," Caitlin said. She had no

idea why she was even talking to this guy. Just a minute ago, she'd been ready to toss the next guy who hit on her through a window.

But this one wasn't hitting on her. Not exactly . . .

"Theorists suggest that brain chaos helps to define aspects of personality and behavior, including decision-making. That chaos is a direct sub-set of connectionism." He finally looked over, but he didn't smile. "Boring stuff, huh? Sorry."

He walked away. Caitlin hurried after him.

"Hey!" she said. "I never said I was bored. Did you hear the word 'boring' coming out of my lips?"

He raised a single eyebrow, as if she were toying with him. "You had this look."

"I'm not bored," Caitlin said. It was true. She couldn't remember the last time she'd had a truly *intellectual* discussion. Not since college—and the creation of Gen^{13}. "Really."

"Then you're the first."

She glanced at a clock against the far wall. "I haven't had dinner yet, have you?"

He shook his head.

"You know of anyplace close?"

"There's Jo Jo's. It's not far."

She smiled. "Then what's stopping us?"

Kat, an inner voice said, *my goodness, girl, you are* picking *him* up. *What is this world coming to?*

Hush, she thought.

On the short walk across Fifth Avenue, she learned that his name was Russell Crews, that he lived for physics, and that he was an assistant professor at Rutgers.

She also learned that he owned two cats and that he had a habit of blathering about science when he was nervous or excited.

So which is it? she wanted to ask. *Do I make you nervous?*

Or excited?

She kept the question to herself. The evening was going far too well to start steering things *that way*.

Even though he was kinda cute...

They reached Jo Jo's. Somehow the crowds on the street, the noise, the looks she received—none of it bothered her when she was with Russell. The restaurant was set in a Parisian-style townhouse. Caitlin peered into the crowded and noisy first floor dining room and was beginning to lose hope of being seated any time soon when Russell asked for a table upstairs.

They were led to a beautiful Victorian-style parlor on the second floor, where several tables lay open. The rush of laughter and music from below quickly faded.

"I love this place," Russell said. "It was created by chef Jean-Georges Vongerichten from Restaurant Lafayette. The food's amazing, inventive—and not a budget buster."

He blushed. "Sorry. That was a stupid thing to mention."

"I invited you," Caitlin said, laying her purse on the table. She took out one of John Lynch's credit cards. "Um—*Daddy's* platinum. I've been saving it for a special occasion, so... the sky's the limit."

They feasted. Russell regaled her with tales of college life and the bizarre experiments his students constantly proposed. She found herself laughing so hard she was practically in tears.

"We had one of those at my college, too," she said. "Some guy who brought in the box, brought in a cat, and said, if it's good enough for Schrödinger—"

She stopped the instant she noticed her companion tensing up. *He has cats. Stupid, stupid...*

She let him talk.

"Particle physics is probably the most frustrating area," Russell said. "Students discover something like QCD and get fixed on it, despite the ridiculous mathematics behind it."

She nodded.

"Sorry," he said quickly. "Quantum Chirodynamics. The idea that quarks are held together by a color force, or charge, of three colors each, and that similar colors attract while dissimilar ones repel."

"Right," Caitlin said. She knew all about QCD *and* QED, Quantum Electrodynamics; she hardly needed the principles spelled out for her. But it was a pleasure bordering on intellectual ecstasy to find someone who actually could.

"Antiquarks have anti-colors, all that," he said. "It's just tough when they get a notion in their heads based on appearances and you've got to shake it loose, that's all."

Caitlin understood.

Did she *ever*.

She held out a glass of vintage red wine, chosen by Russell since she had little experience with such things. They toasted to strange attractors.

An hour later, they were at a small get-together thrown by one of Russell's friends in the city, putting in an appearance. The apartment was small and cramped. Expensive tribal art lined the walls.

Everyone dressed casually. Topics of conversation drifted from politics to science, and from the influence of the media on the masses to the sociological impact of Saturday morning cartoons.

"It's all crashing together," a woman dressed all in black muttered. "Who needs Armageddon when we've already had Wyle E. Coyote *in* office?"

Russell tapped Caitlin's arm gently. "Something I want to show you."

He led her from the apartment to a narrow flight of dimly-lit stairs. They trudged up to the roof, which looked out on a magnificent view of the Queensborough Bridge.

"Isn't it stunning?" he asked.

The golden lights of the bridge seemed to shimmer as a soft breeze gently lifted her hair, as subtle and welcome as a lover's caress. Caitlin murmured in agreement. She was only vaguely aware of how close Russell had come to her, yet—somehow, she didn't mind. She felt so comfortable and relaxed with him. He was so open about his life and his views . . .

"Have your students gone down the sociobiology rabbit hole yet?" Caitlin asked. "My roommate in college did. I'm not saying E.O. Wilson's work with ants and other social instincts was anything less than brilliant, but applying his theories to people, saying that language, group structures, and the disciplines of time and space all come down to biological urges is a little—"

"Can I ask you something?"

Caitlin looked over and was surprised to see Russell staring at her and not the view.

And the *way* he was staring—like a predator that had just trapped its prey.

"Russell?" she said, hoping she was just being paranoid again.

His hands found the front of her blouse.

Her *fist* found the bridge of his *nose*. A sharp high crack sounded in the night and Russell fell back against the roof's filthy ledge. His hand had closed over his nose and mouth. Blood stained the cuff of his sweater.

"What the hell's wrong with you?" he shouted.

"Lousy judgment, apparently," Caitlin said. "I thought you were interested in *me*. In what I thought. In what I had to say. Not just . . ."

She hugged herself as she watched his gentle façade fell away. He got to his feet and stared at his bloody hand. Then his gaze found her. The red glow of a nearby billboard made his eyes look incandescent. He was enraged.

Damn, damn, damn! Why couldn't this have worked out? she asked herself. *Why, for once, couldn't a guy have been what he seemed?*

She turned to leave.

"You think you can just *hit* someone and walk away?" he hollered.

"Things will be a whole lot better for you if I do just walk away," Caitlin said. "And I didn't hit you. That was a tap. If I'd hit you, you wouldn't have a face."

He lurched forward, his hand on her wrist. Blood soaked the white silk cuff of her jacket.

"You're not walking away from me, you slutty little tease!"

She froze him with a glance. "What did you call me?"

Russell didn't let go. "Come on. Lookin' like that. Dinner. Daddy's Visa. A special occasion. Strange attractors."

She yanked her arm free with enough force to make him yelp in surprise.

It was still *nothing* compared to the force she could have used . . .

"So this is why you do all the talking," she said. "If a woman's got something to say, it better be something short and simple. Like, 'yes.' And if a woman's got an opinion, you'll tell her what it is."

He took a step back. "Fine. Just go."

She shook her head. "Oh. Now it's all right. Because you say so."

"Someone should put you in your place."

Caitlin smiled. "I was just thinking the same thing about you . . ."

This time when she struck him, she was airborne.

Fifteen minutes later, Caitlin stood on a dock overlooking the East River. Her jacket was ripped in three places, the seams shot.

Crap.

The bridge hadn't looked so sparkling and romantic up close and personal. Graffiti was scrawled everywhere, and many of the lights had been shot out or shattered by rocks thrown from moving vehicles. She'd had to duck one of them on the trip back down.

A shrill voice cut above the gentle wind. And a figure kicked and screamed as it dangled from one of the bridge's highest struts. Drivers honked and hollered.

All was right with the world again.

Caitlin turned away, allowing Russell's plaintive cries to fade as she turned up 63rd and hailed a cab. Getting in, she heard sirens and saw the flashing lights of rescue vehicles.

That was quick, she thought. Then she saw that the lights were heading the other way.

Well, they'll get to him. Eventually.

The driver either didn't notice or didn't care about the blood on her sleeve and the rips in her clothing. Part of her uniform peeked out from a gash that had gone clean through her blouse. A metal spike near one of the bridge's many struts. It hadn't broken the skin.

He asked for a destination—and it made Caitlin pause. What was her destination, anyway?

She gave the name of the luxurious hotel in which Mr. Lynch had leased a suite for the team and settled back. The cab smelled of old cigars, newspapers, and half-eaten sandwiches. The driver had his radio tuned to a fire and brimstone radio station. A nearly hoarse preacher screamed that damnation waited for the sinners who played any Lotto numbers with more than two sixes involved. Outside, a couple of street kids shouted at the passing cab and a hooker flashed the driver.

She tuned it all out.

What *was* her destination? Where was she heading with her life?

As much as she hated to admit it, even to herself, she'd *enjoyed* those hours with Russell, and with his friends. They were a beautiful lie, of course, and the way it had all turned out would make the evening stand out as one of her less fond memories in the city.

But for a short, wonderful span, she had felt like her old self. A science nerd lost in the wonders and complexities of theory and discovery.

Russell may have proven himself to be just another groping, sex-obsessed jerk, but he had woken something in her, a part of her that had lain dormant for far too long.

She could take classes. *Maybe I'll even get a job at one of the labs—*

The sudden blare of the driver's horn made her jump.

Caitlin looked up to see that they had caught up to the police and rescue vehicles. Some major league ruckus had broken out at a club about a block down.

A sharp beam of golden ivory energy ripped from the side of the building and put out three windows in the building across the way.

She only knew of one weapon that left a trace signature like that one: an I.O. Decimator model 3-aught-3.

"Let me out here," she said, fishing a twenty out of her purse.

She was out of the cab, standing on a sidewalk where a handful of cops scrambled to put up a barricade, when it occurred to her that she had nowhere to change and hide her purse.

"To hell with it," she said, walking around the officers, toward the mass of screaming yuppies and Goth club hoppers flooding from the front door. She didn't give great odds for any part of her ensemble surviving the coming battle . . .

But at least she'd worn flats.

CHAPTER 2

Roxy Spaulding ducked as another blast from the I.O. Decimator seared the air above her. It struck the back wall of the club, scorched it, and released a torrent of destructive energies into the night.

Around her, dozens of leather-clad twenty-somethings screamed and scrambled. They had come to The Trench dressed like extras from *The Matrix*, looking for a fun night out. Instead, they'd gotten caught in the crossfire between a bunch of Mafia-types right out of the Sopranos and another crowd of creeps wearing high-tech armor and carrying weapons Roxy had hoped she'd never see again.

The band had been between sets when the first shots rang out. The extended dance mix of Madonna's *Ray of Light* thundered from the speakers linked to the DJ's booth. Dry smoke filtered through the air while strobing multi-colored lights spun crazily from above, lighting up one pocket of bad guys, while dimming down on another batch of potential victims. The place smelled of sweat, blood, nicotine, whiskey, and fear.

"Get down!" Roxy screamed as a hail of bullets from a Mac-9 reached for an orange-haired couple who'd run directly in front of one of the armored warriors.

They didn't get down. They couldn't. There was no time.

Roxy felt time slow and all but stop. These people were going to die unless she did something. They were going to be cut to pieces!

TIME AND CHANCE

Focusing her power, Roxy felt her head go light as she reached out and took hold of the bullets, altering their gravity just enough to change their trajectory. They showered directly in front of and behind the fleeing couple, missing them by centimeters.

Two bullets bounced off one of the armored warriors. One struck the thigh of the orange-haired guy and spun him around. His girlfriend grabbed him and hauled him out.

Roxy studied the maddened crowd. Somewhere in that terrified, soon to be trampled or fried mass, was her date.

"Mackey!" she hollered.

The drummer didn't respond. Nor did she see his long panther-like jet-black hair or the shock of the purple tee he'd worn tonight to honor her.

Roxy brushed her matted magenta bangs from her eyes and took in the battleground. The Trench had once been an old church. A balcony ringed the huge dance floor. The Sopranos had come pouring in from the kitchen behind the stage, guns raised, several sporting bloody wounds already. The Battletech guys had entered through the front door. The two groups had taken up positions on the right and left flanks of the dance floor, leaving the way clear for some people to escape. Others had been pinned down and were using tables for shields. A small group had escaped out of the back.

There were still way too many civilians for comfort.

Roxy looked down at what was left of the major-league hottie outfit she had bought for tonight. The soft black lace over her leather corset had been sliced in four places. Her mini-skirt now had a slit up one side all the way up to her hip. Her Donna Karan original boots were stained with beer, grease, and some stuff she'd just as soon not think about.

So much for a simple night out with her boyfriend in the band . . .

The petite fighter floated up to the balcony, where she found at least a dozen more party-goers huddled and pressed against the walls. Stray bullets and sizzling bolts of energy riddled the walls, pinning everyone in place.

So far, so good. None of the combatants had taken the higher ground.

A couple of guys with cute goatees argued in one corner.

"I'm tellin' ya, man, it's a quantitative study kind of thing—who's more boss, Puff Daddy or Jigglypuff?"

Roxy frowned. She actually had an opinion on that and was kinda frustrated that she couldn't voice it.

She looked down and tried to spot Mackey.

He was on the dance floor, his skinny tattooed arms over his head. Two people who'd been grazed by bullet fire had fallen over him and weren't moving.

He was all right.

For now.

Another sizzling white bolt of energy struck the wall beside Roxy as she hovered above the action.

"Time to go Carrie White on your backsides," she whispered, corralling her power as she looked around at what items she might use to put an end to this craziness.

Percival Edmund Chang's first indication that maybe, just *maybe*, something was up at The Trench wasn't the sight of terrified people fleeing out the rear entrance. Nor was it the sound of sirens and screams and gunshots in the distance.

Nope.

"Hey, it's a party night and this is a party town and things get a little crazy in these parts, no big," he said to his date Therese as he ushered her from the back alley into the club's fortuitously unguarded kitchen entrance. His big meaty hand slipped down her bare back and grazed her amazingly round and perfectly shaped butt as he guided her ahead. She glanced over her shoulder at him, her smoldering dark eyes and thin smile letting him know that he hadn't crossed any boundaries she wasn't down with when he touched her like that.

Oh, I am having a biochemical reaction, yes I am, he thought. Looking around, he made sure he didn't touch anything else, like brick or concrete or steel. Normally, he had complete control over his Gen-Active power to absorb and replicate any complex molecular structure he touched. But there was something about Therese that made him feel like he could lose that control, lose all control...

That was something he wanted. Desperately.

And something he secretly feared.

"Yeah, just let the door hit me in the face," Bobby said behind him.

Grunge looked back. "Dude, don't be so uptight."

Bobby frowned. His hands were sunk into his long coat and his shoulders had been pointed due south for the last six blocks. Sulking didn't look good on the man.

"Okay, so passes for Gargantuan Sweetbread turned out to be bogus," Grunge said. "Doesn't mean the night's like a total loss or nothin'."

Bobby nodded in the direction of the dark-haired, sultry wannabe model who swayed and sashayed before them. She was tall, thin, and stacked. The top half of her dress consisted of two strips of red satin crisscrossed and tied around her neck like the bow of a Christmas present Grunge was dying to open.

Damn.

"Maybe not for you, studboy," Bobby said. "But I could have been with Sarah."

"Yeah. Trying to stay awake." Grunge waved his fist in the air. "Save the canned ham! Porpoises have purpose!"

Bobby shook his head and smiled. "Jerk."

"Loser."

They laughed and cut through the kitchen. In moments they emerged at the outskirts of the dance floor, where all hell had not only broken loose, but was literally bringing down the house.

It was at this moment, looking at the gangsters on one

side of the club and the goons in the I.O. gear on the other, that Grunge conceded to himself that bringing his date here maybe wasn't the smartest thing he could have done.

Better late than never.

A sudden warmth came from beside him. A brilliant burst of golden flame flared and Bobby "Burnout" Lane flew forward, the fires that were his to control having incinerated his street clothes and exposed his costume. He scooped up a young, heavily pierced bald guy and flew him out of harm's way as the baddies exchanged fire.

Next to Grunge, Therese was frozen. Behind her, the lights in the kitchen flickered and flared out.

"Listen, babe, just go back out the way we came in, just turn and run."

She didn't run. She stood, staring at Bobby as he circled back and attacked two of the I.O. armored guys. She looked transfixed. Transcended.

Way turned on.

Grunge raised an eyebrow. "Hey, you think that's something, check this out!"

Crouching, Grunge put his hand on a fallen microphone stand and felt the change overtake him. He was too excited at the thought of Therese becoming excited to more than barely register the feelings racing through him, the tingling, the racing of his heart, and so much more.

He stared into her eyes as his flesh changed into steel.

Her lips parted.

Slightly.

They were moist.

"Got yer motor runnin', huh, sweetheart?" he asked. "Wait'll you see me in action against these losers!"

He waited for her to respond, grinning ear to ear.

His grin faded as she began to scream. "Hey, what?" he asked.

Her arms crossed over her chest. She shuddered and stumbled back. "Freak. . . . You're a freak and I let you touch me and I was gonna—with you—and—"

She cupped her hand over her mouth, turned, and ran into the shadows. Grunge moved to follow her, when tremulous shapes from the kitchen emerged and came flying at him. He barely had time to get out of the way as knives, frying pans, cooking pots, and huge chunks of metal shorn from ovens came flying toward him.

It was Julia Child meets *Bedknobs and Broomsticks*!

He stood back as the possessed cutlery went sailing over the dance floor, the knives striking I.O. weapons with surgical precision, slicing at trigger fingers, jamming firing mechanisms, while the rest of the debris flew in the opposite direction, clobbering the badly dressed Godfather types.

Only one person he knew of who could do that.

"Roxy?" Grunge said, looking up.

Sure enough, there she was, hovering like an angel. A good kid. Smart, too.

"Get that stinkin' witch!" one of the I.O.-looking guys hollered.

Grunge saw the uninjured, unimpaired soldiers train their energy weapons high on his floating teammate and sometime girlfriend.

"No!" he yelled, launching himself at them.

But he only covered a few feet before they had opened fire.

Caitlin burst through the crowd and saw Bobby and Grunge heading from opposite directions at the armored mercs. She also saw Roxy—Freefall—hovering above, arms open wide, eyes squinting, a sparkling field of energy surrounding her.

And she saw the beams of light rip upward before she had any time to react.

Roxy flew like hell, narrowly escaping the barrage of sizzling power that punched a dozen holes in the wall where she had been, collapsing it and letting in a view of the stars outside.

"Grunge, Burnout, keep those guys busy!" Caitlin

shouted, instantly taking on her role as team leader. "Freefall, the others must have some kind of dampening or disrupter field, it's the only way they could have survived this long considering their firepower. Take it out and help me get these people to safety!"

Caitlin grabbed at an overturned table and hauled it off a small group of terrified club-goers. Her skintight green and purple outfit gleamed as a spotlight struck her at random, turning her and the people she had just loosed from cover into instant targets.

She tossed the metal table at the closest of the I.O. guys, taking a definite satisfaction in the crunch of their armor plate as the table hit. The spotlight moved off and she hauled the cowering club-goers to their feet and shoved them toward the door.

"Move! Go!" she shouted.

Not one of them hesitated.

Caitlin tore through the dance floor, grabbing at people, getting them to safety. From the corner of her eye, she took in Burnout releasing a burning tide upon the mercenaries while Grunge took several on in hand-to-hand. Gathering up a couple of wounded, Caitlin saw Roxy using her gravity power to haul their guns from them, then to levitate the entire group of plainclothes gunmen and spin them around as if they were trapped in the rinse cycle of a washing machine.

She heard a group of *thuds* coupled with groans of pain. Then Roxy was pushing past her to put her hands on a skinny tattooed guy who was hugging the floor.

"Mackey!" she yelled. "Mackey, come on!"

He looked up. "Rox?"

She grabbed his arm and led him toward the front of the club.

"This isn't over!" one of the armored guys hollered. He was one of the few to still have working artillery. He aimed his Decimator at the ceiling and fired in a wide but controlled arc.

"Oh, damn," Caitlin whispered.

TIME AND CHANCE

She hated when they pulled this.

There was a loud creak, then a snapping, and suddenly the ceiling and the walls of the club were collapsing! Screams sounded as the balcony fell.

"Grunge, Burnout, Freefall, we've got to protect these people!" Caitlin yelled.

She saw Grunge beating an I.O. guy so hard that his visor had nearly cracked. His teeth were clenched, his eyes wild.

"Grunge, I mean now!"

Debris rained down. Caitlin caught a few of the largest pieces and tossed them aside, then smashed others to kindling. Roxy used her powers to levitate a collapsing wall. Bobby blasted huge pieces of falling wood and stone into cinders and slag. Grunge happily covered a trio of huddled, wounded young women with his steel encased body as a rain of stone covered them.

When it was finally over, the building looked as if someone had used a wrecking ball on it. Caitlin unearthed Grunge, who was unhurt, and helped the others sift through the wreckage to aid those who could be rescued.

Of course, not one of the gun-toting gangsters or the I.O. armor-plated mercs turned up. They had all escaped.

"So what was that all about?" Caitlin said, shaking her head as Grunge and Bobby flanked her.

"No clue," Bobby said.

"Maybe someone welched on a bet," Grunge murmured. He looked distracted, miserable, and not at all himself. "You never know how people are gonna react to things..."

Roxy was standing with her drummer. He smiled weakly and introduced himself.

"Look, you guys have stuff to sort out," he said finally. "Rox, you give me a call."

She nodded, smiling, then turned to Caitlin and filled her in on everything she had witnessed.

"This was something major," Caitlin said. "Who were those guys with the guns? And those others..."

Roxy nudged her arm. Several police officers were heading their way. "We're not the only ones with questions. Time to fade."

Caitlin led the group through the wreckage. They avoided the police and were soon several blocks away.

"I'll have to tell Mr. Lynch to cancel my credit cards," Caitlin said. "I had to toss my purse up on a roof back there. I'll bet someone's found it by now."

Roxy volunteered to go look for it. Her bag had been reduced to atoms by an I.O. plasma burst.

Caitlin watched as she stopped and looked back to Grunge. His mood was darker than Caitlin had ever seen it.

"Hey," Roxy said. "You wanna come with? Maybe we can stop and get some Thai—"

" 'Nother time," Grunge said. He hung his head and took off on his own.

Roxy followed him with her impossibly wide purple eyes. Her yearning was apparent to every one of them—except Grunge.

Sure, she was dating, but it was Grunge she wanted.

And he didn't have a clue.

"Who did that to him?" Roxy asked, anger clearly rising up in her. "What happened?"

Bobby put his hand on Roxy's shoulder and gently massaged it. "I don't have any idea. But I'll try to find out."

He sighed wistfully.

"Are you thinking about Sarah?" Caitlin asked as she scanned the street ahead for a cab.

"Yeah," Bobby said. "I just hope she's having a better night than the rest of us . . ."

This isn't a rally, Sarah thought. *It's a disaster. It's a farce.*

The organization sponsoring it was called the Coalition for Appropriate Public Lands Use, and the issue at stake was how best to manage the forty to sixty million acres of undeveloped, roadless national forest lands that still remained in the United States. CAPLU wanted the land preserved for wilderness use, while others wanted to build roads into it, log it, use it as a source of wood fiber and motorized recreation. Sarah supported CAPLU's stance.

But somehow, the rally had started off on the wrong foot and gone downhill from there. Maybe it was the cold—fully half the folding chairs set out in Central Park were unused, and the people who were there sat huddled in little clumps, as if to share body warmth. Speaking to the too-small crowd were too many speakers, each of whom went on too long, and each with his or her own agenda to promote. There were politicians from the local and national stage, none of whom seemed to share common goals. There was the National Director of CAPLU, a charismatic woman from Wyoming, but she had defeated the head of the local New York chapter for the job, and the chapter head aimed a few choice barbs her way during his introductory speech. There was a minor Hollywood celebrity, someone whose sitcom had lasted less than a single season, and he seemed to have been invited purely for the name value as he could barely manage to string a sentence together that wasn't about himself.

At least, she thought, *I was able to drop a few bucks into the fund-raising coffers when I got here.* She doubted that anyone who managed to sit through the speeches would feel much like contributing after.

The media director of a different environmental group was droning on now, and Sarah realized she was barely hearing him. "... furthermore," he droned on, "leaving land stewardship issues to the Wise Use and Sagebrush Rebellion forces of the West is like..."

Easterner, she thought. *Thinks because he's addressing a New York crowd he can lump everyone who lives west of the Mississippi into the same reactionary crowd.* She knew people in Arizona and New Mexico and Colorado whose environmental credentials, and policy successes, would make this guy look like a kindergarten student.

GEN[13]

And now I'm doing the same thing the rest of them are, she thought. *Making the struggle be about power and influence instead of working together to further the cause.* Disgusted with herself and the rally, she got up from the cold metal chair.

At least the rally took place in the Park—the one spot in Manhattan where she could find any semblance of nature, even though it was a nature that had been shaped and organized by man. It was a far cry from the windswept mesas and still canyons of her youth, but it was as good as she was going to get around here.

She wandered off into the park, trying to stay on grass and off pavement, as much as possible. Behind her, the amplified voices of the rally's speakers blurred into insignificant buzzing.

Good thing Bobby didn't come, she thought. *It'd just give him more ammunition to complain about me and my social ideals.* If he had wanted her to finish the evening in an amorous mood, that clearly wasn't going to happen now—instead, she was angry and frustrated.

The whole ordeal made her think much more favorably on her experience at the Mary McCardle Shelter. There, at least, she was making a difference. It was on a much smaller scale, but a small scale often meant a human scale. There were real people there whose lives she could improve with a meal, a bed, some meaningful conversation. After a hard shift there, she went home tired but fulfilled, satisfied that she had spent her day making the world a slightly better place.

Gen[13]'s members believed that they were doing good work—*but really,* she observed, *all they ever seemed to do was fight. Who knows what kind of energy that gives off to the world?*

The crisp, cold air and the day's winds made the Park feel fresh and alive, and with a nearly full moon overhead she could see nearly as well as in full daylight. The moon silvered the autumn leaves, still clinging fearfully to limbs or scattered and whipping into whirlpools on the ground.

TIME AND CHANCE

Grass crunched under her feet, so much better than concrete. Somewhere in the dark just ahead of her would be The Lake—already, she thought, she could smell the water on the air. Sarah was tuned into nature more than most people could ever be—weather spoke to her, wind and rain and sunshine whispered in a secret language, a communion of elements that she could share with no one.

This was where she came to escape the city's crowds—not for solitude, but to reconnect with Mother Earth. It was as spiritual a place as there could be in the middle of nine million souls.

So when someone screamed there, it was as startling and out of place as a scream in church.

Sarah didn't hesitate. She ran straight toward the frightened voice she had heard. Female, for sure. Young, sounded like. And very very scared.

She came over a hill and found them, on the other side.

They were just kids.

Her age or younger. Early teens, maybe a couple of them as old as twenty. No one older than that.

They looked like gangs, to her. She hadn't paid that much attention to inner city gang warfare, but these kids seemed to be wearing what could pass for gang uniforms.

One bunch of them, the group standing nearest her, was wearing jackets and jerseys with the numbers 21 emblazoned on them, and she seemed to remember hearing something about a gang called the Downtown 21ers. She'd read an article in the Times about them once—the number referred to the twenty-one members of the gang killed in the defense of a particular neighborhood, a few years before.

The other group, running now, scattering and disappearing into the night, was wearing a wider variety of clothing, but each member had something yellow on—a headband, an armband, shoes, a ski parka. She couldn't remember having heard of a gang that used yellow as its colors, but that didn't mean anything. She was no expert on gangs, and the evidence was right there in front of her.

Both gangs consisted of boys and girls—more of the former, but more gender-balanced than she'd have expected. An unanticipated side-effect of the feminist revolution, she figured, was that girls now felt it acceptable to fight and die in gangs, as well as the boys.

She moved a little further down the hill. The 21ers were blocking her view, but there seemed to be something going on behind them. Some of the 21ers were huddled together on the ground. She couldn't see what they were looking at. But over the muffled conversations taking place, she could hear wet sobbing. *Someone's hurt—?* she wondered.

"What's going on?" she demanded. Loud and forceful. *Take control of the situation from the outset,* she told herself.

One of the 21ers spun around, a large knife clenched in his fist. "None of your business, lady," he said.

"I'm making it mine," she replied. She gestured toward him and loosed a tiny lightning bolt, barely visible in the bright moonlight. He jumped back when it hit him, shocked but not injured, and fell to the ground with a sharp yelp.

"Hey!"

"The next one will hurt," she warned. "Get out of my way."

The others were aware of her by now. No one knew quite what she'd done, but her manner was convincing. They parted for her.

And on the ground before her was a girl, maybe seventeen. Her leather jacket had an embroidered 21 over the heart. She was bleeding from several wounds in her chest and head. She was conscious, in pain, chest heaving as she was racked with sobs.

Sarah glanced about, but beyond a few knives and a single automatic pistol, saw no weapons that could have done this specific type of damage. The automatic's entry wounds would have been bigger, and the girl would be dead.

"They did this?" she demanded, nodding toward where the yellow gang had been.

There was no response at first. Sarah found that odd—she'd have expected that if their enemies had done it, they'd have no problem saying so. She figured that gangs held to a code of silence, but that was to protect their own, wasn't it?

"Who did this to this girl?" she asked again.

"Watkins done it," a voice in the crowd said.

"And who's Watkins?"

A boy came out of the crowd. He was maybe fifteen or sixteen, tall and gawky, with short dark hair. Big hands and feet and head indicated that he would grow into an imposing figure of a man.

If Sarah let him.

He held something in his hands, dark and bulky. He wore a heavy cable-knit sweater, and over the sweater a hockey jersey with a 21 on the chest.

"You're Watkins? You did this?" Sarah asked.

"I didn't mean to," Watkins said. "Nat's my girlfriend, man. I never meant to hurt her or nothing."

The picture started to become clear. "You shot her by accident?"

"The gun . . . it just went off," he said, voice quivering. "I didn't know . . ."

"Let me see it." Sarah held out a hand, and he put the big weapon in it. She held it to the moonlight.

She was right. It was an I.O.-issue Stinger, an electrically-operated weapon that fired a rain of sharp, tiny needles at its victim. If he had really been aiming it at her, she would have been dead. Probably he had been fooling around with it, not sure how to operate it. It was a tricky gun. How it got into the hands of a juvenile gang, she couldn't have said.

She threw it to the ground and blasted it with lightning. There was a sharp crack and the scent of ozone in the air, overwhelmed in a moment by the acrid stench of burning steel and grease.

"You get any more of those, turn them in," she said. "They're more dangerous than you realize. Trained soldiers take special classes in how to work them. You're lucky she's not dead."

"It's just a gun," one of the boys said.

Sarah grabbed his collar in her fist, pulled his face close to hers. "And I'm just a chick," she said. "You wanna take your chances with me?"

He was silent.

She let go. The girl needed medical attention. The gang would have to come second.

There were times, she knew, when having superpowers came in handy. This was one of them.

She scooped the bleeding girl into her arms and took flight.

Sarah was nowhere near the flyer that Bobby and Roxy were. She could manage, by creating powerful enough, tightly focused winds that would take her where she wanted to go. But she was somewhat lacking in grace and sophistication next to them.

And sometimes her landings were a little rough.

When she brought the girl down in the ambulance bay of the Lenox Hill Hospital, the gust of wind that preceded her was powerful enough to blow over several gurneys. Fortunately, none were occupied at the time.

And fortunately, this was New York City—the ER doctors on site had seen superheroes plenty of times before.

"What do you got?" one asked her.

"Know what a Stinger is?"

Another doctor broke in. "I used to be an I.O. medic," she said. "I've treated Stinger wounds. How did this one get it? Doesn't look like an enemy agent to me."

Sarah handed the girl off to the doctor, who laid her on an up-ended gurney. The doctor's name badge identified her as Doctor Lara Koljonen. "Her name's Nat—Natalie, Natasha, something. Her boyfriend accidentally shot her with a Stinger. I destroyed it."

TIME AND CHANCE

"Good," the doctor said, fastening the gurney's straps. "Nasty weapons."

Sarah followed the doctor into the Emergency Room. "If you don't mind, I'd like to stick around, ask her some questions when you've got her stabilized."

"Fine with me," the doctor said. "Police'll be asking her some as well. We have to report gunshot wounds. Even from Stingers."

"Or especially," Sarah said.

"Right. Just have a seat. I'll find you when she can talk."

Sarah found a molded plastic chair that wasn't facing the waiting room's blaring TV. None of the magazines looked interesting. She leaned her head back on the hard chair, closed her eyes, and tried to take herself out of the building, out of the city.

"Miss?"

Strong hands shook her shoulder.

She opened her eyes, and looked into the kind face of the former I.O. medic.

"She'll be fine," Doctor Koljonen said. "She's going to hurt for a while, but he didn't hit any vital organs."

"That's good," Sarah said, stifling a yawn.

"Would you like to see her?"

"Yes," Sarah replied. See her, and find out where her boyfriend got an I.O. weapon. Those weren't commonly available on the streets, as far as Sarah knew. The dissolution of International Operations could have meant that some of its weaponry was ending up on the open market, though, and that would be very bad news indeed. Sarah hoped that wasn't the case.

The doctor led Sarah to a window-enclosed room. Inside, the girl sat up in a bed, a glum expression on her face. Doctor Koljonen opened the door, smiled at her patient. The patient didn't smile back.

"Natalie, this is Sarah," she said. "Sarah saved your life by bringing you here."

"I wouldn't've died," Natalie said, her voice flat.

"You might have," the doctor said. "You were losing a lot of blood, and you were in shock. You stayed out in the cold park much longer, you could easily have died. You owe this young lady a great deal."

"That doesn't matter," Sarah said. "You don't have to like me. What I would like from you are some answers."

"What kind of answers?" the girl asked. Her tone was hostile, as if Sarah hadn't done her any favors by saving her life.

"That gun that Watkins shot you with. It's called a Stinger. It's made for an organization called International Operations. Where did he get it?"

Natalie stared at a spot on the wall behind Sarah. She didn't speak.

"Natalie?"

"Huh?"

"I asked you a question."

"I don't talk about stuff like that."

"I'm not trying to get him in trouble. But if those weapons are hitting the street, people are going to get hurt."

"That ain't my problem."

"Yes it is," Sarah argued. "You've already been hurt. What makes you think it won't happen again?"

"He wouldn't do that."

"Maybe not. But what if that other gang had some Stingers? Then how many of you would have been hospitalized? How many killed?"

"Doc, I don't want to talk to her no more," Natalie said.

"Natalie, listen—"

"Doc!"

Doctor Koljonen put a firm hand on Sarah's arm. "We need to respect her wishes," the doctor said. "Besides, the police have the legal standing to question her, and they'll do a thorough job of it, I promise."

"They'd better," Sarah said. "Or it won't be a pretty time to live in New York."

She left the room, stalked out of the hospital into the street. It was very late. She caught herself wondering briefly if Bobby and Grunge had had a good time at the concert.

But that curiosity was short-lived, pushed aside by her distaste for the kind of society in which a girl would consider keeping her mouth shut about her gang's illegal weapons purchases more important than human life—even her own. *How do you live in a world like that,* she wondered. *What's up and what's down?*

And she found herself thinking, not for the first time today, that all the superheroes in the world weren't powerful enough to do anything about the real problems they faced. The real problems lay much deeper, inside the human heart and the human soul.

Places that, sometimes, an individual could reach. But places in which super powers had no impact.

If anything, those powers created a gulf between the so-called hero and the people—the planet—the hero meant to serve.

Maybe it was time to hang them up.

CHAPTER 3

The transaction took place in the vast empty parking lot of a factory that had been abandoned for at least a decade. The factory stood on the shore of Jamaica Bay, where once it had taken in vast quantities of steel and turned it into office furniture for the military, olive and brown desks and filing cabinets and chairs. The kind of furnishings that no one admitted to liking, but after a lifetime of sitting in those chairs and working on those desks and filing in those cabinets, every retired military person who looked a table or chair of that color felt a small twinge of nostalgia.

Carlo Bertolucci felt no such twinge. He had spent most of a year in the Army, before the unpleasant matter of the sergeant with no sense of humor had raised its ugly head, followed by the time in the brig and the court martial and the dishonorable discharge. But that was okay. Carlo had realized the military wasn't really for him anyway, and the military seemed to agree.

Standing outside the black Lincoln in the cold night, he wouldn't have known what the factory had once made anyway, if Teddy, the driver, hadn't mentioned it. Teddy was from Brooklyn, and, while no one in his family had ever worked for the factory, Teddy had fought with kids whose parents had.

To this day, Carlo thought, *that's what Teddy's good for. Fighting, driving a car. Not much in the smarts de-*

partment, but good to have around when you just need meat.

Still inside the Lincoln with Teddy was Tony Inciardi. Also muscle. Tony was one of the new breed of gangster who empathized with Tony Soprano, idolized Don Corleone, and patronized Brooks Brothers. He complained constantly that his gun ruined the cut of his sport coat, to the point that Carlo often wanted him to leave the gun at home.

At which point, he'd end up wearing the sport coat in his casket.

One thing Carlo couldn't stand, it was a complainer.

Anyway, Carlo was more of a Banana Republic type, even though it infuriated his uncle Niccolo, the tailor. He liked simplicity of line, the modern cuts, the contrasting hues. Tonight he wore a black cashmere sport coat under a black wool overcoat, with white wool slacks. His shirt was white silk, as was the white scarf draped once around his neck, outside the sport coat. His black hair was slicked back and pulled into a tight ponytail. Some of the guys told him he looked like one of the Colombians, or maybe even a Cuban. When they said that, he just smiled. He knew they thought the Colombians were dangerous.

He liked to be thought of in that category. To further promote the image, he always traveled with muscle.

Chances were, he wouldn't even need muscle tonight. It was to be a simple transaction, cash for merchandise. The Lincoln's trunk held the cash.

The Range Rover rolling across the parking lot toward him carried the merchandise. Carlo just hoped that it was only bringing merchandise, and maybe a couple of big dumb guys to lift it.

He wasn't in the mood for a firefight, especially after the things he'd been hearing about the fiasco at the Trench. A perfectly legitimate dispute between opposing business interests, broken up by a bunch of super-powered do-gooders who didn't know how to mind their own business.

This city was built by people who could mind their own business. You take care of your own problems, Carlo thought, *and you let other people take care of theirs. Unless, of course, you are their problem.*

The Range Rover pulled into position twenty yards from the Lincoln. Carlo glared at its unseen driver until the SUV's lights blinked out. When he was no longer in the spotlight, he walked forward, until he was ten feet from the Lincoln's hood, and stopped there.

The rear passenger-side door of the Range Rover opened, and a man got out. He was tall and broad-shouldered, with short curly hair. He wore a leather jacket over a polo shirt and khakis.

Carlo almost laughed. *If you are going to play in these leagues,* he thought, *you should at least dress seriously.*

The front passenger door swung open, and another man stepped down. This one was even more laughable. He looked like a technician, a scientist maybe, or the guy you call to come over and hook up Internet service for your kid. Thick glasses, short disappearing hair, a bit of a paunch. And nervous—Carlo could practically see his knees wobble from here.

If this man wasn't here to sell him a million dollars worth of weapons, Carlo would have shot him just on principle.

"You bring the money?" the egghead asked him.

Carlo shook his head sadly. "I am a businessman," he said. "You, I take it, are also a businessman, no? When you do a business transaction, you do not ask if the other party has the money, correct? It is assumed that if you're there to make a deal, you have the money. Otherwise, what would be the point?"

"I guess so," the guy said.

"Let's start over," Carlo said. He walked a couple of steps closer to the Range Rover. "My name is Carlo. Carlo Bertolucci."

"Sam Perrine," the egghead said. He stuck his hand out, as if to shake across the distance. Carlo held his hands close to his sides. His right was ready to snake underneath his cashmere jacket for his Beretta automatic if it became necessary.

He didn't think it would. But it bothered him that Perrine was so unprofessional. Anything could happen when amateurs played.

"A pleasure to meet you, Mr. Perrine," he said. "My understanding is that we can help one another out."

"Sounds like I have something you want," Perrine said. "And you're willing to pay a fair price for it.

"That is so," Carlo said. He smiled, and he knew that his smile was considered charming by almost everyone who saw it.

Perrine returned it with a shaky grin.

"I have two associates in my car," Carlo told him. "And the 'fair price' you mentioned is also in my car. I assume that the merchandise is in yours?"

"Yup," Perrine said. "Along with two men of my own. Plus Jake there." He indicated the polo shirt guy on the pavement.

"A reasonable precaution," Carlo said. "If I might make a suggestion. Your driver has parked the car so that its nose is facing my car, which adds to the distance the merchandise will have to be hand-carried. It's fairly heavy, isn't it?"

"Weighs a bit, now that you mention it," Perrine agreed.

"Why not have your driver back the Rover up to my trunk?" Carlo offered. "You and I can stay here and chat as he does so."

Perrine thought about it a moment. Carlo could almost see his brain ticking, calculating the chances that this was some kind of trick or set-up. It wasn't—Carlo was genuinely worried about the ability of Perrine's men to lift the merchandise, and he didn't want his own people to be holding anything but their own guns, in case there was some kind of double-cross.

Finally, Perrine nodded. "I guess he can do that, all

right," Perrine said. He went back to the still-open passenger-side door and said something to the driver. Then he shut the door, and the driver backed away cautiously. When he was far enough back, he put the Rover into drive and pulled it behind the Lincoln. He backed up again, until the rear ends of the two vehicles were about ten feet apart. In the red glow of the back-up lights, Carlo could see a man squatting in the cargo space of the Rover, with a rifle or shotgun in his hand.

"Cold night," Perrine said while they waited.

"Very," Carlo agreed. "But after we're finished you'll be able to afford to visit the nicest restaurant you can think of. Sit by the fire, enjoy a lobster or some fine beef, some good wine, a cup of espresso after."

"Sounds nice," Perrine said. "You really know how to live it up, huh?"

"Money's pointless if you don't use it to enjoy life," Carlo replied. "It is never an end in itself, to me. Only the means to get what I want."

"Which, tonight, is ten I.O. Atomizers," Perrine said.

"That is correct."

"You going to want a demonstration?"

"I know how they work," Carlo answered. "I want to see that they do."

"Figured you might." Perrine moved closer to Carlo. Carlo let his hand drift toward his jacket.

"Don't sweat it," Perrine said. "Now we've moved the Rover, I've got to walk past you to open the back. You do want the back open, right?"

"I do," Carlo said. "And I want that shooter in the back to come out of the car before you open it. I'd also appreciate it if your man in the leather jacket moved closer to the Rover, so my back isn't to him during the transfer."

"Done, and done," Perrine said. "Jake," he called. "Do me a favor and stand over there by the front of the Range Rover, okay?"

"Got it," Jake replied. He jogged past the Lincoln, took up a position off the Rover's front right fender.

TIME AND CHANCE

Perrine crossed to the back of the Rover, tapped on the window. "Larry," he said, "come on out the back door."

There was motion inside the dark vehicle, and after a moment, the rear passenger door opened again, and Larry climbed out. He was just as tall as Jake, and more muscular. He still held the rifle in his hands. Carlo noted with some pleasure that it was an Italian carbine.

"Is that really necessary?" he asked Perrine.

Perrine shrugged. "Put the hardware away, Larry," he said. "We aren't gonna need that tonight."

"Thank you," Carlo said as Larry complied. "Now, the back."

Perrine opened the back of the Rover. Inside it was a single wooden crate, about four feet long, two feet wide, a foot and a half tall.

"Here they are," he said.

"Please open it," Carlo asked.

"Glad to." The crate was held closed by a hasp, but no lock. Perrine turned the swivel eye and lifted the strap. The top of the crate swung open easily.

Carlo stepped closer. They were there. Ten International Operations Atomizer AE-4s. They looked more like vacuum cleaner tubes than weapons—flat steel cylinders, ridged about halfway down like corrugated cardboard. At one end, there was a small instrument panel, and a trigger button. At the other, instead of being an open tube, they tapered to a point, and there was some kind of crystal embedded in the very tip.

"May I?"

"Be my guest," Perrine said.

Carlo lifted one from the crate. He held that away from the wooden box, then reached in and chose an Atomizer from the second row. Just to be cautious. He put the first one back into the crate.

"You said you know how to work it, right?"

"I have never actually fired one myself," he said. "But I've seen it done, once."

"Let me," Perrine said. He pointed to the instrument

panel. "Power switch is here. Most of the controls are heat sensitive, so you just have to have your fingers in the right spots, but not that one. Press that little switch."

Carlo pressed.

The Atomizer hummed softly. "All charged up and ready to go," Perrine announced. "See that display screen? That shows you your target, reads distance, wind velocity, atmospheric conditions, and so on. That display make sense to you?"

"Let me pick a target," Carlo said. He turned slowly. About a hundred yards off, across the empty parking lot, was a tall metal light pole. The lights were no longer working, and the thing stood there like a child's forgotten toy in an overgrown backyard. "Okay, I've got it."

"Once you've acquired the target, then rub your index finger over that little panel that says "Lock."

Carlo did it. On the flat plasma display screen, he saw an image of the light post. It was clearer than he could actually see the post from here.

"That tells the AE that what it thinks is your target really is your target. Then the display onscreen settles down. Those distance numbers are accurate to within .05 millimeters. Thing can't really read wind and atmosphere at a distance from itself, but it can estimate based on the conditions where you're holding it, and any visual cues it might pick up. But the beauty is, the AE's blast is self-guiding, so if it should encounter a sudden gust or something, it won't matter. It'll correct its course. It knows you've selected that target, and by God it's gonna take out that target."

"And the trigger?"

"That other panel," Perrine said. "Like I said, it's heat and pressure sensitive. Once you've locked a target, all you have to do is touch the panel and she's triggered. Just don't be standing in front of the focusing crystal when you do that."

"I imagine that would be unpleasant."

"Putting it lightly. Some versions of this weapon were

made using quartz, emerald, ruby. Even cubic zirconium. These babies are diamond, all the way. Nothing works like the real thing." He watched Carlo. "Go ahead, do it."

Carlo looked at the plasma display, ran his finger over the trigger panel. The Atomizer seemed to wriggle in his hands—or maybe that was his imagination. A pure white beam shot out from the end of the weapon, raced across the distance, and enveloped the light pole. It flared brightly, and then was gone.

So was the pole.

There was no sound, no smoke, no mess. Just . . . gone.

"Where does it go?" Carlo asked.

"Nowhere," Perrine explained. "The AE just alters its atomic structure, destroys the stuff that holds things together. That light pole was composed of a bunch of atoms clinging to each other like babies to their mommas. Without the cling, the atoms disperse. I could get more technical if you want, but . . . "

Carlo waved a hand. "Not necessary," he said. He smiled at the cylinder in his hands. "I don't care how it works, as long as it does that every time."

"Guaranteed," Perrine said.

"Now, now, now!" Frank Parkhurst shouted into his microphone. He was airborne in a Buzzer, a small three-person copter that Wager had bought the design for and manufactured to his own specifications. They were fast and agile and deadly, and there were five of them descending on the parking lot that had once belonged to the Lummis Desk Works.

Wager's sources had told him that a deal was being made here tonight, and that Wager would probably be interested in the goods that were changing hands. Frank, leading the assault, had kept the Buzzers out of sight of the participants, watching through binoculars until the demonstration was over. At that point, instructed by Wager, watching via comm-link, that he really did want these weapons, Frank ordered the pilots to take the copters off stealth mode and move in loud and fast.

The five of them swooped down like angry birds defending a nest, from five different directions. The chop of their rotors filled the night air, kicking up trash and debris from one end of the vast parking lot to the other. As his Buzzer closed on the vehicles, Frank gripped the trigger joystick and squeezed. Tracers flew from the side-mounted guns, sparking on impact with the pavement. The fury of the guns competed with the din of the copters.

In each of the other Buzzers, a gunner followed suit, strafing the ground and cars with large-caliber tracer rounds. *This is going to be a breeze,* Frank thought. *And when its over, I'll have delivered Wager's two most powerful weapons to him. Let's see how useful Suzanne Sawyer seems after that.*

Carlo heard the helicopters coming a moment before he could see them. They appeared, as if from nowhere, out of the blackness of the night sky. He barely had time to register them as a threat when the guns began to fire.

"Trap!" he shouted. He hit the ground and, still clutching the Atomizers, rolled underneath the big Lincoln. He knew it was armor-plated, but he figured the Range Rover probably wasn't.

The first spray of tracers tore up the pavement and pounded against the car. He heard someone scream, and between the Rover's wheels, saw Jake hit the ground bleeding from a couple of wounds.

Either they shot their own guy, or Perrine wasn't in on the set-up. A third party was in play.

The copters buzzed away, then banked and came back in for another strafing run. This time, Teddy and Tony returned fire with their AK-47s. Larry, Perrine's guy, had jumped back into the Rover for his rifle, but it wasn't going to do him much good against those helicopters.

Carlo had the perfect weapon. The only problem was, how did you use it against a moving target? And what kind of a shot could he get from underneath a car?

While he was debating that, he heard an engine start up. The Rover! Perrine was going to make a run for it— with his merchandise! He aimed the AE-4 at the Rover's wheels, but then realized he didn't know enough about how it worked. Would it atomize the whole car, including its contents? That was no good—he wanted those other Atomizers.

He took a chance, and rolled out on the driver's side of the Lincoln. He pounded on the door with his fist.

"Teddy!" he called. "Stop that car!"

"How?" Teddy asked.

"I don't care how!" Carlo roared. "Kill the driver, whatever. Just stop it!"

Teddy stepped from the Lincoln, raised his AK-47 to his shoulder, and aimed down its length at the departing Range Rover. He fired, and one of the SUV's tires blew. He fired again, holding down the trigger, chewing up metal and shattering glass.

But the Rover kept going.

Then a burst of tracer fire tore up Teddy's leg and torso. He dropped the AK-47 and hit the pavement. Another copter skimmed by overhead, another spray of tracers, and Teddy's head exploded.

Carlo threw himself back under the Lincoln. This was all going wrong.

From underneath, he hammered on the Lincoln's skid plating. "Tony!" he cried. "Hey, Tony!"

But there was no answer. Tony was either dead, or paralyzed with fear. Either way, he'd be dead all over again when Carlo got hold of him. Leaving him here underneath a car with those freaking helicopters strafing everyplace . . .

Through his anger, he realized that the pitch of the choppers' rotor blades had changed. They'd landed. He looked out from his position beneath the car, and saw four of them, blades spinning slowly, spread out around the parking lot. They had surrounded the Lincoln, but they'd landed a good distance away.

Probably thought everyone in the car was dead by now.

In the distance, Carlo could hear the fifth one racing away. Following the Range Rover, he guessed.

He knew he was a dead man. He only had one chance to pull out of this, and that was with the weapon that he had clutched through the entire attack. The weapon he'd only used once, with instruction.

On a stationary target.

Carlo shrugged. You did what you had to do, in this world. He eyed the plasma screen, pointed the diamond tip at one of the teams of men who were even now advancing from the copters. Two men from each one, and he figured each had a pilot who stayed with the ship.

When the first pair was visible on screen, he touched the "Lock" panel. The numbers on the screen stabilized, except for the distance number, which was getting smaller as the men approached.

He touched the trigger.

The bolt of white light hit the men.

They didn't even have time to scream.

But Carlo knew that he had just targeted himself by taking out those two. There was very little question of where the light had originated from, and he was a sitting duck under this car.

He scooted out between the front wheels, rolled onto his stomach, and sighted on another pair. Locked, and fired.

They were gone.

Still moving, he leapt onto the Lincoln's hood, rolled over it. Lead slapped the Lincoln's armored sides.

He laid the cylinder down across the car's roof, sighted, locked, fired.

Another pair was bathed in bright light, and then vanished.

Two of the copters took to the air, their pilots unwilling to face the Atomizer.

Carlo took aim.

TIME AND CHANCE

• • •

"Kill him!" Frank shouted into his collar microphone. "He's just one punk with a fancy gun!"

"You kill him, then!" someone retorted in his earpiece. "I'm outta here!"

Frank emptied the clip of his Mac-10 at the Lincoln, even though he could see his bullets bouncing harmlessly off its armored hide. He saw the guy turn and point the tube at him.

Behind him, the Buzzer he'd arrived in kicked into gear and lifted off the ground.

As Frank hit the pavement, he saw the gunman raise his sights. The white blast of light flew over Frank's head, enveloped the Buzzer. It vanished, and Frank darted across the dark parking lot toward another Buzzer.

"I'm coming!" he called into the mike. "Move out, move out!"

The Buzzer's blades started to whir. When Frank reached it, it was almost off the ground. One door was hanging open, and he hurled himself through it. "Go, dammit, go!" he screamed.

The Buzzer lurched once and lifted off. From across the parking lot, Frank saw the burst of light that meant another one had been vaporized. Just this one left, and the one that had gone after the Range Rover.

He didn't breathe until the Buzzer was miles away from the Bay.

Samuel Perrine sat doubled over in the front passenger seat of the Land Rover as bullets slammed into its tail and punched out its rear window. Lead whizzed over his head.

He was sorry he'd ever come here.

Lindsay had been a professional NASCAR driver, and Perrine had hired him for exactly that reason. He put all his skill to work now, threading the Rover across the parking lot, around the occasional lamppost, heading for the street beyond. Once there, it was just a short hop to the Shore Loop Parkway, and Perrine figured the helicopter wouldn't try to gun them down on such a populated road.

He figured wrong. Traffic was light, this late, and the copter stayed above them, blasting down at them with its guns.

"Larry," Perrine finally said. "Do something about that."

Larry reached back into the cargo compartment. The crate was still open, and he removed one of the AE-4s. "Hold 'er steady," he told Lindsay. He thumbed the window open, stuck the AE-4's end out, located the copter against the dark sky.

He locked it down, fingered the trigger.

The pursuing helicopter vanished.

For twenty minutes, no one spoke. Finally, when Perrine thought he could trust his voice again, he looked at Lindsay and at Larry.

"I gotta get me a new trade," he said.

CHAPTER 4

Roxy stared at the phone in stark disbelief. Sitting in her room, alone on her bed, she moaned imploringly at the impassive black receiver.

Then she slammed it onto the cradle, nearly smashing it.

Hugging herself, she rocked back and forth, feeling vulnerable and small, wounded and frightened. Her Malibu 8 tee-shirt—one given to her by Grunge, a memento from a visit to the set of one of his favorite buxom-blondes-with-guns-on-the-beach TV shows, was stretched down to her ankles, and her bare feet were cold.

Mackey had told her to call. She had.

The number he had given her was bogus. The people on the other end had never heard of him.

She'd never called him before, never been to his place. They met at clubs, they snuggled at the apartments of his friends and band-mates. Roxy had never questioned this. Things had been moving along at a nice comfortable pace between them. He had been sexy and sweet, tantalizing and wise, and he had treated her the way she had always wished Grunge would. He had shown her respect and desire. She had even wondered if they were falling in love.

"Just a mistake," she chanted as the first rays of early morning sunlight stole over her. "Wrote down the number wrong or something, that's all. It was crazy there."

She clutched her knees and rocked harder, fighting back the tears. The room surrounding her seemed to engulf her with its vast spaces. She'd never had this kind of room when she'd been growing up. Never. Her mom's entire trailer could fit in this place.

God, she wished she were home right now. She felt like such an—

"Idiot!" Grunge shouted at his reflection in the bathroom mirror. "Miserable butt-lickin' good-for-nothin' idiot, that's what you are!"

He stood naked before the glass, his hands curling into fists, his long hair dripping wet from his steaming hot shower. He hadn't slept. Hadn't been able to stop thinking about what had happened with Therese at the club.

Snarling with rage, he drove his hand toward the mirror and somehow stopped the blow just in time. The skin of his largest knuckle touched the glass and his out-of-control emotions did the rest. The change came swiftly, numbing his brain, sending his heart racing out of control and causing every nerve in his body to explode with a shocking energy.

He saw his body turn to glass. He watched as he became completely transparent, his skull and bones, his organs and nervous system entirely exposed.

The door opened and Bobby gave a stunned bleat of surprise at the sight of the amazing transparent man.

"Get out!" Grunge shouted.

Bobby moved so fast he nearly burst into flames. The door slammed. Grunge reached down and locked the door. Then he looked down at his hand.

You can see what I am, he thought. *No hiding. No secrets. You can see everything.*

He pictured Therese staring at him in horror. Thought of what she had called him. The things she had said.

Freak.

He wasn't normal. Couldn't be normal, not ever again.

Shuddering, he forced his body to take on the appearance of human skin and tissue once more.

As he stared at his flesh, he wondered if it was real.

He had taken on the molecular composition of so many things since he had become Gen-Active, it was possible that he really wasn't human at all anymore, that he had no true face or form, just the memory of it. And if he forgot—

If he forgot—

Grunge squeezed his eyes shut and shook his head. He wouldn't forget.

He wouldn't.

No way would he—

"Forget it, I'm telling you," Sarah said.

She sat at the table of the hotel suite's small kitchen, Bobby in his oldest, rattiest robe across from her. He called it his comfort robe, and had clutched at it tightly ever since he had returned from the bathroom. Now he was seated, and staring at the soyburger she had made for him as if it contained worms.

"Really," he said. "I should have been with you. I was a jerk to go off with Grunge like that."

She took the plate away from him and pretended not to notice his sigh of relief. "I'm worried about that girl. I called the hospital and they said she's getting better, but there are things I could feel about her and her life that no amount of western healing can fix. These kids are in trouble and there's no way to help them."

Bobby was still staring down at the table, at the blank space left by his plate.

"Hello?" she prompted.

"Sorry. Distracted a little." His lips curled up in distaste. "Ever get an image in your head and you like, just can't pry it out, no matter how hard you try?"

"Well—"

He shuddered again. "No. *Hard* was a bad word to use. Makes it more difficult to get rid of that image."

"Can't be that bad," Sarah said. "It's not like you walked in on Grunge in the shower or something."

"Right . . ."

She sat down and went to work on the soyburger, sipping her herbal tea between bites. "The image I can't get out of my head is the look that girl gave me. The hatred in her eyes."

Bobby was looking at her now. He really seemed to be interested, to be listening.

If only I could trust that look, she thought.

"I know being Gen-Active doesn't mean we have the right or even the responsibility to use our powers to put an end to things like gang warfare or the oppression of the poor," Sarah said. "But as a person, I feel like I'd sleep better at night knowing I had done something. That I had made some kind of difference. I just felt with her last night that nothing could make a difference."

Bobby covered her hand with his. She felt something within her melt.

"Do you think it's possible?" Sarah asked. "Do you think there are some people who are just beyond hope, past all helping? I mean, if that's true—"

"It's not true," Bobby said. "People give up. They lay down and they tell themselves they're ready to die. But they're not. Anybody can be brought around."

"You really believe that?" Sarah asked. She was impressed. Bobby had that same fire in his eyes that normally only shone after he had been talking with Mr. Joe at the shelter.

"You bet I do," he said. "It's not exactly—"

"Brain surgery," Caitlin whispered, surveying the web site she had called up. "Now that's a possibility . . ."

She had been up for hours, thinking about her "date" with Russell and the battle at the club. The fight had been good in a lot of ways—they had saved innocent lives, and she had been able to get rid of the rest of her pent-up fury at that royal jerk.

Yet . . .

It had left her feeling empty. Was this what she wanted to do with her life? She was twenty-one years old. She would be in her senior year right now if she hadn't left college. Gearing up for graduate school.

There were so many areas that interested her. Theoretical physics. Medicine. Sociopaleontology. The possibilities were endless.

Only—they weren't. Not for Caitlin Fairchild, "leader" of Gen[13]. She looked at herself in the mirror by her vanity.

What about for Caitlin Fairchild, normal person? she wondered.

There was such a thing. Or, at least, there could be. She was certain of it. I.O. was history, despite what they had seen last night. No one was chasing them anymore.

It was time to really think about what they were going to do with the rest of their lives. Running around in a butt-cheek baring skin-tight battlesuit and fighting bad guys was one thing for now, but what about when she was thirty? Or forty-five?

Or *sixty?*

What if she wanted to get married? Have kids? A normal life?

The here and now, she thought, *just try to live in the here and now.*

But her eyes had been open. She had been asleep. Dreaming. And now she was wide awake. Thinking.

And now that she had started, she wasn't about to just—

"Stop!" Roxy hollered over all the screaming.

The other four members of Gen[13] turned to stare at her. They were in the living room and every member of the team was in a foul mood.

Roxy was suddenly aware of four very intense stares that had been turned on her. Everyone was dressed and *everyone* was acting like they had just mainlined a triple mocha-chino. Caffeine city. Jeez.

"We need to come up with a plan," Sarah said.

"Yeah, that's it," Grunge said, sprawled on the couch,

TIME AND CHANCE

the wide screen TV's remote in his hand, a lite beer in the other. He was flipping through their 103 channels so fast it was impossible to tell what was on. "We need a plan. 'Cuz we're Gen-freakin' 13 and we gotta put an end—blah, blah—to this horrible evil—blah, blah—that's like overtaking the city—blah, blah . . ."

Sarah gestured and a thunderclap sounded inside the hotel. A torrent of rain fell, soaking Grunge and the couch.

"Yeah, very mature," he said, taking another sip from the can. "You can explain all the water damage."

"Sarah!" Caitlin yelled.

The tall, raven-haired beauty growled and made the rain cease. "We *are* Gen^{13} and *yes,* we need a plan."

Roxy sighed. Ever since Sarah had heard about the incident at the club she'd been going crazy. She was certain there was a link between the armored guys she and the others had fought, and the I.O. weaponry that had gotten into the hands of the gang members last night.

And then there was the way Grunge was acting. Totally un-Grunge like. It was kinda creepy. She couldn't remember ever seeing him like this.

"I don't think I.O. is re-forming," Caitlin said. "This is something else. Fallout from the organization's demise. We should have seen it coming. All that equipment and weaponry had to end up somewhere."

"It's ending up in the hands of children," Sarah said. "And those children are killing each other with it!"

Caitlin put her face in her hands and said, "We should ask Mr. Lynch. He'd be able to tell us how to handle this."

Roxy cleared her throat. She'd had about enough of this. "Mr. L. said it was time for us to start running our own lives. Thinking about our futures. If we go running to him every time there's a problem, how are we going to ever learn to deal with things on our own?"

Bobby came forward and finally spoke up. "Roxy's right. Maybe we should get involved, maybe not. I dunno.

I don't even know if there's anything for us to get involved with. Right now all this stuff seems pretty random. No clear connections. Even if we wanted to do something, where would we start? And if we decide to get involved, it should be because it's something we all want to do."

Sarah looked up sharply. Her gaze narrowed. "So, as usual, you think we should do nothing. Just party and look the other way?"

"That's not what I'm saying. Just—look at us. The last week, has there been one single thing the five of us could agree to do together? Even one?"

The room fell silent. A hiss of static rose up to fill the vacuum and everyone looked over to see that Grunge had put the TV on a dead channel. He stared at it with a strange mix of contentment and disgust.

"Hell'd they ever do with test patterns?" Grunge asked. "I used to love test patterns when I was a kid."

"That's it," Roxy said. "Some fresh air. Now. It does a body good and there are five of us here that could use it."

The other team members reluctantly followed Roxy's prompting and prodding, and before long, she had them out on the street.

"See?" Roxy said. "There's something we all agreed on. Bobby's argument is dead in the water. Case closed. So—is this a deal Gen[13] should be handling or not? What does everyone think?"

No one replied. They all looked like they were having one of the worst "morning afters" in history and she knew that it wasn't from drinking.

"I think maybe the world don't need no stinkin' Gen[13]," Grunge said in his best John Belushi, Killer Bee voice. Only there wasn't even a trace of mirth in his tone. "And maybe none of us need it, either."

Roxy couldn't believe she was hearing this. No Gen[13]? What would they do with their lives?

What would she do?

"Something to think about," Caitlin said, looking away.

Now Roxy was doubly stunned. *My own sister—half-sister, really—is going along with this?*

"Waitaminute. So some of us had a bad night," Roxy said. "That doesn't mean we have to start talking about hanging up—"

A scream tore through the cacophony of honking cabs and swearing residents on Fifth Avenue. Roxy looked up and saw a young woman in a black skirt and gray sweater running after a guy who was racing away with her purse.

"Help! Somebody help me!" the woman yelled.

The guy was across the street, weaving through the mix of yuppies, darkly clad "artistic types," and flat-out wackos lining the sidewalk. A few looked over from cell phones. Most ignored the situation.

Roxy focused her power. It would be easy enough to pluck that guy from the crowd and leave him hanging in mid-air until he dropped the purse. God, if he wasn't dressed the part of an early morning purse-snatcher. Bulky jacket. Ski cap. Rollerblades. Stubble. A rat-like little face.

Yeah, taking care of this creep would be just the release she needed right now.

Energies surrounded her and she held out a single gloved hand—

Only to see a short, long-haired, muscular guy in a black mesh tee with torn jeans race across the street, leap over the hood of an oncoming cab, and tackle the creep.

"Grunge?" Roxy said, stunned. The other team members were silent, but staring in equal wonder.

Grunge leveled the guy with a single punch to the jaw and jerked the purse out of his hands. He walked over and held it out to the woman—who bypassed him completely and kicked the purse-snatcher right in the face as he was getting up. He crumpled and rolled into the gutter.

Then Roxy saw something she had wished she could have brought about.

Grunge smiled.

The woman whose purse had been taken came over to

him, shaking her head. He gave her the purse and turned to leave. She slipped something into his hand and then hurried off.

Grunge came back, grinning ear to ear. "Huh. Didn't even have to use my powers. And check this out!"

He held out the woman's business card. "She said to call her and we could have lunch. It was the least she could do. Pretty classy, huh? And I *loved* the way she kicked that guy."

"It's great," Roxy said.

"I'm going to the shelter," Sarah said.

Bobby hurried after her. "I'll come with."

Grunge sauntered off, happily checking out his reflection in the window of every shop he passed.

Roxy turned to Caitlin and said, "I was thinkin', there's some new shops open in the Village, maybe we could—"

"I'm gonna hit the library and a couple of the universities," Caitlin said. "I've got some stuff to sort out."

Don't we all, Roxy thought. "Sure," she said. "I understand."

Caitlin kissed her on the cheek and gave her a hug. "Thanks."

Roxy watched her blend into the crowd—as much as Kat ever blended anywhere. It took a while, but finally she disappeared from view, leaving Roxy alone . . .

And wondering if Grunge may have been right.

CHAPTER 5

Joe felt like he'd won the lottery.

At least, that's how these people were treating him. They'd taken him from the lab where he'd been tested right into a stretch limousine. Inside the car, he'd been toasted with champagne. Suzanne, the statuesque woman with the short silver hair sat next to him in the back. On the seats facing them were Raymond, a barrel-chested guy with small hard eyes and tree-trunk arms that strained the sleeves of his sport coat, and Lee, the slender and bespectacled doctor who had administered the blood test.

Joe didn't know what was in his blood—he'd have guessed cheap wine and failure—but Lee saw something there, and that, Joe was told, was what this was all about.

The lottery.

He was, finally, going somewhere.

New York City is full of brownstone buildings, block after block of them. Most are single family homes sharing common walls on two sides, a few steps up from the street, three or four stories tall.

But not all of them.

The limo cruised past miles of them, up First Avenue, over the Harlem River and the Bronx Kill, into the South Bronx. Finally, in Hunt's Point, across the East River from Riker's Island, there was a corner building, part of a block that looked like a hundred other blocks in the city.

The car came to a stop. Suzanne gave Joe an open-mouthed smile.

"We're here, Joe," she said. "Home sweet home."

He had been paying scant attention to the world passing by outside the limo, but emerging into the bright sunshine, he realized they were in a neighborhood that he wouldn't have considered desirable or even safe. The brownstone Suzanne stood looking at appeared abandoned—boards nailed over glassless windows, no signs of habitation of any kind. The only person on the street was carrying a bottle in a paper bag and wearing rags. Joe knew the homeless had to sleep where they could, but even he had never come to a place like this to squat.

Raymond and Lee exited the car, and the chauffeur took off. *Wise,* Joe thought—*leave it sitting in this area too long and you'd find the wheels gone even though you were still inside it.*

He'd been under the impression that these folks had money, though. The nice car, the expensive lab equipment . . . what were they doing at this abandoned tenement?

"This is home?" he finally asked.

"Don't judge a book by its cover," Suzanne said. "Or in this case, a home by its outer shell."

Joe shrugged and watched her climb the six stairs to the front door. She put a key in the lock and turned it, and the door swung open. Raymond touched his arm and he went up the steps behind her, into the building's entryway. The stench was overwhelming—decades of waste and decay and hopelessness had left their mark.

Inside, it looked pretty much like he'd expected it to look. There was trash everywhere, years' worth of old newspapers, broken bottles, rusting cans. In a room just off the foyer that had probably once been a formal sitting room there were three paper-thin mattresses, stained and torn. More trash surrounded them, like the sea around an island chain.

A staircase led up from the foyer, but the first six steps

were gone, leaving a jagged-toothed mouth that opened into black emptiness.

Graffiti covered every wall inside—huge letters spelling out gang names, obscene phrases, meaningless symbols and drawings.

Raymond and Lee followed him inside, and Lee shut the door, locking it from within.

"This is a nice place," Joe said sarcastically. "Ritzy."

"I told you, don't judge it," Suzanne said.

Whatever, Joe thought. *If it gets better, let's see it.*

Suzanne led the way again, down a tiny hallway next to the staircase and through a darkened doorway. Joe followed, Raymond and Lee bringing up the rear. Inside the doorway was a room that had probably once been a half bath—pipes for a toilet and sink jutted from the floor. But the fixtures were gone, and even here they waded through the filth of years of neglect. The far wall of the bathroom was gone, replaced by a seemingly random accumulation of plywood sheets and two by fours.

Suzanne pushed on one of the plywood boards and it swung open as if on a hinge. Joe suppressed a shiver—there was more to this place than met the eye. But he couldn't shake the impression that it was a sinister place, somehow. He felt like he was being watched...

Carl Malone needed a quiet place to hole up and finish his bottle. He'd had to panhandle all morning to afford it, and when he got back to the overpass under which he usually slept, he found that it had been occupied by three other guys, young ones, who had stolen his bedroll. They'd chased him off with rocks.

But he'd held onto his Thunderbird, so it wasn't all bad.

And so he'd wandered, looking for someplace warm and private. Taking an occasional slug from the bottle as he went. When he saw the huge black car, his first thought was that he was hallucinating. He'd rubbed his eyes and squinted through the harsh sunshine. Still there. And there were people getting out of it. When the car drove away, they went into the end brownstone.

He could barely remember knowing that there were people with that kind of money. He'd seen them, of course, on TV. Rockefellers and Kennedys and the like. But Carl had spent more than a decade on the streets, his last job disappearing in the last recession. He knew it wasn't just the job—he had some kind of mental problems, he figured, he drank to shut out the voices he heard, he got into fights now and then. He had never fit into society, so he'd left it behind.

People with money scared him. He didn't want to go down to the end of the block where they might see him. The brownstones along this block all looked abandoned, so he decided to check one out, see if maybe there was a place he could squat for a night or two or three.

He looked up and down the block. There was no one around. He climbed the steps to one, tried the door. It was locked tight, and boards were nailed across it.

But there was a window level with the door. The glass was gone and there were a couple of boards nailed up there. Between the boards he could see inside—wallpaper peeled from the walls lay in curled strips on the floor, along with a threadbare brown blanket and a dozen empty Sterno cans. Someone had claimed the place once, but everything seemed covered in layers of dust, as if it hadn't been used in some time.

He reached for the boards, yanked them from the window frame, and dropped them inside. Then he climbed through the gaping window.

Once inside, he tried to reposition the boards, hammering the nails into the rotting wood of the window frame with his fists. No sense advertising that there was someone in here. It stank, but then, so did he. This place was out of the wind and it was quiet, and there was even a blanket, of sorts, for the night. He'd have a look around the rest of the place; who knew what treasures it might yield?

Right after he finished his bottle.

"Alarm," Beckwith said. He was a light-skinned black man with pale eyes and short curly hair, dressed in a dark sweatshirt and jeans. At his hip he wore a Browning 9mm in a leather holster. He sat before a bank of video monitors showing him black-and-white images of a dozen rooms. Some of the monitors kept a constant location in view, while others switched randomly between multiple cameras.

"Which unit?" Telford asked him. "I'll take it." Anna Telford was short, just over five feet. But she worked out with free weights five days a week, ran six miles every morning. Her arms were bigger around than most men's thighs. Her copper hair was clipped short, out of her face. She was strong and she liked to fight. It wasn't unusual for her to volunteer to deal with intruders, and it wasn't unusual for Beckwith to let her have her fun.

"Twelve zero six," he said. "Unarmed, at least partially intoxicated." He smiled. "Be my guest. I'll alert Wager."

"Right back," Telford said. She pushed up from her chair in the security office, grabbed a small needle gun, and climbed a concrete stairway.

The security office was down one flight from street level. Most of the serious work of the complex took place on the level below that, two stories down. There were three of these stairways and one elevator, all leading to the main complex, which was mostly located beneath the "yards" that ran behind the brownstone buildings.

From outside, even from the air, Telford knew, the block looked like any other block of abandoned brownstones. The poorer sections of the Apple were loaded with 'em. Looking down from above, you'd see a row of houses facing the street, each with its own small fenced-in yard. Those yards butted up against those of the houses facing the parallel street.

What you couldn't tell from outside was that Wager had bought, under a wide variety of names and through an assortment of dummy companies, the entire block.

TIME AND CHANCE

He'd knocked out walls, hollowed out passageways, and built a maze of tunnels connecting the houses to one another. Beneath the yards, he'd dug a deep pit and constructed a vast concrete bunker, dozens of rooms filled with scientific and research equipment, staffed by legions of scientists and aides and administrators.

Ventilation shafts were cleverly hidden in the brownstones. Emergency exits led into the sewers, so in the unlikely event of evacuation, people would come out more than a block away. The nearest vehicular access was a garage two blocks away, so people coming and going usually parked briefly on the street in front.

Security was very high-tech. Video cameras and motion sensors watched every brownstone. Guards, on duty twenty-four hours, watched the monitors and responded to any breach with swift efficiency.

Telford was one of the guards.

"Mr. Wager."

Wager looked up from his monitor, glanced at the intercom unit on his desktop. He was online, tracking the fluctuations of global currency. He'd invested seven hundred thousand dollars in Japanese yen today, feeling a great likelihood that the yen would take an upswing. So far, it had gone up by almost four cents on the dollar. His profit, if he bought dollars now, would be in the neighborhood of twenty eight thousand dollars.

Not big money. But not bad for a few minutes' work, requiring no effort on his part and even less risk.

Wager didn't deal in risk. He dealt in probabilities, and there was no one alive who understood them like he did.

"Yes, Beckwith."

"Just wanted to let you know, sir. There's an intruder on the premises, but he's being dealt with."

"And how is our friend Joe coming along?"

"He'll be to you in about four minutes, sir."

"That's fine." Wager turned back to his screen. A soft click indicated that Beckwith had signed off.

Wager didn't like anyone inside his private sanctum, except for Suzanne Sawyer. It was a tiny room, to begin with—one wall of video monitors, a desk, a big leather chair, all squeezed into a room slightly less than nine feet square. It was almost dead center in the complex, built of unadorned concrete blocks.

He felt safe there. He tilted back in his chair, savoring the sensation. Took a sip of cranberry juice from the glass on his desk.

Another four minutes, and then he would meet his future.

The chances that it would be an improvement over his past were one hundred percent certain.

There had been a time when Wager had been known as Thomas Carlisle. He'd been a small man, a weak man, a frightened man.

He was still small. The other words no longer applied.

Within a week, two at the outside, he would be the undisputed ruler of New York's criminal community. Not weak or frightened anymore.

Thomas Carlisle had been a gambler, and a successful one. He played the odds. Most of the time, he beat the odds.

He traveled constantly—Las Vegas, Atlantic City, Monte Carlo, Macao—anyplace there was a game of chance, a deck of cards, a roll of dice to place a bet on. He was perfectly capable of blowing a quarter of a million dollars in the space of a single evening, because he knew—knew, not just believed—that the next roll, or the one after, would be the one that would reverse his fortunes. He believed in going home a winner, and he did so, night after night.

He partied with movie stars and gangsters. Beautiful women vied to spend time with him. He was not big, not muscular, not especially handsome. But he was rich, and there was an undeniable energy to him. He was charismatic in the truest sense of the word.

TIME AND CHANCE

Until, one night in Reno, Nevada, he made a mistake.

Thomas hardly ever bothered with Reno. It was decidedly low-rent. The stakes were small. The hotels left much to be desired, and the women were brash and unrefined compared to those of the world's gambling capitals.

But there was an event, a poker tournament with a one million-dollar purse that he didn't want to miss. Not because he was especially a poker fan—too much of the human element, and not enough reliance strictly on odds. But he could play the game, and he could use the mil.

A week of bad luck had put Thomas Carlisle in debt to some of his "pals." He wanted to pay it off before the friendships turned sour and he ended up with broken bones, or worse.

He knew the chances of winning the poker tournament. He also knew the possibility of winning a cool million at any other form of gambling in the space of twenty-four hours. The tournament won out.

He played enough roulette to cover his entry fee of twenty-five thousand, and he bought himself a chair. In the first rounds, he did well. He was a contender.

The night wore on. Thomas knew the odds. He made his choices. He folded when he had to, bumped up the pot when he could, bluffed when he thought it best.

At the end of it all, he had won.

He took the million dollars. Passed out substantial tips to the waitresses, the dealer, the casino security people who escorted him to his suite, the bellman he asked to find him a woman for the night.

Thomas Carlisle had averted catastrophe. He didn't want to celebrate alone, but he didn't know any women in Reno, and the ones in the casino hadn't been glamorous or beautiful enough to bother with. He told the bellman he wanted the most stunning woman in town, never mind the cost.

When she arrived, she was indeed stunning. He negotiated a price with her, handed her the money, in advance.

And she showed him her badge.

An undercover cop, working on Reno's efforts to tame its reputation.

Trying to bribe an officer only made things worse. He was taken into custody. Tried, and convicted.

Six months in the care of Nevada's finest.

In prison, his money did him no good. Most of it went to pay back his debts, which weren't forgiven just because of a little unexpected incarceration. The tax man collected a large chunk as well. He had some left, but no access to it from behind bars.

In prison, he was small and weak and frightened.

The other prisoners took advantage of that.

Thomas Carlisle was traumatized by the treatment he got in prison. Life there was so different from life on the outside. Violence loomed around every corner. There was no place that was truly safe. Eventually, he took to thinking of his cell was a sanctuary, because, even though they could still get him in there, it was the closest he had to a private spot. At night, with the cells locked down, he had only his cellmate to worry about, and his cellmate was a white-collar criminal with no interest in brutalizing Thomas. Nor did he do anything to help protect his cellmate.

Thomas retreated into himself, into his mind. The terror and the pain and the anger worked on him, twisted him, changed him into something else.

It began simply enough. A guard was filling out a lottery ticket near Thomas. The man made a remark about Thomas's rep, his abilities as a gambler. Jokingly, the guard asked Thomas to choose his numbers for him.

The guard won a quarter of a million dollars.

Word spread. Soon it became clear that Thomas had a gift. Something special. And his services were quickly in high demand. Prisoners wanted to know the odds of escape plans they had made. Or of their own survival should they follow one course of action over another.

Thomas obliged them—and the abuse stopped. More than that, he began to gain privileges and status. The war-den gave him a private cell in return for a little favor involving the "accidental" death of his wife...

And Thomas never, *ever* had to leave his cell. His meals were brought to him. He was given a phone, a television, whatever he wanted.

Of course, by the time he was released, he was diagnosed as an agoraphobic—afraid of being out in the open, in public places, or, really, anywhere except his own private space—the smaller, the better.

And his powers of computing odds were improved a thousandfold.

Where, before, he would have been able to tell the odds of a roulette ball landing on red five spins out of seven, he now could watch the ball and instantly compute its chances of falling on any given number. He knew at a glance if a blackjack dealer was going to bust, just by watching the way the cards played out. He could determine, before it happened, the chances of any given airplane crashing, or rain falling from the sky, of a police detective's being able to solve a particular crime.

All life was odds. Probabilities. And Thomas Carlisle had become the master of probabilities. Something had clicked in his brain, something that enabled him to figure the odds on any event he considered.

He was always right.

He began to call himself Wager. He made a lot of money, fast. Hired associates.

And he developed a plan.

He'd had to beg for his life, his safety, from the criminals he met in prison. Had to put up with their abuses, their brutality. At least until his powers had manifested. But Thomas feared the day his powers would fail him. It was a terror that weighed on him constantly. He could think of only one way to ensure that he would never again suffer at the hands of criminals and thugs, he vowed. Instead, he would own them, control them. Rule them.

He started by coming to New York City, America's

marketplace, where anything could be had for a price. Anything at all.

And then, he set out to buy the unthinkable. He would pay whatever price it took, but he would own a man.

Carl Malone shoved a pile of wadded-up newspapers out of the way, pushed a flattened cardboard box up against the wall to provide some protection from the cold seeping up through the building's hardwood floor, and sat on the cardboard, back against the wall. He opened his brown paper bag, unscrewed the lid from his bottle. The sharp tang of his wine bit his nostrils. He inhaled deeply.

And heard a sound.

Looking up, he saw a dark figure emerge from a wall.

Maybe he didn't need to finish this bottle after all.

Anna Telford recognized that violence was not a reasonable solution to problems.

But it made her feel good. If that was sick, then she was sick. And she wouldn't be seeking medical help for this disease.

Through a peephole, she took another look at her next victim. Telford loved this kind. While it was true that with the syringe she carried and the "magic elixir" it contained, she could make anyone her prey, old or young, weak or strong, wealthy or poor, she was drawn to wrecks like this one. This man had made his choices and ended up here, where she could do whatever she wanted without fear of consequences. It made her feel god-like. Or at least like an avenging angel.

A part of her regretted having to use the solution she carried. She'd rather this scum remember what had been done to him. Unlike civilized people, who didn't respond well to physical violence, filing lawsuits, alerting the police, he had nowhere left to go, no one he could complain to.

She sighed. Regardless of her personal wants, she had a job to do. At least she would remember. Her flesh would be alive with the memory for some time to come.

She touched the button that activated the wall panel. It swung open and she stepped into the outside room of the brownstone.

"You're trespassing," she said.

The man rubbed his eyes. "I'm sorry, lady. I didn't think . . ."

"Save it."

She advanced on him, drawing her nightstick from a loop on her Sam Browne belt. She slapped her palm with it.

"I'll go," he said. "No problem. Forget I was ever here."

"I won't be the one who forgets," she said. He struggled unsteadily to his feet, as if preparing to leave. She faced him. He was taller than her, close to six feet. But he was intoxicated, weakened from poor nutrition, worn out from the streets. He didn't have a chance.

She slipped the nightstick back into its loop. She'd use her hands for this one.

She started with a sharp jab to the belly. The man doubled over, and she met his chin with an uppercut. His head snapped back. She followed it with an open hand, caught him beneath the jaw, and slammed his skull against the hard plaster wall.

His eyes glazed over, knees buckling.

Then she went to work.

For this, Wager exited his sanctum.

They met him in the larger sitting room, just outside. Comfortable leather sofas lined two walls, a low table with a bowl of nuts on it between them. A couple of chairs faced the sofas. The lighting was indirect, from floor lamps facing toward the ceiling. Drinks could be served from a bar in one corner.

Suzanne held the man's left arm. Raymond held his right. Lee stood just behind him.

The man smiled, but without real humor. *Polite,* Wager

thought. *And subservient. That's good. That'll make this easier.*

"You may call me Wager," he said. The man started to put his hand out to shake, then pulled it back, probably noticing that Wager had not offered his. "And you are Joe, they tell me?"

"Joe Monteleone," he said. Wager observed, happily, that Joe Monteleone was in good physical condition, especially for someone who lived on the streets. Probably he had not been without a home for very long, and he'd taken care of himself in his former life. He was a handsome man, in his mid-thirties, Wager guessed. He'd have sandy blond hair, when it was clean. He was in need of a shave and a bath now, and he could use some dental work, but he appeared to have a strong jaw, a straight, slightly prominent nose, and clear brown eyes.

"It's a pleasure to meet you, Joe Monteleone. Please, have a seat. Care for a glass of water? He can have water can't he, Lee?"

"Water's fine," Lee said.

Suzanne and Raymond released Joe's arms and he sat on one of the couches. She took a seat close by while Raymond went to the bar. Lee chose one of the chairs, and Wager sat in the other one.

"Do you have any idea what you're doing here, Joe?" Wager asked.

Joe scanned the room, the faces, all with a curious expression. "No, I guess I don't," he said.

"You're making history, Joe. Did you ever think that you would make history?"

"There was a time I thought I might," Joe replied. "But that was a very long time ago."

"Recapture that feeling, my friend. Because you will. You are. I am a very wealthy man, Joe. And I am about to make you an offer, in the terms of that old movie, that you can't refuse."

"What kind of offer?"

Raymond returned with a silver tray on which ice

cubes clinked in four tumblers of water and one of cranberry juice. He served the juice to Wager first, then passed out the waters.

Wager took a long drink from his glass before answering. "I would like to buy you."

"Excuse me?" Joe asked.

"To purchase you. To own you."

Joe started to rise from the sofa. "I think you've got the wrong guy," he said. "I'm not for—"

But before he could even get all the way to his feet, Suzanne put one hand on his right knee. Exerted pressure. The knee gave and he dropped back into his seat.

"You haven't even heard my offer," Wager said. "Trust me, it will be to your liking."

"I don't think so," Joe said.

"Take a look at yourself," Wager urged him. "What are you? Homeless? A drifter? A bum?"

"I've been called that."

"And do you have a family, Joe?"

"I—yeah, I do. Haven't seen much of them lately."

"But you'd like to provide for them. Make sure that they're taken care of."

"Well, sure. Who wouldn't?"

"You might be surprised, how little regard some people have for their families, Joe. But I'm glad you're one of the good people."

"I don't really have anywhere better to be, Wager," Joe said. "But even so, if you'd get to the point."

"Very well, Joe. I can understand your curiosity about this. It must all seem very strange to you."

"You got that right."

"I am something most people only hear about in the newspapers, or in whispers, Joe. Something that doesn't come along very often in this world. I am a true criminal mastermind. I am on the verge of owning New York. And I don't plan to stop there."

"Sounds like delusions of grandeur to me."

Wager's face darkened. No one dared intimate that he

was anything less than sane, ever. Who was this—

But he checked himself. He needed Joe. He'd have Joe, one way or another. But having Joe's cooperation would be the easier way.

"Not at all, I assure you. I only need one more thing to make it all happen, Joe."

"What's that?"

"You. I need you."

"Why me?"

"The reason I say I want to own you, Joe, is that I need you to do as you're told without question, with blind obedience. I need you to accept whatever is done to you, willingly and immediately. I need you to follow orders. To submit your will to mine."

"I'm not really that kind of guy."

"I can't promise that you won't be hurt. In fact, you might not survive it at all. But if you do, you'll be a changed man. Stronger, more powerful than you have ever dreamed of. In so many ways. And whatever happens, whether you live or die, your family will be taken care of. They'll live in high style, for the rest of their lives."

"You can guarantee that?" Joe asked.

"I can, and do. You have my word on that. I already have a legal contract written up to that effect, which I will sign as soon as we agree to the deal."

"What do I have to do?"

And Wager had him, as simple as that. Once he asked that question, there was less than a one in ten million chance that he would try to back out. Almost a statistical impossibility.

"Nothing to it," Wager said. "It turns out, Joe, that your biochemistry and mine are almost identical. We could practically be brothers. Closer than brothers, in some ways. Isn't that right, Lee?"

"That's right," Lee replied. "Matches in the ninety-two percent range."

"I love percentages," Wager explained. "I use them. I

play them. They help me get what I want. Ninety-two is a good one, and it'll help you get what you want too."

"That still doesn't answer my question," Joe said. "What do I have to—"

"I need to test something. A substance I acquired recently that will bestow upon its user powers unimagined. I intend to take it myself, but not before I know approximately what it will do to me. I don't want to accidentally take a lethal dose, but I want to take enough to guarantee a successful transformation."

"So you're looking for a guinea pig."

"Aptly stated. A guinea pig whose body's responses will closely resemble my own. What I'm going to give you will most likely make you an immensely powerful being. Once that happens, even though you will be physically stronger than me, you will still belong to me, do you understand that? You must swear to me your absolute allegiance, as long as you live. Otherwise, the deal is off, and your family will not only not be taken care of, they will be killed. Remain loyal to me, and your family thrives. Betray me once, and they die. It's easy to remember, wouldn't you say?"

"I think I got it."

"Good. Then what do you say?"

"Where's that contract?"

Four hours later, Carl Malone woke up in an empty gravel parking lot in New Jersey. He ached everywhere. When he touched his face, he flinched from the soreness. And there was a stinging on the inside of his elbow. Rolling up his sleeve, he saw a little mark, like he had given blood.

He couldn't remember how he got here. Or where he'd been. He scoured his memory, but the last thing he could clearly bring up was the night before, drifting to sleep inside a cardboard box near a train track. It had been cold and damp, he recalled. After that, though—nothing.

Next to him, he noticed, stood a brown paper bag. He looked inside.

A bottle of Thunderbird, brand new, unopened.

Life was good.

CHAPTER 6

After a little more than an hour, some of the missing started to drift back into the Mary McCardle Shelter. Sarah sat with a cup of bad coffee that had cooled while she waited. Bobby was in the kitchen, talking in low tones with José. When the bell on the door tinkled, though, he shoved through the double doors and joined Sarah on the floor.

The first one in was a woman named Marcia. She was a regular, and they both recognized her. She came in through the glass door, stopped just inside the dining room, and looked around it as if it were all new to her.

"Hello, Marcia," Sarah said.

"Hello," Marcia said. She blinked a couple of times, staring at Sarah's face.

Sarah gave her a smile, trying for welcoming and concerned at the same time. "Is everything okay?"

"I guess so," Marcia said.

"Where've you been?" Sarah asked. "Did you go somewhere with the others?"

Marcia stroked her chin with the stubby fingers of her right hand. Her left held the brown plastic grocery bag she used as a suitcase/purse. She blinked again. "I don't think so," she said. "Maybe. I don't remember, really."

"Are you hungry?" Bobby asked.

"I hadn't really thought about it," she said. "But now that you mention it . . ."

Bobby turned, stuck his head back through the kitchen

doors. "José," he called. "See what you can get started. I'll come back and help in a minute."

"Gotcha," José responded.

The bells chimed again and a couple more people walked in. Each had a similar expression to Marcia's—something like confusion. *Like they know they're supposed to be here,* Sarah thought, *but aren't exactly sure where "here" is.*

Sarah went to the door, opened it, and looked outside. The cold air hit her like a brick of ice. Down the street, she saw more of them coming, walking back slowly, as if just strolling randomly in this direction. But she recognized all of them. They were just about the only people on the street, and they were all headed toward her.

When they reached the door, she held it open, and tried to greet each one by name. "Hi, Pat," she said. "Terry. Hello, Elizabeth. Hi, Linda." They gave her blank looks, or forced smiles, but none of them seemed quite sure who she was.

As the parade wound down, Sarah went back to the kitchen to find Bobby working with José on a vat of spaghetti. Bobby was watching a simmering pot of meat sauce.

She sniffed the air. "You couldn't use a vegetarian sauce?"

"Hey, they need protein," Bobby argued.

"There are other sources of protein," she said. "Anyway, let's not get into a dietary debate now. I need to talk to you." She cocked her finger at him and he followed her from the kitchen. She led him toward a quiet spot near the hallway.

"I don't know what's going on, but something freaky has happened to these people," she said.

"You mean, in addition to them losing their homes and loved ones?"

"I mean today, just now. They act like they don't even know who I am."

"But every one of them has been here before, Sarah," Bobby pointed out. "They've all met you."

"That's what I mean, nimrod. They've met me, but they're looking at me like they have no memory of it. Something's happened to them, some kind of mass hypnosis or something."

"Have you tried asking them?"

"Not yet. I thought maybe we should both talk to a couple of them, so one of us doesn't miss something."

"Okay. Want to do it in the office, or what?"

"I'll see if Jennifer will let us," Sarah said. "Be right back."

She started toward the office, then stopped, looked back over her shoulder at Bobby. "You didn't put any pork in that sauce, did you? Or organ meat?"

"It's all beef," Bobby assured her.

"Probably rain forest beef," she said with a sneer. She went into the administrative office.

Ten minutes later, they sat in the office with Tyrone. He was a tall African-American man in his late fifties, with a grizzled salt-and-pepper beard and shoulders as wide as a city bus. He'd worked construction until a falling I-beam broke his back. After that, he'd become addicted to painkillers, and, unable to find steady employment, had gone through a number of part-time jobs. He ended up unemployable, and on nights he couldn't get into a shelter he slept on top of a subway grate. He was big enough that he was allowed to sleep pretty much wherever he wanted, and the other homeless people in his neighborhood didn't object when he took the best spots.

"I remember a man comin' in here," Tyrone was saying. "No, it was two folks, two men. They talked to Ms. Stone for a minute—" naming the tall silver-haired woman who had recently begun volunteering and who, Sarah noted, had not been seen since these people left the shelter. "—and then one of them, he got up in front of the room, right where Jennifer or Elaine stand when they want to talk. This guy, he said something about how he had an opportunity for us to earn a little spendin' cash, we wanted to go with him. Well," he chuckled, a low, throaty laugh. "Figure that went for most of us, so we followed him out the door."

He tapped his temple with one finger. "I can't quite recollect where we followed him to, though. Or what we did, once we got there. But I looked in my pockets, just a few minutes back, and I can tell you what ain't there. Spendin' cash. Not a nickel."

"I'm sorry you were used like that," Sarah said. "Without getting the payment you were promised. If you can remember anything about where you were taken, I swear we'll collect on that promise."

"It was a building," Tyrone said. "Like an office or some such. But I can't remember any more than that. It all just goes dark, until I was almost back here. First thing I can recall after that was seein' you standin' there in the doorway, Ms. Sarah."

"Do you feel any different?" Bobby asked. "You weren't hurt or anything, were you?"

"My arm feels pretty sore, now you mention it," Tyrone replied. "Like someone punched it pretty hard."

"Can we see?" Sarah asked him.

"I'm a little shy about takin' my shirt off in front of you, Ms. Sarah," he said. "I ain't had a real shower or nothing for a while."

"We can probably get you a shower tonight," she said. "I'll talk to Jennifer, see if we can't get showers and beds for everyone who went with those men."

"That'd be nice."

"In the meantime, if you want to just show me your arm," Bobby said, "I'm sure Sarah won't mind stepping into the hall."

"I can do that," Sarah said. She rose from her chair, went out the door, and shut it gently behind her. When she was gone, Tyrone pulled off his coat, then peeled a sweater over his head, and started to unbutton his ragged blue work shirt.

A few minutes later, Bobby met Sarah in the hallway. "He's been injected with something," he said. "Or had blood drawn, one of the two. He's got a needle mark right here." He indicated the inside of his elbow.

"And it's fresh?"

"He says it is," Bobby replied. "Still sore. Must have just happened."

"Let's talk to some of the others."

"I'm with you."

"Needle guns, Sunbursts, plasma blasters—this stuff is all I.O. issue, Mr. Lynch," Caitlin said. "But it's all over the streets of New York, and God knows where else."

Jack Lynch sat in his desk chair, which he'd swiveled to look out the window at the city beyond. The view from here was staggering, the kind that people paid vast amounts of money to claim for themselves.

Lynch was paying it, too. He didn't mind. Money was only good if you spent it, and he'd cheated death too many times to want to hang onto any. He could keep the kids in some degree of comfort here in an opulent Manhattan hotel suite, keep them supplied with whatever equipment they needed, and oversee their work.

Not like he'd done before, though. In the early days of the team he'd been coach, cheerleader, owner, and medic. They were all dealing with being kids, having incredible powers they could barely comprehend, and being on the lam from International Operations grunts working for those who had caused their powers to manifest in the first place.

Gen^{13} were the sons and daughters of Team 7 members, of which Lynch was one. His own son, Bobby, still used the name Lane—one of his many foster families—instead of taking Lynch for his own. Caitlin and Roxy were half-sisters, daughters of Alex Fairchild with two different mothers.

They'd all been taken away to a secret installation in the California desert, trained, and experimented on, in an attempt to bring their hidden powers to the fore. And it had worked. The kids became superheroes. But Ivana Baiul, who ran Project Genesis, didn't care much for the "heroes" aspect of that. She wanted the kids to work for her, super-soldiers or super-enforcers of her will. They rebelled against that idea, and her, and went on the run. I.O.'s Keepers chased them as long as they could, but Lynch managed to hide them out in La Jolla, California, for a while. Then they went on the move again, to the Florida Keys, and finally here to New York.

And Lynch had decided, moving here, that he would step back. The kids had matured. They needed to find their own ways in the world, and not look to him for all the answers. He didn't have them anyway.

He remained available in an advisory role, and once in a while he went into action with them when it was warranted. But mostly, he stood back, observing, keeping tabs on them and on the greater world picture, pointing them in the direction of trouble or injustice when he could.

He'd brought enough grief into the world. Through these kids, he thought maybe he could make some of it right.

"Mr. Lynch?" Caitlin said again.

"Sorry," he replied. "Looking at the view."

"Where do you think these weapons are coming from?"

He turned the chair slowly back to face his den. Caitlin sat on a visitor's chair, her impossibly long legs folded under her. Manifesting her powers, in her case, also meant undergoing a physical transformation that changed her from being a slight, near-sighted, frail girl into a tall, voluptuous, muscular goddess.

Behind her, Grunge leaned on the door jamb. He wore a black tee-shirt over his thickly muscled chest and broad shoulders. His straight hair hung down into his eyes, but it didn't seem to bother him.

Roxy sat on a couch nearby. Her tight sweater was a

magenta shade that nearly matched the streaks in the front of her black hair, with blue jeans.

"Yeah," Roxy said. "Because, like, if we're going to go up against people with weapons that can kill us, I'd rather just stay home and watch TV or something."

"A kitchen knife could kill you, Rox," Grunge pointed out.

"It'd have to get close enough," Roxy said. "Fat chance. But someone with an I.O. plasma cannon could take me out from the other end of Fifth Avenue when I'm coming out of Tiffany's."

"Like you shop there," Grunge said.

"I browse."

Lynch cleared his throat, and the conversation stopped. "Remember when Max Faraday went insane, with his Divine Right power?"

"And threatened to reshape all of reality to fit his image of what it should be?" Grunge asked. "Hard to forget."

"As part of that reshaping," Lynch went on, "he shut down International Operations. The organization was one of the few institutions that understood what he was, that knew about the Creation Equation. I.O. might have been able to rally its forces and stop him. Unlikely, but they had a better shot than the FBI or the CIA or any of the other alphabet soups in D.C. He couldn't have that, so he willed the dismantling of the entire organization, office by office."

"Right," Caitlin said. "And it hasn't been put back together. Congress wasn't willing to fund it anymore, right?"

"One of the only intelligent decisions Congress has made in the last decade," Lynch replied. "But when those offices shut down, there were people—lots of them—put out of work. Some of those people were angry about it. And some of those angry people had access to information, equipment, even weaponry."

"Weren't there any precautions—" Caitlin began.

Lynch cut her off. "Sure there were. But they assumed

that, if the agency ever were shut down, there would be some time. It takes months, years, even, to wind down a government bureaucracy like that. No one anticipated that it could be done overnight by an insane pizza-delivery boy with the power to alter the fabric of reality."

"Some people just don't think ahead," Grunge observed. "Me, I've never trusted 'em. Come to your house, who knows what's inside that flat box?"

"Yeah, that's usually what comes to mind when I order pizza too, Grunge," Roxy said. "Who worries about whether or not they remembered the pepperoni or the extra 'shrooms? They're just as likely to go berserk and kill you with a razor-studded pie as they are to get your order right."

"Hey, I don't make fun of your phobias," Grunge said. "Well, yeah, maybe I do. But that doesn't mean you have to make fun of mine."

"If I could go on," Lynch said.

"Sure, dude," Grunge offered.

"Thanks. The point is, ever since I.O. was shut down, the world's black markets have been awash in former I.O. secrets and technology. There hasn't been an intelligence garage sale like this since the KGB went belly up in the '80s. I'm not surprised that we're seeing I.O. armaments on the streets now. I'm surprised it took so long."

"But you'd think some of the people using it wouldn't be able to afford the prices it must get," Caitlin said.

"True," Lynch agreed. "It must be going for cheaper than I'd expected. I thought it would fetch top dollar, but I guess not, if street gangs are getting their grubby mitts on it."

"Maybe they make it up in volume," Grunge suggested.

"Do you know who or where the likeliest sources for these guns would be, Mr. Lynch?" Caitlin asked. "If you were a New York street gang, where would you go to buy this stuff?"

Lynch turned to his computer, punched a couple of

keys, scrolled down with his mouse. "I can give you a few names," he said. "I don't know anything for sure, but I can point you in some possible directions. You'll have to do some legwork, though."

"Kat's got the legs for it," Grunge said with a laugh.

Roxy sighed. "If you were closer, I'd slap you. Just consider yourself slapped."

"Ow," Grunge said. "Feel better?"

"Much."

Lynch sent his list to the printer next to his desk. *This is good,* he thought. *That kind of weaponry shouldn't be on the street. If the kids can clean this up, that'll be one black mark erased from the permanent record of my soul.*

If I live another thousand years, I should be able to get the record clean.

Wager stared at the array of screens before him with breathless anticipation. His test subject sat in a steel reinforced chair in a sterilized chamber. Joe Monteleone had been stripped naked and scrubbed, every hair removed from his body, every potential contaminant flushed from his system. He had been fed with bursts of high caliber nutrients, he had endured stoically as subliminal texts were hard-wired into his consciousness to ensure that he possessed all the knowledge necessary to undertake his mission.

He now knew the names and locations of every crimelord in New York City. He knew their every proclivity, their routine habits, their endearing qualities, and most importantly, he knew how to get to them.

All of them.

And now he was ready. He sat in the white chair, his legs and wrists restrained.

Wager stared at the man. Joe was scrawny and weak, despite the stimulation and strengthening his muscular-skeleton had already received. Wager secretly despaired that the man would not survive the injection.

Of course, he knew the odds; he understood that there

was currently a fifty-seven percent probability that the subject would not only live, but thrive.

Still, he couldn't relax. He was tense—and excited.

He watched as one of his white-robed, blue-masked doctors approached the man, his *property*, with a syringe. The doctor looked up to one of Wager's many cameras, nodded, and plunged the needle in the man's arm.

The test subject flinched at what Wager imagined to be the brief sting of the injection, but, other than that, revealed no emotion as the Gen-Active serum was delivered into his system.

Wager studied the subject's face. He used a digital controller to zoom in.

At this close range, it became clear that Joe was fighting to rein in his fear, and that gave Wager some assurance—as well as a perverse thrill. Wager studied Joe's face and saw the muscles contract and expand. Joe suddenly shuddered and began to quake as if G-forces had sprung up from nowhere and were now tearing at him.

Wager pulled back the digital enhancer, returning his view to a full body shot. He didn't want to miss any of what was happening. He had to understand the full scope of the process to which he was still debating on subjecting himself.

Before his eyes, the test subject changed—and while the metamorphosis occurred, Wager felt like a god.

Joe bucked against the restraints as every gram of fat in his body turned to muscle, then even more muscle manifested seemingly from nowhere. His forehead bulged and the veins in his arms, legs, and temples rose up from his flesh and looked as if they were going to explode.

He became something incredible.

His skinny arms and legs mushroomed into Olympian proportions. His torso became broad and incredibly defined.

The hair grew back on his head and in other regions.

He became . . . *younger*. Virile, strong, and—

The restraints burst as he threw his head back and screamed!

Just then, a well manicured, feminine hand reached before Wager and tapped the control panel in his lap with a single lovely finger. The image before Wager froze. A time code appeared before the frozen digital recording.

"He was quite entertaining, wasn't he?" Suzanne Sawyer asked.

Wager looked over his shoulder at her. If it had been anyone else, he would have had them executed immediately. Yet there was something about Suzanne, the proximity of her, the smell, even the taste, at least, as he imagined the taste to be, that made him forgive the intrusion.

He hadn't realized until now how he had been panting, his face flushed, his every nerve tingling and alive.

Suzanne bent low, her blouse falling open to reveal her generous cleavage. "That will be you. The final tests are in. There are no signs of rejection. And his power readings are—impressive."

She turned and hopped up on the control board, crossing her long legs, which were revealed by her short skirt. "When will you take your injection?"

"When I feel the odds are with me," Wager said. "The subject hasn't been field tested yet."

"The subject," Suzanne mused. "I'm sure we can come up with a more colorful field name for him... What about Cipher? It works on several different levels."

Wager nodded. "Very well."

"I think things are going to change for us both very soon," Suzanne said. "I just finished briefing Cipher. He's been outfitted and waits only for you to engage the vid and audio links. Then the real fun can begin."

Wager tapped a button on his control panel and the digital recording of Cipher's creation was relegated to storage.

"It's interesting," Suzanne said.

"What is?"

"You. I understand that your basic preoccupation is domination and submission, but there is more. Your desire to own another human being, to have every aspect of that person's life under your control. It must be quite a thrill."

Wager raised a single eyebrow. "What are you getting at?"

She smiled and leaned back a little. It was a practiced, yet still perfectly effective and provocative move. "Nothing. Except that there is something to be said for voyeurism."

"I'm not a voyeur," Wager said uncomfortably. "I have to know what's going on at all times."

"You like it," she said in a breathy whisper. "Why do you think I'm drawn to you?"

"The healthy paycheck and stock options."

She shrugged and tossed her hair. "Have you ever considered that exhibitionism is the flip side of voyeurism?"

Wager was . . . intrigued.

"Come on. Do you honestly think I'm not aware of the microfilament cameras in my bedroom, and that I couldn't have put them out if there were things I hadn't wanted you to see?"

"Things," Wager said, gripping the arms of his chair and shifting around. He thought about the body he would soon possess. The beauty of it, the power . . .

"Like that night with that young guard or all the other times on my own—"

"Two," Wager corrected. "There were two guards."

She smiled. "How I remember. Yessss. Just checking to see if you did." Her hands brushed his console. It jumped slightly in his lap. "Do you save all your favorite moments?"

He swallowed hard and didn't answer.

"Good." She leaned down and only barely brushed her lips with his. "To the future."

Wager busily engaged the vid and audio links hooking him to Cipher. "To the present."

• • •

Joe Monteleone studied the chiseled, godlike being staring back at him from the silver mirror in the mission launch room.

He almost didn't recognize himself.

And he felt damn sure that Margaret, Elyse, and Joe Jr. wouldn't recognize him at all. At least, not from any stray video footage that might be picked up by one of the news stations or some reporter with a 35mm in his pocket. He was going to be visible. Major league visible.

That was part of the plan.

Drawing a deep breath, Joe ran his hand over the emblem on his chest—a snake eating its own tail. He looked at his silver and black gloves, the visor and headgear he wore, the armlets circling his biceps and thighs, the boots and gleaming trunks. He truly looked like something out of one of his son's comic books.

"I'm ready," Joe said.

He waited. There was no reply. He tapped his earpiece and waited. There was still no reply.

The launch room was a small, deserted ruin of an office. It reminded Joe of something from a '40s detective movie. There were gadgets hidden everywhere, but at a glance, it just looked like another hollowed out section of this soon-to-be-condemned length of brownstones.

"Wager?" Joe asked. "Hey, is anyone—"

"Speak when you are spoken to, not before," came a familiar voice. The voice of his "master."

He took that voice very seriously and fell silent.

Joe was kept waiting, in the room, in perfect stillness, for eighteen and a half minutes. He knew it was precisely that long because of an array of digital readouts in the interior of his visor.

Wager was teaching him a lesson.

"You have been informed that your code name will be Cipher," Wager said at last.

Cipher waited.

"Respond."

"I was told the name was pending your approval, sir."

"You know what a cipher is, don't you?"

"There are several meanings."

"But only one applies to us. And that is, 'a person or thing of no value or importance.' You are easily replaced. Keep that in mind."

Cipher nodded. "Yes."

"Now you will go about your function. Engage your cloaking abilities."

Summoning his power, Cipher felt his nerves jangle a little as his body—and costume—faded into his surroundings.

"Exit the room."

There was no door. Nor did there need to be one. Cipher walked through the walls, into the glaring sunlight of mid-day.

Three people walked *through* him without ever noticing that he was there.

"Proceed to Milo Face's domain."

Cipher walked a dozen blocks and soon stood before the entrance to a posh hotel.

"Make your presence known."

Allowing himself to become tangible and visible, Cipher walked to the curb, picked up a taxi, shook it twice on its side to dislodge its screaming passengers, then hurled it toward the front door.

The doorman leaped out of the way as the cab smashed through the double glass doors. A half-dozen armed security men had appeared before the mangled cab had even stopped bouncing in the lobby, and before all the shattered glass had stopped falling like snow in a Christmas globe.

"Deal with them," Wager commanded. "Non-lethal force."

Cipher broke several bones and left all the guards unconscious in less than eight seconds. He was quick, as well as strong.

"The penthouse. Go there."

Cipher entered the hotel. He ignored the screams. A

guy in a black suit drew down on him and unloaded a full clip from an automatic into Cipher.

The bullets were trapped by his dampening field, and fell harmlessly to the ground. They wouldn't have done him harm in any case, but they might have injured the equipment linking him to his benefactor.

He was the only one to take the elevator. It stopped one floor short. Cipher reached *through* the control panel and manipulated the circuitry to prompt the elevator to continue on its journey.

When he reached the penthouse, he held his head high, impassively, just like the Terminator. That was his role in this. Stoic. Unmovable.

He played the part well.

Tendrils of searing white force reached out for him as the doors opened. Cipher became intangible with plenty of time to spare.

"Excellent," Cipher said.

Cipher stepped into the penthouse apartment of one of New York's leading crimelords. He didn't even look at the guards who were leveling the precious antiques and setting fire to priceless original paintings in their efforts to fry him with various bits of I.O. weaponry they had acquired.

He moved through them like an avenging spirit, become tangible only long enough to disarm the various guards.

"Hurt them some. I like when the bones crack," Wager said.

Cipher obliged. He tried not to think of these people as human. When they had passed him on the street, they had certainly not seen him in those terms. They were obstacles, nothing more. Unpleasant objects to be moved out of the way so that he could perform his function. Nothing more.

Still . . . The smell of urine as one relieved himself, screaming at a bone jutting from his bleeding arm, feces from one he had all but crippled with a single blow, the salt of tears from another who begged for his life, unaware that Cipher was not here to kill anyone.

Though...

What would he do if that became part of the deal? He hadn't thought of that when he had made his agreement.

"Tell them what you want," Wager said.

"I want to see Milo Face," Cipher said. "I know he's here."

A shower of bullets came at him now, along with screams and the blasts of a pair of sawed-off shotguns.

All useless.

He brushed aside the spent slag and turned to his new assailants. The pale, moon-shaped face of his target was now in full view. Milo Face wore a silk kimono and was surrounded by three heavily armed and startlingly underdressed Asian women.

"Oh, now it's going to become tiresome," Wager said. He sighed in Cipher's ear. "Let them exhaust themselves."

All three women launched themselves at Cipher, punching and kicking. He didn't become intangible. Instead, he allowed the field to take every hit.

Soon, the women stood panting, sweating running down their faces.

"Tell them why you're here," Wager said.

"I'm here on behalf of Wager," Cipher said. "From this minute forward, you will give a tithe to Wager. Forty percent of your gross from legal and illegal activities. Your books will be open for our inspection at all times, and agents will be placed..."

Milo Face brought up a handgun and emptied it at Cipher's head.

Once the noise had ceased, Cipher continued. "Agents will be placed in all of your corporate holdings and they will be assimilated into your protection, arms, and drug operations. This will ensure that you are unable to follow your nature and attempt to renege on our deal. Respond."

The crimelord stared at Cipher with dark, beady eyes. He glanced to his companions. All three women shook their heads. They, at least, seemed to understand the futility of resistance.

"Show him why he must comply," Wager said. "No violence."

Cipher became intangible and walked through Milo Face. The man went into a hysterical fit.

Then Cipher became invisible, and whispered threats in the crimelord's ear. He spoke of things Milo Face was certain no one knew. He made it clear that the man would never feel safe, never know peace, unless he gave in to Wager's every demand.

Finally, he said the words that pained him. "The boy in Texas. We know about him. What does his life mean to you? Would you like him to go through existence paralyzed? Or worse?"

Face was on his knees, in tears. On the verge of breaking.

"Very good," Wager whispered. "I had calculated a ninety-eight percent probability that this tack would be successful. Finish it."

Cipher hesitated. Then he said, "Or he could disappear. You would never know if he's alive or dead. You would never be able to find him, never help him."

Face broke into wracking sobs.

"Respond," Cipher commanded.

The crimelord crawled toward the bedroom. Cipher fully materialized and followed him. The man revealed a hidden safe behind the wall of a closet, opened it, and began to pile money and jewelry into a bag.

With trembling hands, he gave it to Cipher.

"Petey will be all right now, won't he?" the man asked. "Tell me. Please!"

"This is the beginning," Cipher said. "Only that. Respond."

The crimelord hung his head. "I understand. I understand. I . . . obey."

Cipher turned invisible and intangible, taking the bag with him. He was on the street soon after.

In his ears, he heard Wager's laughter.

In his mind, he heard a father's frightened sobs.

CHAPTER 7

Sarah and Bobby had questioned everyone who had been taken from the Mary McCardle Shelter and experimented on—everyone except Mr. Joe.

They sat on the steps behind the shelter, Bobby staring at the graffiti covering the rear walls of the dilapidated office building just ahead. A wild dog, a Rottweiler, prowled around the garbage dump. He came dangerously close to a sleeping bag bearing an old woman known only as the Lady. She refused to ever enter the shelter, and always spoke to the volunteers as if they were the hired help at a posh restaurant.

The volunteers had often remarked that it was a miracle she had never frozen to death out there. But she had always been healthy.

Bobby noticed the animal and loosed a bolt of flames in its direction, searing the dumpster. It whined and ran off.

The Lady turned over in her sleeping bag, seemingly oblivious.

"It was simply *hungry*," Sarah said. "It would never have attacked her."

"Whatever," Bobby said. His knees were up by his chin.

"I have an understanding of the natural world. I know about these things."

"Fine."

They sat in silence. Finally, Sarah put her hand on

Bobby's arm. "This is about Mr. Joe, isn't it?"

He pulled away from her and stood up. Stretching, he looked away from her and didn't answer.

"We don't know that he was one of the people used in the testing," Sarah said. "He's probably at another shelter."

"I've phoned them."

"You what?"

"I called them. All of them. And visited every one of them within two miles of here. No one's seen him."

Sarah nodded. She had to hide her delight that Bobby had finally taken such an interest in the well-being of someone other than himself. "Maybe if we work together, we can find him. José mentioned something about him having a family somewhere. We can—"

A sudden scraping from off to her right made her stop. Sarah and Bobby turned to see the Lady approach. Her heavy boots scraped as she dragged her weak left leg behind her.

She was in her sixties, and wore sweaters layered five deep, discarded baggy running pants, and a pair of mittens with the tips of each index finger worn through. Her hair was white and frizzy, her cheeks rose red. Her eyes were dark, almost violet. And her lips were pulled back in a smile that might have revealed wisdom—or madness.

"You won't find Mr. Joe that way," the Lady said. "Why don't you ask your boss?"

Sarah frowned. How could this woman know about Mr. Lynch? And why would she think he had any idea where to find one homeless man in New York?

"You don't have to pretend with me," she said in a raspy voice. "I've seen. I know what you are."

Bobby looked at her sadly. "And what's that."

She leaned in close. Her breath stank. "Seraphim. Angels."

"Really," Sarah said, suddenly very uncomfortable. "We're not—"

"Fire comes from this one's hands," she said, pointing

at Bobby. "Winds from yours. I've seen it."

Sarah and Bobby exchanged worried glances.

"Don't think I'd tell on you," the Lady said. "I know the difference between minions of the dark and the light. I've fallen victim to the dark angel Sabnack, who causes the bodies of mortals to decay. The only man I cared about was taken by Dantalian, who changes the thoughts of mortals from good to evil. And I've struggled with Zepar, the fallen seraph who brings women to the brink of madness and beyond." She hung her head. "And I've seen children sacrificed on these streets to Moloch, who revels in any mother's tears. He had mine, damn him."

Sarah tugged on a strand of her long hair, twisting it uncomfortably. "We're really not—"

The Lady's eyes gleamed as she looked up suddenly. "I've been chosen as messenger. As herald to those chosen to uphold the light!"

"What kind of message?" Bobby asked uncertainly.

"The family name is Monteleone. The man you seek is Joseph Monteleone." She fished in her pockets. "He was good and kind. He gave me this to watch over while he was gone."

She pulled out a crumpled newspaper clipping. It was a listing of Joseph's marriage to Margaret, fifteen years earlier.

"Mr. Joe looks so young, so healthy," Bobby said. He was amazed.

The Lady smiled. "The will of the light has been worked through me. I am truly and heartily blessed."

She turned and went back to her sleeping bag.

Sarah tapped Bobby's arm. "Come on. There's enough information here for us to get started with. The library's open until late."

"All right," he said, staring after the old woman. He shook his head. "Angels."

"It depends on how you look at things, I suppose," Sarah said. "Maybe in the right light, almost anyone can look like an angel."

TIME AND CHANCE

• • •

Three full hours were taken up by the trip to the library, but by the time Sarah and Bobby left, they had the address of Margaret Monteleone's sister, Illiana Pruit. A cab took them to Long Island, and a small town called Massapequa.

"This here town's famous," the cab driver said. He was bald and pierced in every visible location. "This is the home of the Baldwins and the Guttenbergs. You want the best pizza in the world, I'll take ya to Pappalardo's, they's gots signed pictures from Steve when he was doin' them *Police Academy* movies and all. Y'know, people forget he did some classy stuff, like *Cocoon* and *The Day After*. And that guy, y'know, the guy, from the movie, that *Born on the Fourth of July* guy, he was from here. I could take you by his old place. They didn't shoot the movie here, though, said it didn't look right no more, went to somewhere in Texas for Long Island, you believe that?"

Right now, that pizza sounded awfully good to Bobby. He had settled in the back with Sarah for the long drive, and had been able to tune out most of the driver's chatter. The presence of Sarah's hand, firmly held in his, her hair so close, her body . . .

It was a little like heaven.

Soon, the cab pulled up before a broken down two-story house. It was lime green with brown shutters, desperately in need of a paint job. There were two broken windows and the porch looked ready to collapse. They had traveled through several middle class neighborhoods to get here, but it was clear this little side street had seen better times.

"Wait for us," Sarah told the driver.

He giggled and looked at his meter. Bobby looked at the amount they had racked up and figured the return trip would pretty much make the driver's day.

"Heck, yeah!" the driver said. "And you folks, you take your time." He settled back and pulled a romance novel from beneath his copy of the *New York Times*. It was Tina Wainscott's *Dreams of You*.

As they approached the front door, a fifty-year-old woman in a red and white business suit came burst from the front door, a sign with a wooden stake attached to it in her hands. Bobby and Sarah had to leap back to avoid being impaled!

"Excuse me," Bobby said.

The woman screeched as she looked up finally and saw that she was not alone. Then she composed herself. "May I help you?"

Bobby took in the realty sign in her hands and felt his shoulders drop. "We were looking—"

"For a fixer-upper," Sarah interrupted. "We're getting married soon."

"Well, the place isn't really ready to be shown," the woman said. She fished a card out of her jacket pocket. Her picture was on it, along with her name, Rose McClendon. "But if you can come back in a week—"

Bobby looked around at the other houses on the block. Several had "For Sale" signs. "Are you handling all of these?"

She set the post down and looked at Bobby with greater interest. "All?"

Bobby wished out his wallet and took out one of the cards his father had given him. "We're representatives of Bryce Electronics. It's my father's company, actually. We're looking for a prime location to build a housing community for our top execs. Somewhere exciting and unusual. With character. History."

Rose flushed as she studied the uptown address on the card. "Really?"

Sarah looked at Bobby and crossed her arms over her chest. She looked impressed by Bobby's line. "Yes, really."

Bobby frowned, pulling slightly on his stubbly goatee. "Of course, what we'd need is to speak with someone who can supply us with information. The names and status of all the property holders from the street entrance to the cul-de-sac back there. Even the ones who've recently moved."

"Oh?" Rose asked nervously. "Why so?"

"We would like to know *why* they moved. Fear of crime, gangs, vandalism, perhaps..."

"No!" she said quickly. "Oh, no, nothing like that. Why, the family that was living here just came into an inheritance. The owner, Illiana Pruit, just bought a condo in Boca Raton, and her sister is living at the Regent Hotel in Manhattan. Her and her adorable children. I can get all that information together for you, there are no worries of the kind you mentioned, none, this area just needs a face-lift, that's all. I can show you some of the other houses, if you'd like."

Bobby shook his head. "No, we've got your card. I just wanted to see the area for myself. I'll make a report and get back with you."

"Do!" Rose cried in a panic bordering on ecstasy. "Oh, please, do!"

When they returned to the cab, the driver was weeping openly, his tears staining the pages of his paperback. He reached for the meter. "Lemme just finish this chapter. I'll turn off the meter and everything."

Bobby sighed and nodded. Well, he'd shown *some* backbone and ingenuity today. No sense over-exerting himself.

Sarah leaned over and kissed his cheek, then nuzzled close.

This wasn't like heaven, it *was* heaven. No wonder Mr. Joe hadn't come back to the shelter. He was rich now!

The drive back seemed to take a third of the time they had spent getting to the island, even with traffic. Bobby and Sarah listened as the driver talked about the plot of his novel and how much he was hoping to go to the Romance Writers of America conference this year. He had two manuscripts to publishers and was keeping his fingers crossed.

"Sure, there's a cab driver in both of them," the guy said. "Publicity platform, that's what they call it in publishing. Hey, here's this cabbie writing about cabbies.

They can put me on *Good Morning America, Howard Stern*, whatever. The main thing is the message, y'know. *Love is everything, and even better when you can share it.*"

"That one of yours?" Sarah asked.

"Naw!" the driver said. "That's Wainscott. But man, she sums it up."

Bobby leaned in and kissed Sarah. She kissed him back, softly, sensuously.

It sure was the message, Bobby thought. It sure was . . .

They got to the Regent Hotel and put the fare and the driver's tip on one of the five platinum Visas Bobby carried. The driver nearly cried again when he saw how generous Bobby had been.

Soon they were in the lobby of the posh hotel, ringing the Monteleones on the desk phone. Bobby gave his name to the woman who answered, and explained that he was a friend of her husband's.

The line went silent for an instant, then the woman gave him her suite number and told him to come up. She sounded worried and excited at the same time.

In the elevator, Bobby told Sarah about the exchange.

"Maybe she thinks you're disadvantaged, like her husband used to be," Sarah said. "From the street."

"I should have mentioned the shelter. Our work there."

Sarah grinned and kissed him again.

"What was that for?"

She hugged him. "*Our* work."

The elevator took them to nearly the top floor. The doors opened and Bobby led Sarah to the Monteleone's suite.

"I can't wait to see Mr. Joe again," Bobby said. "I bet he was planning on coming back to the shelter all cleaned up and—"

Before they reached the door, it opened and a small, anxious woman appeared. She wore a peach colored designer dress and her hair and make-up had been done by top professionals. Her jewelry glittered.

Her lovely brown eyes looked tired—yet lit with hope. "Have you seen my husband? Please tell me he's all right!"

With those words, Bobby felt the comfortable little world he had built up in his mind for his friend collapse in on itself. Whatever good fortune had recently come to the Monteleones, it had nothing to do with Mr. Joe. Nor had he benefited from it.

He explained the situation, leaving out the bits about the homeless being taken away for some kind of bizarre testing.

Margaret Monteleone's petite frame trembled, and she looked away, taking a moment to put herself back together before letting Bobby and Sarah in so they could talk some more. Her children were in the living room. A nine year-old boy sat before a Play Station, while his older sister paced back and forth with a cell phone in her hand. The boy wore commando camouflage pants, black boots, a black tee-shirt, and shades. His hair had been buzz cut. The teenager had a long and lithe body clad in tight jeans and a midriff baring white tank. Her blond hair spilled to the middle of her back.

"That's right, a dance academy, honest to *God*," the teenager said. "Can you believe this? It was some guy on my father's side who passed away. He left us—I don't know how much, but a lot. A real lot..."

The boy noticed Bobby instantly. The teenager barely even looked his way.

"Hey, you wanna see my new game?" the boy asked. "I'm Joe Jr. My dad's a secret agent, like in this game. You wanna see? You wanna?"

Bobby smiled and let the little guy show him the game while Sarah and Margaret talked.

"My dad had to go on a secret mission," Joe Jr. said. "That's what he told me the night he went away. He's gonna come back, though."

"Yeah, he is," Bobby said. His determination to find his friend returned. "You bet he is."

By the time they had left the suite and were riding the elevator down, there was a fire in Bobby's eyes that had nothing to do with his incredible powers.

"We're gonna find him," Bobby promised. "I don't care what it takes."

Sarah was holding his hand. She brought it to his lips and kissed it. "I believe you."

He felt the warmth of her affection rush through him.

They held each other as the elevator raced ever downward, delivering two angels fallen from the perfect grace of their belief, but stronger than ever because they had taken the journey together.

CHAPTER 8

Samuel Perrine lived in a high-walled estate on the Hudson River, about an hour north of the city. A wide driveway led up to the main house, which was built of red brick with what looked like freshly-painted white wooden trim. The expanse of lawn between the wall and the house was bright green, and looked recently mowed. The whole place was as neat and clean as an architectural magazine's spread—*you'd never believe,* Caitlin thought—*that anyone lives here.*

Well, maybe except for the three guards at the gate.

There was a wrought-iron gate, also painted white, spanning the driveway. Next to the gate stood a small guardhouse, a red brick structure with white-framed windows and an open door. Inside the guardhouse she could see two men in jeans and thick dark sweaters. They both carried automatic rifles.

A third guard stood just behind the gate, wearing a green parka and a Yankees cap. His rifle was held loosely in his hands, as if he wasn't expecting trouble from three kids. Caitlin had driven the rented car up here, had almost passed the house, then stopped, backed up, and turned straight into the driveway. The guard standing before them looked like he was just waiting to see what destination she'd ask directions to.

"We can take these mooks," Grunge said from the backseat.

"Sure we can," Caitlin said. "But we don't want to. They haven't done anything to us."

"Mr. L. said Perrine might not be too anxious to see unannounced visitors," Roxy reminded them. She rode shotgun, and had spent most of the trip fiddling with the radio as stations drifted in and out of range.

"Why didn't we make an appointment, again?" Grunge asked.

"Because Mr. Lynch said the only thing worse than showing up unannounced would be letting him know we were coming," Caitlin pointed out. "Perrine would be in Canada by now if he'd heard we were on our way."

"It's not like we want anything from him," Grunge said.

"We want information," Caitlin said. "For years, when he was with I.O., that was what he bought and sold. It's a valuable commodity in his world."

"You think these clowns with the guns are I.O.?"

"Probably," Roxy said. "They have that abused loser look to them. You can smell it on ex-International Operations goons. Like you can tell when leftover turkey's been in the fridge too long."

"Or a grilled cheese sandwich that you find behind the TV, and you're not sure if it's just dusty or if it's got actual mold on it, so you have to taste a corner of it," Grunge added.

"Okay, more than I wanted to know, big guy," Roxy told him.

"I help you kids?" the guard at the gate asked.

Caitlin thumbed her window button. As it slid down, she stuck her head out. "We're looking for Sam."

"You on the list?"

"I doubt it," she replied. "We're friends of a friend. He doesn't know we're coming."

"Then he ain't here."

Grunge opened the rear door, stepped out of the car. This move prompted both of the guys in the guardhouse to come outside. The sound of their weapons being cocked was loud in the rural silence. The only other noise was the car's engine idling.

"Grunge," Caitlin hissed. But it was too late. The move had been made.

"Look, dude," Grunge said. "We know he's here. We just wanna shoot the breeze with him for a coupla minutes, then we'll motor. No big."

"I told you, *dude*," the guard at the gate said. "He ain't home."

"You told us he lives here, which was stupid to begin with. Now you're gonna get out of our way before you get hurt."

The guard raised his weapon, turning it to point out through the gate. "I don't think I'm the one who's going to get hurt."

"C'mon, Rox," Caitlin whispered. "This could get ugly."

"When you're talking about Grunge," Roxy said, "it's almost a guarantee."

The girls left the car. The other guards brought their guns up. Caitlin could see the play of emotions across their faces—they were looking at three young people who seemed to be unarmed, and didn't really look like much of a threat. But could they take that chance? Most people would've turned tail as soon as the firepower came out, and been halfway back to Manhattan by now.

"I think you should listen to our friend," Roxy told them. "Just let Mr. Perrine know we're here, and we can all still be pals."

"We never were pals," the gate guard said. "We won't start now."

Grunge leaned back, casually, and touched the car with one hand. A wave of familiar sensations passed over him—a slight salty taste in his mouth, a faint ringing in his ears. His stomach flip-flopped once, then began to calm again. His heart sped up.

He was changing.

As everyone watched, Grunge went from being encased in flesh to being wrapped in automotive-grade steel. His molecules mimicked exactly the surface of the car he had just touched—so close that the most sophisticated lab equipment wouldn't be able to find a difference.

His skin wouldn't stop bullets fired point blank, he knew. But it might deflect any that came at him glancingly. And it would be disconcerting enough to the guards that their aim might be thrown off anyway.

"Oh," one of the guards said, his voice sounding unconcerned. "Gen-Actives." He flicked a switch on the stock of his gun, and the weapon began to hum. The other two guards followed suit.

Convertibles, Caitlin thought. *These guys are tougher than they look. If we were normal, their bullets would have been good enough, but they've just converted their guns to plasma mode.*

Nasty enough to kill us.

Mr. Lynch was right about this Perrine guy. He doesn't take chances.

Grunge held up his hands. "Listen, maybe we got the wrong house," he said.

"Yeah, and maybe you think you can just waltz in here and push people around," the guard came back. "Isn't that the way you super-clowns are?"

"We don't want any trouble, really," Caitlin said. "We just really need to talk to Mr. Perrine. Like we said, we're friends of an old friend of his from I.O."

"Then you should have made an appointment." The guard raised his weapon to firing height. Aimed it at Grunge. Squeezed the trigger.

And suddenly, the ground disappeared from beneath his feet. "Hey!" he shouted.

Roxy had used her anti-gravity powers to float him into the air before he realized what was happening. Without giving him a chance to regain his equilibrium, she tumbled him through the air and against the brick wall of the guardhouse.

Grunge took advantage of their momentary distraction

to lunge through the bars of the cast-iron gate and grab the barrel of another guard's weapon. He changed again, instantly taking on the properties of that weapon and effectively fusing himself to it. He yanked.

The gun came through the bars. The guard remained on the other side, face smashed against the cold iron. Grunge flicked one metal finger against the guard's chin, and the man fell sprawling to the drive.

Caitlin took out the third one with even less subtlety. She kicked the gate, in the center where the two sides were held together by a lock. The lock shattered and the gate swung on its hinges, into the third guard. He braced himself for the impact, but he wasn't counting on Caitlin's additional weight. Just before it hit him, she jumped onto the swinging gate and rode it.

The gate hit him with the force of a speeding truck. He was slammed off the driveway, winding up in the lush grass beyond.

Grunge reverted to his human form. "They got the guns, but they didn't get the training," he said. "These guys worked for Ivana, she would have had 'em canned before lunch."

Roxy was pushing the gate the rest of the way open when they were surprised by a voice from the guardhouse. It sounded electronic.

"Bravo," it said. "Well done."

Caitlin turned toward the brick structure. "Mr. Perrine?" she ventured.

"You said something about knowing a friend of mine?"

"His name's John Lynch," Caitlin said. "He's kind of our mentor."

"Lynch, sure," the voice said. "Come on up to the house."

"What about these guards?"

"I'll send some replacements down, have these guys hauled off to a medic," Samuel Perrine said. "Don't you worry about them."

• • •

"That was some nice work," Perrine said.

They were seated in a cozy office, decorated in a very masculine fashion, lots of leather and dark wood, mahogany, maybe, Caitlin thought. Perrine sat behind a heavy desk with a computer on top, a couple of telephones next to it, and a pad of legal paper to one side. A steaming mug of coffee sat on a coaster. He didn't seem to fit the office, as if he'd rented the house furnished. He looked like a scientist—thick glasses, an unruly shock of thin, graying hair, a small mouth with a weak chin. He was thin and short, with a bit of a potbelly and tiny hands that looked as if they'd be at home rummaging about inside a computer. The office said successful manly guy, but Perrine was techno-geek.

Of course, in an age where the richest people are techno-geeks, Caitlin reflected, *the two aren't necessarily mutually exclusive.*

"Sorry about the gate," Caitlin said.

"Don't worry about it," he assured her.

"Guards could be better," Grunge observed.

"They try," Perrine said. "Maybe they'll have learned something." He took a sip from the coffee cup on his desk, tilted back in his swivel chair, and regarded them. "I'm sure you didn't just come here to knock my guards around, though."

"You're right," Caitlin said. After quickly introducing the team, she got right down to business. "Here's what's happening. A lot of weaponry that used to belong to International Operations is winding up on the streets of New York. You know these weapons, right?"

"I invented a lot of 'em."

"That's what Mr. Lynch said. So you know that it's deadly stuff. That even I.O. agents were carefully trained before they were assigned it."

"That's true."

"But the kids using it now have had no training. Some of them have never even held a .22 revolver, and suddenly they've got a Stunburst or a plasma blaster or something like that in their hands."

Perrine massaged the bridge of his nose. "That's not what they were designed for."

"Right," Caitlin pressed. "But it's what's happening."

"I still don't see what this has to do with me."

Grunge lost his temper. "Dude, you're selling it!"

Perrine looked shocked. "You think I'm selling I.O. armament? That would be illegal. I'd have had to have stolen it in the first place."

"Mr. Lynch thought you were one of the most likely prospects," Caitlin added. "He said if there're I.O. guns out there, Samuel Perrine is part of the process."

"Just because I created weapons doesn't mean I deal in them," Perrine protested.

"Your guards have some pretty this-week firepower," Roxy said.

"Sure, I kept a few pieces," Perrine said.

"Look, Mr. Perrine," Caitlin said. "We aren't here to arrest you or anything like that. I happen to think selling arms is wrong. And selling arms to people who aren't checked out to use them is even worse. But what we want now is to get a line on who is buying and selling the guns to the kids in the city. If you are selling, I doubt you're dealing directly with the gang members. We want to dry up the supply in Manhattan, but to do that we have to find out who's moving the stuff. What you do to make a living now that I.O. is gone, however awful it is, is your own business."

"Ms. Fairchild, I assure you that I never expected any of my pieces to end up in the hands of children, or criminals of any age."

"Dude, you're heinous, but we can look past that," Grunge offered. "Just let us see your customer list or whatever so we can track down the guns."

Perrine threw his head back and laughed. "Customer lists?" he asked. "There are no customer lists, young man. Guns are a cash business, at least on the level you're talking. You don't keep records, you don't ask for I.D., you don't tell the government anything. You deliver the merchandise and you take the money. With luck, nobody pulls a gun on anyone else, and everyone goes home with what they came for."

"So you aren't denying it anymore?" Roxy asked.

"Why bother?" Perrine said. "You can't prove anything. You have no jurisdiction, no authority here. Yes, I may have sold some guns. I may have had access to I.O.'s New York armory in the last days. But I assure you, I thought those guns would wind up in the hands of law enforcement professionals, or people who wanted simply to defend their homes."

"Don't law enforcement professionals usually buy their weapons through legal channels?" Caitlin asked. "Never mind that. Here's what I really want. There's a weapon I saw the other night. It was firing energy blasts that practically ripped the walls of the building."

"Sounds like a Decimator," Perrine said. "Maybe a 3-aught-3. Not many of those around."

"That's what I thought," Caitlin said. "Even Mr. Lynch didn't know for certain. Do you think you'd remember who bought something as rare as that?"

Perrine steepled his fingers, touched his chin with them. "I might."

"Try really hard," Grunge said, a threatening edge in his voice.

"I know this much," Perrine said. "I didn't deal directly with the client."

"How does that work?" Roxy asked. "You just toss the gun out the window of your car, and he throws money at you?"

"Not quite," Perrine replied. "He had someone make the transaction for him. Two men. They seemed like underlings to me, no one of much importance in his operation."

"Operation? You think it's a big organization?" Caitlin asked.

"I don't know how big," Perrine said. "But I'd guess well-financed."

"Why?"

"Whoever was in charge was watching the whole thing, and giving instructions, via a highly sophisticated video link device. The men I dealt with were both wearing tiny cameras concealed in their clothing. They had microphones, and earpieces. It was apparent that their employer could see and hear everything that went on, as if he were right there in the room with us." Perrine smiled. "I wouldn't have minded getting a look at their gear, I can tell you that."

"You have a fondness for high tech, do you?" Caitlin asked him. "I.O. must have been your dream job."

"Even dreams have to end," Perrine said. "You always wake up sometime."

"The kids your weapons have killed won't," Grunge said. "I were you, I'd stop thinking so much about how to make them kill better and start worrying about the end results. These ain't video games you're making, man. People really die."

"I understand that, Mr. Chang."

Grunge gave him a look. "I hope you do," he said.

CHAPTER 9

Cipher had been given a partner. It was about the last thing he wanted or needed, but this was Wager's will, and he did not question the commands of his benefactor.

His partner's name was Jay. He was a trim, good-looking guy in an Armani suit with short-cropped black hair and dark blue eyes. Cipher stood beside him, invisible, intangible, unseen and unknown, while Jay "chatted" with a trio of equally well-dressed gangsters. They stood on the pier, near a garbage reclamation dump. A trawler drifted away on the sparkling waters, bearing waste that would be dumped at sea rather than stuck in another landfill.

Cipher knew that he should be paying attention to the words of his partner and the crimelords. But Wager had made their roles clear. Jay was the mouth, Cipher the muscle. If things got brutal, if Jay's very reasonable arguments did not win over the punks before them, it would be Cipher's turn to convince them.

His words were lost on Cipher. He looked to the sea and thought of his time on the water. The peace. The adventure. The sheer joy of being out there...

Shaking himself, he trained his gaze on Jay. His partner possessed a Rolex, Raybans, a cell phone, pager, and the other piece of standard equipment Wager's operatives carried: a titanium blade, electrified. Thin latex gloves that looked and felt just like skin and carried untraceable fingerprints. A Kevlar-style vest no thicker than a tee-shirt that could stop Teflon rounds if necessary. Two firearms, neatly hidden, one braced near his ankle, the other beneath his left armpit. Flesh colored stingers mounted in his palms—just by shaking his wrists, he could choose between any of ten drugs ranging from sedatives that would mellow his victim out to poisons that could paralyze instantly. With a handshake, he could deploy them.

Jay didn't seem like the typical thug. He was easygoing and friendly, a great listener, and a very intelligent man. He had a B.A. from Harvard Business and had minored in Psych. He could talk about any subject, and put anyone at ease.

Cipher's new partner could also make it very clear that when he spoke, he was laying down the law. Wager's law. The only law that mattered.

Jay had just finished dictating terms to the trio of neatly groomed crimelords and was waiting politely for a response.

All three laughed in his face. They sat on one side of a picnic table while Jay sat on the other.

Jay sighed.

Suddenly, Wager's voice thundered in Cipher's ears. "Make them understand!"

Cipher moved into action. He became visible and tangible, startling the crimelords. He didn't know their names. In an hour, he would barely even remember what they looked like. It hardly mattered to him. All he cared about was keeping track of their positions—and the positions of the snipers and other gunmen these three had stationed all around them.

"He's—he's *real*," the closest of the targets hissed. He was bald with a dragon tattoo that was mostly hidden by his dark suit, but the tips of its wings spread across his neck and the sides of his face. He wore a single gold earring and his teeth had been capped. His eyebrows had been shaved and his skin was perfectly tanned.

He grabbed at his lapel, as his to speak a command into a hidden microphone.

Cipher didn't give him the chance to speak. He smashed the picnic table with a single blow. He had struck it at precisely the spot Wager had commanded and with exactly the correct amount of force to achieve his goal. As Wager had predicted, bits of wood and steel exploded like shrapnel, missing Jay completely, seemingly miraculously, while slicing into the bodies of the crimelords.

The bald man who had been closest to Cipher lost two fingers, an ear, and sustained a scar that ruined his tattoo. The others were impaled in the stomach, legs, shoulders, and hands. Wager had predicted the odds of exactly these wounds to the last decimal.

Jay grabbed two of the wounded, dazed men and pulled them close, as shields. The snipers and other shooters wouldn't dare fire at him for fear of hitting their employers.

That meant the rest of the play was up to Cipher. He leaped at a stack of crates piled thirty feet high, landed on top of them, and took the gun from a sniper. Clubbing the man unconscious, he fired at six of the remaining ten gunmen spread out among the pier. His shots disarmed them with pinpoint accuracy, leaving a half-dozen wounded, bloody victims—all of whom would live.

Four left. The heavy-duty hitters.

Cipher casually dropped back down to the pier. His opponents came at him with precisely as little finesse as he had come to expect from their kind: untrained, undisciplined, probably Special Forces washouts. One carried a rocket launcher, another an I.O. Cobra-Covert Ion Gun, the last two simple bazookas. They came at him from four directions, firing all they had.

Cipher became intangible. The weapons fire found other targets. Explosions and carnage rocked the pier and a section of planking twenty feet across crumpled and fell into the water.

All of this had been anticipated, of course. Wager had predicted the exact moves of his opponents with ninety-eight percent accuracy.

TIME AND CHANCE

A stealth chopper swept in from over the roof of a manufacturing plant several thousand feet away.

"The other two percent," Wager said, amused. "Cipher, that looks like a pretty toy. I want it. Intact."

Cipher nodded. He looked to the bald crimelord. "Do you accept Wager's terms?"

The bald man shrieked a defiant command into his lapel. "Alpha! Alpha nine nine—"

Jay shot him.

The bald man sank back, his body relaxing in death. Cipher stared at his partner. He hadn't been prepared for this.

Yes, he had allowed the other four guards to kill one another, and he had hurt many people, but he hadn't considered how easily, how casually, this could lead to murder.

He also wondered what the hell was going on? Wager had given *him* the order to bring the chopper in . . .

Jay knelt beside the dead man and spoke two simple words into the bald man's lapel microphone. "Land it."

The chopper swept in closer, men stationed with high tech weapons out of its left flank. Jay turned his gun on the next crimelord.

The man blanched and grabbed his lapel. "Land it!"

The chopper circled once, then came in for a landing on the pier. It hovered slightly above the fragile wood planking. Cipher stared at the chopper. It was a beautiful machine.

"The pilot stays," Jay said. "Everyone else comes out, unarmed."

The crimelord repeated Jay's commands. The gunners and the co-pilot emerged from the sleek black chopper.

Jay hauled the wounded crimelord to his feet. The man moaned and clutched at his stomach, where shrapnel had struck him.

"Get the other one," Jay said.

Cipher grabbed the remaining crimelord. This guy was smaller than the one who'd been killed, with long blonde hair tied in a ponytail. His wounds weren't nearly as grievous as those of his associate.

Wager had fallen silent. At least to Cipher. Was he commanding Jay's actions?

They boarded the stealth chopper and were out of the area long before the authorities arrived. The chopper cruised over the waters, the surviving crimelords whimpering and clutching at themselves in pain.

Jay smiled and leaned in close to them. "Do you accept Wager as your personal savior?"

Both men acceded without any further encouragement. "Your friend's holdings, personal and business, legitimate and illegitimate, will be divided between you two. Any further discord and you die, your families die, everyone dies. Understood?"

The crimelords bowed their heads.

Three hours later, after two more "meetings," Cipher stood with Jay on the roof of one of Wager's new holdings.

Cipher wanted to ask Jay what had happened on the pier. But Wager had been talking in his ear ever since that incident, and hadn't sounded even mildly put out. So what right did he have to question?

The building was fifteen stories high. It housed the corporate offices of nearly sixty businesses, all subtly entwined, all formerly under the control of Luis Pendarro. That man was now a figurehead, and a grateful one, at that. At least he still had his life. News of the death at the pier had spread and was making their job much easier.

"It's beautiful up here, isn't it?" Jay asked.

Cipher felt the wind sweep across him. It carried a chill.

"I loved that ride in the stealth CPT-2099," Jay said. "There's nothing like flying if you really want to feel a sense of freedom. Of being in control. Your own man."

A soft breathing sounded in Cipher's ears.

Wager.

The breaths were short and hard. Cipher could almost feel the man's anger.

He waited.

"Throw him from the roof," Wager commanded.

Cipher felt a knot tighten in the pit of his stomach. He didn't move.

"You heard me," Wager said. "Do it."

A shudder passed through Cipher—and for a moment, he wasn't Cipher at all. He was Joe Monteleone. He was a man with free will, capable of making decisions, a human being with a past and a future.

And he was not a killer.

"I own you," Wager said. "That was our deal. I wished to own another human being, and you accepted those terms. That means you will do anything I say. Even take your own life if I so command it. If I'm forced to clarify this even one more time, or if I must repeat an order again, I will consider our contract null and void, and there will be consequences for all involved."

Joe Monteleone closed his eyes. *For all involved.*

His wife. His son and daughter...

Jay was still speaking when Cipher grabbed him. He screamed as he was thrown from the roof.

Cipher heard him screaming for several seconds more. Then the wind swallowed up his screams.

"This is not an organization in which initiative is rewarded," Wager said.

The lone man who stood on the roof, struggling to convince himself that he was Cipher, and only Cipher, grimly nodded.

The cab screeched to a stop behind a pack of stopped vehicles.

"Mother of God, did you see that?" the driver hollered.

Bobby and Sarah were in the backseat. They had been so intent on one another that they hadn't been aware of anything else.

"What?" Bobby asked.

"A guy just hit the sidewalk. Must of jumped out of a window or something." The driver was grizzled and overweight. He stank of sweat and cigarettes. His eyes were wide. "He just, like, exploded. Jeez, I mean, I think I saw his jaw go through the window across the street!"

Bobby and Sarah looked at each other.

" 'Course, in this town, it kinda makes you wonder if he fell or if he was pushed," the driver said. "Especially with everything that's been happening today. Friend of mine said some weird lookin' guy, body builder or something, came outta nowhere in his undies and just picked up his cab, shook him and his ride loose, and tossed the cab clean through the lobby of this hotel. Then there's all that gang stuff, the mobs, high tech weirdos flying around, I dun . . . it really makes ya think, like, maybe Jersey's not so bad, y'know, retire, get a little place in Somerville or whatnot. Y'see what I mean."

"Maybe," Bobby said. He paid the man and got out, Sarah quickly following.

Bobby motioned to an alley. "We can hide our clothes there."

Sarah put her hand on his chest. "No time. I'll go."

"But—"

She spread her arms and a sudden wind carried her up. She sailed gracefully upward.

His eyes narrowing, Bobby balled his hands into fists and burst into flames. The fires carried him upward while they burned his clothing to cinders.

Speeding around Sarah, he streaked over the rooftops before her. There was no sign of a struggle anywhere, and no one standing around suspiciously.

He flew onward, Sarah calling to him and racing to catch up. Finally, he landed in a playground several neighborhoods away.

Fires were still crackling all along his body when Sarah touched down beside him.

"What was that?" she asked.

Bobby looked away sullenly.

"I'm serious," she said. "What was that?"

"I don't understand you," he said. He wouldn't look at her.

"*You* don't understand *me*," she snapped.

He nodded.

"We both had the same idea, didn't we?" Sarah asked. "Maybe that guy didn't jump, maybe he was pushed, let's check it out before whoever did it could get away?"

"Yeah."

She came around in front of him, gesturing at her clothing. "I said I'd go first because I didn't *have* to duck into an alley, take my street clothes off, and hide them, before I could go up. That was it. That was all."

"Just wanted to save time," Bobby said. He looked down at his battlesuit. It was made to withstand the fires he controlled.

"Yes, so if anyone was up there, they wouldn't have time to get away." She frowned. "And so we wouldn't have to risk having our clothing and valuables stolen when we left them behind. Of course, you figured out a way around that, didn't you?"

He had toasted not only his clothes, but his wallet as well. It had been a dumb, impulsive move and he wasn't sure why he'd done it.

No, that wasn't exactly true . . .

"You want everything both ways," Bobby said.

Sarah arched a single eyebrow. "Exactly *what* are we talking about?"

Bobby's shoulders slumped. The bi-thing. She thought he was bringing that up again. "What I mean is, one minute you want one thing, the next, you want something else."

"Oh. That's helpful. That clears up everything."

Some kids walked by and pointed at Bobby through the fence. Even in New York, he looked a little out of place in his costume.

Sarah took off her ankle length jacket and handed it to

him. "I'm not even going to ask if you thought to toss your wallet before flaming on."

Bobby took the jacket and slipped it on. "Thanks."

"You want to thank me, give me an explanation."

He hesitated, then, "I keep trying to be what you want. But you keep changing what that is."

Her beautiful face revealed no hint of emotion. "Go on."

"I thought you wanted me to be involved with social causes, like you. So I started volunteering at the shelter."

She said nothing.

"You know what it was for me? I'll tell you. A pain in the butt. And that was it. At first, anyway. But then I met Mr. Joe and things changed..."

"I see that."

"And now, today. I start acting more like my dad, I start getting take charge and all, and you're all over me. So, I'm figuring, yeah, that's what she wants."

Sarah didn't even blink. "This is quite a dilemma. For you, I mean."

"Then we get out of the cab, and I'm saying what we're gonna do, and you just blow me off and do whatever the hell you want to do. I just don't get it. One minute I'm thinking you want me to really be the guy in our relationship, the next, you're acting like nothing I say matters."

Sarah turned her gaze to the street. "So this is all my fault."

"I just don't know what you want."

"I'm sorry," she said.

Bobby was startled. "Well, look, I mean—"

"What I should say is, I'm sorry you feel that way. I've never meant to be anything but completely forthright with you." She shrugged. "It's just that there's a difference between seeing you rise up to your potential and seeing you act like a dominating *ass* because you think that's what'll turn me on. It's kind of like the difference between being a guy and being a man. If you need things spelled out for you, then it's pretty clear which of those categories you fit into."

She started walking. She was all the way to the schoolyard entrance when he finally managed to get his legs moving and head after her.

Dammit. He had tried, really tried, to tell her how he felt. And he had totally screwed things up.

He fell in beside her and they walked down a quiet street. Two-story houses sitting practically on top of one another lined the street. A convenience store and a restaurant waited at the corner, near the light.

"I think we should split up," Sarah said.

"What?" Bobby said. "Wait—"

"We can cover more ground looking for Mr. Joe that way,' " Sarah said. She still wasn't looking at him. Her hand dug into her purse. "Do you want cab money?"

"No."

They reached the corner. At the opposite light stood a gorgeous young woman in a tight red tank top and tight white slacks. Bobby couldn't help but notice her naturally curly hair, spilling down to the middle of her back, her exotic, dark, Salma Hayek style beauty. She looked like a gypsy queen. Just stunning.

What was he doing?

He looked over at Sarah, hoping she hadn't caught him staring at the girl across the street.

She hadn't.

Instead, she was looking at her, too. And in the same way . . .

It was too much. Bobby was about to grab her arm, to tell her that maybe she was right, maybe they should split up, and not just in their efforts to find Mr. Joe, when the restaurant window behind him suddenly exploded.

Bobby and Sarah reacted instantly, instinctively. They spun, his flames melting the glass that might have cut them to pieces, her winds containing the terrible force of blast.

They rushed inside and found a dozen people crawling

amidst the wreckage. Employees and patrons. Two people were on their feet, another struggling to rise before them.

The two who were standing carried weapons that may have started as Uzis, but had been transformed into killing machines with far more power. A man and a woman, both wearing boots, jeans, tight black sweaters, and ski masks. Only their physiques gave away their sexes. The man had a few grenades on his belt. The woman only had one.

That had been the source of the explosion.

On their knees before them was a man wearing the same I.O. armor the shooters in the club had worn. His armor had been cracked open and his face revealed. Hard eyes, a deeply lined face, chiseled features that were now raw and bloody.

The gun-wielders aimed their weapons at Bobby and Sarah.

Big mistake.

Bobby leaped at the woman, a fiery trail rushing behind him. He had the gun away from her, a melted slag that had charred her fingers, and had knocked her unconscious before he realized that he'd toasted Sarah's coat. The other gun-wielder slammed against the wall beside him. Bobby could feel the force of the hard air that had smashed into him, driving the air from his lungs, knocking him out practically on contact.

Bobby fried his gun, too.

They turned to the merc in the I.O. armor. He was trying to get to his feet, either to run or to make a stand.

"I don't think so," Sarah said, dropping him with a single kick to the jaw. He crumpled in a heap.

Bobby nodded. "We're going somewhere we can have a nice little chat . . ."

CHAPTER 10

The hotel suite really was big. *Not the size of the house we gave up back in La Jolla,* Caitlin thought, *but for a Manhattan penthouse, it's enormous.* Everyone had their own room, Mr. Lynch had his own office, and he'd equipped one room to function as a kind of lab space. The maids kept out of that one—pretty much only entered the suite under duress as it was, ever since the incident with Bobby and the hotel towel that wasn't really flame-retardant.

Caitlin, of course, was the only one who ever went into it, if you didn't count the time that Grunge decided to see how long it would take to toast a slice of raisin bread using the Bunsen burner.

She was in there now, taking apart a device she'd removed from the helmet of the goon they'd captured. It was clamped into a vice, and she peered down at it through a mounted magnifying glass to see all the detail. It was a marvel of miniaturization.

There was a tiny lens, almost microscopic, at the end of a fiber-optic cable no bigger around than a piece of fishing line. A thin strand of wire ended in a minutely larger item that had to be the microphone. At the other end of the whole construction was an earpiece the thug wore, but that wasn't what interested Caitlin so she ignored it.

Whoever's behind these guys, she thought, *he's got some money. Good thing Mr. Lynch does, too.*

TIME AND CHANCE

She removed the set screw that held a narrow metal plate down, and slid the plate off, setting it onto her spotless work surface. Beneath the plate was what she was really looking for. It was so small and nondescript, most people looking at it would have seen only a little gold dowel with a slightly larger, disc-shaped head, shaped much like a pin or a nail.

Caitlin saw a transmitter.

Bingo.

The magnifier wasn't going to be enough for this kind of work, though. Using micro-surgical calipers, she lifted the transmitter from inside the communications unit, tugged the tiny fiber-optic wire free, and clipped it onto a glass slide. Time for some close-up work. She slid the slide into place on a microscope, and glanced at her watch.

Where is he?

Not coming, probably, she decided. *Don't sweat it. You've got work to do.*

Ten minutes later, there was a knock at the door.

"C'mon in," Caitlin called. She didn't look up from the microscope's display, which showed on a fourteen-inch monitor positioned next to the 'scope.

The door opened. "There ya go," Grunge said. "Just like I said."

"Thank you, Grunge," Samuel Perrine said.

At the sound of his voice, Caitlin finally glanced away from her work. Given the difficulty they'd had getting through his security, it was a little odd seeing him here, unaccompanied.

"Hello, Mr. Perrine," she said.

"Hi, Caitlin," he replied. "And please, just Sam."

"How's it goin', Kat?" Grunge asked.

"Fine, Grunge."

"That thing's really a little TV receiver?"

"Seems to be."

"Can you get the Playboy Channel on it?"

"It's not that kind of receiver, Grunge."

"Just checkin' y'know, on account of Lynch not lettin' us order it on the regular TV."

"I figured, Grunge. Although it seems to me that he didn't shut it off until after you'd run the cable bill up by several hundred dollars."

"How was I to know Pay-Per-View meant you really had to pay?"

"We're going to be a little busy in here, Grunge."

"Hey, never let it be said that I can't take a hint." Grunge bowed once, and left the lab, closing the door behind him.

Caitlin smiled toward Perrine. "I'm glad you came, Sam. I wasn't sure you would."

He scratched the end of his nose. "When I got your call, I wasn't sure I would either. I had to think about it for a while. But I guess finally I thought about what you guys had said, about weapons I built and sold ending up in the city streets, being used against kids . . . well, I decided I couldn't just sit back and not try to help."

"I don't know if this is exactly in your field," she said. "But it sure isn't in mine, and I could use an extra set of eyes."

He tapped the temple piece of his glasses. "They ain't great," he said. "But they're yours for the duration. What've we got?"

She indicated the comm unit still held tightly by the vise. Perrine looked it over.

"This was in one of those helmets?" he asked.

"That's right."

"Makes sense. Remember I told you the guys I met with were in audio and visual contact with someone else? I couldn't see the whole structure, but I'm sure this is the same thing from the bits I could see."

"I had a feeling it was," Caitlin said. She indicated the monitor. "Here's the part I'm most interested in."

"The transmitter," Perrine said.

"I'm thinking maybe there's a way to determine the frequency and trail it back to its source. The guy we took this from isn't talking, and we still need to find out who's running this show."

"Where is he?"

"Our prisoner? We turned him over to Mr. Lynch. He's still trying to persuade him to share a little."

Perrine laughed. "Jack can be pretty persuasive."

Caitlin put a hand over her mouth. "Not in a torturing kind of way."

"That, too," Perrine said. "But that wasn't what I was talking about. The Lynch I knew had a whole range of ways to persuade."

"Good."

"Let's take a look at this thing," Perrine said. He scanned the monitor. "Very nice work. Sophisticated. See that?" He indicated the microscopic conducting blade that carried electricity from the long-life, equally miniature battery.

"What about it?"

"It's one of mine."

"That's yours? You mean—?"

"I invented it. I didn't necessarily build this particular one. But it's my design."

"So what does that tell us?" Caitlin asked.

"Whoever made these comm units has some I.O. background."

"Can you tell who it was? Do you recognize the craftsmanship?"

"There were too many people in and out, over the years I was there," Perrine replied. "No way to narrow it down from just this."

"Then we're back to square one," Caitlin sighed.

"I think your first impulse was the best one," Perrine said. "We get this thing receiving and we find out where the signal is coming from. They wouldn't use a common frequency for it—whoever this belongs to doesn't want cell phones or radio signals interfering with his transmissions."

"Good point."

"So let's see what's what." He rubbed his hands together, eager to get to work.

They spent the next hour like that, working closely together, hunched over the 'scope, watching their progress on the monitor. Caitlin found that she enjoyed working with Sam. He was smart, he was occasionally witty, and he was willing to stand back and let her take over when she was on a roll.

There was no romantic attraction, but, she realized, she definitely enjoyed spending some time with an intellectual peer.

Only one thing bothered her. After a little more than an hour, she felt comfortable enough to bring it up.

"How can you do that?" she asked. "Sell guns, I mean. Stolen weaponry."

Sam put down his tools, looked at her for a long moment. "It wasn't an easy decision," he said finally. "There was nothing automatic about it. I was an armorer for a long time, for International Operations. I mean, I did other things, too, I've always been a scientist and a tinkerer and an inventor. But for I.O., mostly what they had me doing was using my expertise to make weapons.

"Eventually, you start to forget what they're used for. They're machines, they're ideas that you come up with in the night hours and implement when you get to work the next morning. They're tools. They're hunks of metal and wire and chips.

"Do you suppose the manufacturers of cigarettes, or the growers of tobacco, or the people who print the cardboard cartons, think when they get to work in the morning about the people who are going to die of lung cancer that day, Caitlin?" he asked. She shook her head.

"Right," he went on. "They're thinking about their own lives, bills they have to pay, debts, the mortgage, the kids who need shoes and school supplies and college tuitions. They're wondering how they're going to retire.

"Same with me. I went to work and I invented weapons. What they were used for didn't even enter into it, except when my bosses came to me and said they needed something that would accomplish a specific task. Then it became a challenge. 'Make a gun that'll shoot around corners. Make a weapon that'll annihilate everyone in a room but not mark the walls.' That kind of thing."

Sam looked away. "When they asked for something like that, we all just got together and pretended we were designing weapons for a video game. We had a bunch of code names that only us designers knew about. We made up stuff that made Doom look tame. It's what got us through. Our way of disassociating ourselves when reality got too close.

"And I was good at it. I got used to a certain kind of lifestyle, because I was paid well for what I did. The home, the land, the staff, all that kind of shielded me from thinking about the end user of my work. Or the end user's victims.

"Then I.O. shut down suddenly. No warning, no time for arrangements to be made for any of that technology. My babies were about to be orphaned."

He shrugged, and picked up his tools again. He and Caitlin were almost finished with the device they were building. He bent over the table and started driving a tiny screw into place. "What better place for them to go than with their father? I loaded up a few trucks at the armory. There was no one there to stop me—the guards had all filled their cars and taken off already. It takes a certain income to maintain the lifestyle I was used to, and I had the means—my weapons—to provide that income. But only if I went into sales. So I did."

"And you didn't think about the difference between your weapons being used by intelligence operatives, presumably working for our side, and the common criminals you were selling them to?" Caitlin asked.

"I admit, I had some blind spots," Perrine said. "You helped me with that. You and the other kids, Grunge and Roxanne. My eyes were shut to what I was really doing, and you opened them. Thank you for that."

"You're welcome."

"In case you're wondering—of course you're wondering, but you might be too polite to say it—I'm getting out of that particular business."

"What are you going to do?"

"I don't know yet. I'm sure I'll be able to find something. I've got plenty of ideas left in me."

"And what about the guns you already have stockpiled?"

"Maybe Lynch can help them find a good home."

"We'll ask him," Caitlin promised.

Perrine tapped the surface of the small metal box they'd been working on. "Looks good to me," he said. "Let's try it out."

Caitlin took the miniature receiver she'd removed from the thug's helmet and slid it into a tiny slot on top of the box. She flipped a switch, turned a dial, and the box started to hum.

"It's connecting," she said, breathless excitement in her voice.

"Sounds like it," Perrine agreed.

Another moment passed, and then a low-pitched whine issued from the box. "Got it," Perrine said. "Frequency's in use, right now. Let's roll."

"I'll get the others," Caitlin said."

Ten minutes later, the team was assembled, in full battle uniform. They crowded into Perrine's sedan.

"There's got to be a better way to get around this city," Bobby said.

"We could take the subway, but we might attract some attention," Grunge offered.

"I'm serious, man," Bobby countered. "This is lame. What if we needed to be someplace in a hurry?"

"Dude. Umm, you'd fly?"

"Right," Bobby said. "Forgot. Never mind."

"Someone still has to carry you, Grunge," Roxy pointed out. "And Caitlin there is no featherweight."

"Best way to get someplace fast is to get a cab, anyway," Grunge said. "Driver may not take you where you want to go, but he'll get you there in a hurry."

"I think Sam's car will be fine," Caitlin said. "It's a little squishy, but it's private."

"How are we supposed to follow the signal, Kat?" Sarah asked.

"The pitch will change," Perrine offered. He backed the car out of the VISITOR parking space underneath their hotel. "Higher means we're closer, lower means farther away."

"So we just drive all over the city and listen to that box?" Grunge asked. "That could take freakin' forever."

"No, Grunge," Caitlin said. "Listen to it. It's already at a high pitch. Wherever the signal is coming from, it's not far away at all."

"And this will lead us, like, right to the bad guys?" Roxy asked.

"Not necessarily," Caitlin replied. "They're broadcasting on a rarely-used frequency. The box is reading that frequency, and telling us that it's in use right now. That doesn't mean it'll take us to the source"

"Although it might," Perrine interrupted. He pulled the car out of the parking garage and into the street, merging seamlessly with the flow of traffic.

"Right," Caitlin agreed. "We won't know until we get there."

"Wherever 'there' is," Grunge said.

"There" was an office building a few miles away, on the edge of the city's financial district.

The building was new—built in the last few years, on a block where there had been a row of small businesses; shops, a couple of restaurants, a family-owned dry cleaners, all had given way to a towering construction of glass and steel and gleaming marble.

Most of the building was still empty. The street level contained a bank and, around the corner, a couple of upscale chain clothing stores. They'd parked Sam's car on the street behind a delivery truck chugging noxious exhaust into the air and, carrying the whining device—practically screaming now—had found their way into the building's elegant lobby. Elevators lined the far wall, and glass doors on one side opened into a small gourmet coffee shop. There was a directory on a wall, but many of the spaces were blank. None of the names meant anything to them, or, it seemed, to Perrine.

Caitlin turned to the guard station, behind a shining countertop. A guard, rail-thin, with heavy black glasses and greasy strands of hair hanging from underneath his uniform cap, regarded them through disapproving eyes.

What do I ask him? she thought. *Excuse me, but have you seen a bunch of criminals in fancy armor?*

"Help you find something?" he asked.

"I don't know about this," Sam whispered. "We don't know for sure that the guys you're looking for are the only people in town using this frequency. We don't even know if our tracker really works. We could be closing in on someone with a particular brand of cordless phone."

"Little late to think of that, man," Grunge said. "We're pretty much committed here."

"It has to work," Caitlin said. "There's nothing about it that shouldn't work."

"You're right," Sam agreed. "I think we need to go upstairs. Could be down—I can't quite tell yet. We won't know until we move, one way or the other."

Caitlin cocked a head toward the bank of elevators. The building was sparsely populated—a few business types came and went from the elevators, but it wasn't nearly as crowded as the financial district tended to be on weekday afternoons.

"No thanks," she said. "We're fine."

"Okay," the guard drawled. "You let me know, you need any help. That's what I'm here for."

"We'll do that." Caitlin threw a smile at him and crossed the lobby in four long strides. The others rushed to keep up. As they drew near, she pushed the down button on the elevator panel.

"Might as well rule out down first," she explained.

After a moment, the elevator doors opened. The team filed in, and Caitlin pushed the door for the first underground floor, a parking level. As soon as the doors shut and the elevator began its descent, the device changed pitch, dropping an octave.

"Wrong call," Caitlin said.

"No harm done," Perrine said. "When it stops, we just go up."

The elevator reached the parking garage level and the doors opened. Everybody waited for them to close again, and when they did Roxy pressed the "2" button. The elevator started to rise.

The box started to scream again.

"Better," Perrine said.

The elevator bypassed the street level and stopped on the second floor. The box's whine hurt their ears, it was so high.

"Ow," Grunge complained. "Dude, can't we kill that thing now?"

"I don't think we'll need it much longer, Grunge," Caitlin said. "When we've found these clowns, you can do anything you want to it."

The elevator came to a stop and the doors slid back.

Roxy, standing in front of the doors, spoke first.

"Uhh, Kat? I think we found 'em."

Caitlin turned in time to see Roxy using her powers to lift a half-dozen I.O. Stingers from the hands of armor-clad mercs. She took in the room beyond the elevator. It was a spacious, multi-tiered, state of the art communication center. Technicians in white lab coats looked up from clipboards or computer terminals. Men and women in finely tailored business suits pointed at them and ran toward a corridor directly opposite the elevator. A dozen more mercenaries, some only partially garbed in I.O. armament over their black and green shirts, slacks, and boots, flooded the room. A large television screen the size of Caitlin's old dorm room displayed an Ouroboros—the symbol of a snake eating its own tail.

The place looked like something out of a Bond film. Caitlin couldn't believe there wasn't even a reception area, some kind of front. Could anyone just accidentally get off on this floor and witness this?

"Full deployment," Caitlin shouted. "Go! Go!"

The team moved out. Bobby and Sarah flew ahead, Grunge and Roxy flanking them on foot. Caitlin slammed the down button and shoved Sam against the wall, knocking the wind out of him before he could protest. As much as she appreciated all he had done, this was no place for him.

She stepped out and the elevator doors closed behind her.

Showtime.

Caitlin decked the first armored merc who raced at her, then delivered a high kick to another who tried to close on her from behind. Armor cracked and unconscious bodies fell.

Ahead, Bobby torched a handful of control panels and computer screens as he sailed straight at another guard. Sarah lifted her arms and lightning blazed from her hands, striking several guards and terminals.

"We need their records!" Caitlin yelled. "Don't fry everything!"

"Relax, Kat," Roxy said as she levitated two more guards and smashed them together. "Enjoy the party!"

Caitlin ducked a stream of energy from a stinger and flung a desk at her attacker. Enjoy *this?* Her half-sister had been in the superhero game too long. They were here to do a job. Clean-up. And that was it. Fun didn't enter into the equation.

She turned and saw Grunge chasing after the people in the suits and the lab coats. Several guards moved into an intercept pattern. Grunge bowled through them, scattering the mercs with ease.

Finishing off a somersaulting armored warrior brandishing a fiery energy sword, Caitlin ordered the others to follow Grunge's lead. There would be other ways off this floor. The thinkers and the planners, that's who they needed to take down. The muscle was only here to get in the way and slow them down.

Caitlin charged after Grunge. She could see his square shoulders and long, dark hair as he chased his quarry down the long corridor. It splintered to the right and the suits and labs took it.

In seconds, Roxy, Sarah, and Bobby were with her.

A pounding and crashing came from just ahead. She covered the long corridor, turned, and nearly ran straight into Grunge's meaty back.

"I don't get it," he said.

There was nothing before him but a wall. Yet—she had seen those who ran the operation come this way.

The wall had huge dents and craters in its surface. Grunge had apparently attempted to go through it, but had failed. A shiny reflective surface was exposed in one small spot.

Caitlin didn't like the look of this. "Go back!"

She turned with the others—and found another wall.

"How in the—" Roxy began.

"Floors, ceilings!" Caitlin said. "Bobby! Sarah!"

Searing flames whipped past Caitlin and burned into the ceiling while brilliant blasts of lightning hit the floor. Bits of plaster and steel shot up and rained down, exposing more of the shiny reflective surface Caitlin had seen in the wall ahead of her. Roxy used her power to keep the debris from striking anyone.

Glass shattered and the lights above went out. Bobby's flames and Sarah's lightning provided the only illumination. Caitlin balled her hands into fists and launched herself at the wall, striking with all the force she could manage. Again, plaster and bits of metal came loose but the trap imprisoning them was not even scratched.

Caitlin stepped back, surveying the trap. The box in which they found themselves was eight feet wide, twelve feet long, and eight feet high. There were no air vents, no electrical plugs. Kicking at the rubble at her feet, Caitlin saw a small generator that had fueled the lights Bobby had shattered, melted, and fused.

"If we can't escape, we'll run out of air and die," Caitlin said. "Simple and clean."

"Yeah, let's give the creeps who designed this thing extra credit on their homework assignment," Grunge said.

Bobby reduced the fires in his hands to a dim ember. Just enough to see by, but not enough to substantially cut into their oxygen.

"So what do we do?" Roxy asked.

Before Caitlin could reply, a thin red beam of light shot out from the wall beside her. "Down!"

The beam singed her hair as it ricocheted back and forth within the confined space, shooting holes in the remaining plaster on the walls and bouncing off the strange reflective surface underneath.

Other beams fired. Some came from above, others below. They criss-crossed, shot up at diagonals, and began to form a deadly web of sustained, fatal power. Caitlin and every member of the team had to leap and dive to keep themselves from being burned. Sarah snarled in pain as one of the beams raked across her shoulder and back.

"That's it," Grunge said. He reached down and placed his palm on a patch of the reflective metal below. His form shimmered and changed, taking on its exact molecular composition. "This ain't gonna be easy and it ain't gonna be fun, but here goes . . ."

Caitlin watched as her teammate's form stretched and expanded. His body flattened and became featureless, then rose up and reached around the others.

"Grunge, no!" Roxy hollered.

Caitlin understood what Grunge was doing. She watched as his body molded itself to the walls, the ceiling, and finally the floor, preventing the deadly energies from reaching them. Bright crimson bursts lit up all around them—the energies striking Grunge's body and bouncing off. Sounds of pain reverberated all around them.

"It's killing him," Roxy whispered. "Don't let him do this, Kat—it's killing him!"

Caitlin looked away from her half-sister. She had already thought of a way out, but she didn't dare voice it. Too many lives other than their own would be at risk.

Suddenly, she felt a breath on the nape of her neck. She spun, but saw no one.

Sarah glanced her way. "Kat?"

Then Sarah's hair rose as if invisible hands were running through it. "Lovely," a deep, rumbling voice said behind her. Sarah whirled and kicked. She nearly fell off-balance when her foot struck only empty air.

"Be ready for anything," Caitlin cautioned.

"Yes," said the voice. This time it was near Roxy. "Be ready."

For several long moments, the voice did not speak. Caitlin and her friends waited, exchanging anxious gazes.

"Who are you?" Caitlin asked.

Silence.

The reflective steel surrounding them lit up, glowing bright crimson as a concentrated array of energies struck from the other side. Grunge bellowed in pain, but his body did not yield.

She thought of her plan once more. The only way out of this trap.

What if—

A blow that would have shattered any normal human being's spine landed in the small of her back. The shocking, sudden pain made her gasp, and the unexpected impact sent her stumbling forward. She turned to face a hulking giant of a man who wore the same symbol she had seen on the video screen when they had first entered.

"Curiosity gets you killed," the man said. He wore

communication gear similar to what had been taken from the merc they had captured.

It had all been a set-up. A trap.

Bobby and Sarah launched themselves at the man—and passed harmlessly through him. He came for Caitlin and threw a punch that took all of her strength to block. It was only a feint. The real hit came from his other fist, which slammed into Caitlin's stomach and doubled her over.

"No!" Bobby yelled.

Caitlin heard the crackling flames an instant before Bobby loosed them. She wanted to tell him to wait, but the air had been knocked out of her lungs. Instead, she flattened as the flames passed through her attacker and nearly consumed her.

"Too slow," the man said.

He reached out and grabbed at the wall—at Grunge's *body*, and dug his fingers in deep. A cry of agony sounded from everywhere and nowhere at once.

Caitlin swept her legs around, grinning as her feet struck solid flesh. She kicked the man's legs out from under him and made him release Grunge. With a leap she was on their attacker, but she passed through his body once more. He could become intangible with a thought—but he was not infallible.

"Better," the man said. "My employer wishes for you to know his name. He is Wager and this city is his. You *children* should not have challenged him."

He motioned for Caitlin to come closer. With a snarl she launched herself at him. This time, he did not become intangible. He barely defended himself as fists that could punch through steel walls buffeted his head and torso.

"More," he said. "Show me everything."

Caitlin drew back her fist—and realized she hadn't even bruised the man or damaged his communication equipment.

"He's got some kind of field around him," Caitlin said. "A dampener, I think. Classic I.O."

"Don't stop," the man said. "The longer you make the testing, the longer you get to live. Wager has an interest in Gen-Actives."

So *that's* what this was all about. Taking their measure. Analyzing them.

Just like when they were given their powers.

"You want to see what we can do?" Caitlin asked, her rage overtaking her reason.

The man nodded.

"Grunge, come back. Now!"

The sleek metallic surface that had surrounded them withdrew and reformed into their teammate. He looked weak and dazed. An array of sizzling energy beams struck at them and Roxy had to pull him to safety.

"Roxy, hit this box we're in with everything you've got," Caitlin commanded as she took Grunge from her. "Make it weigh ten tons if you can."

Raising his hand, the man said, "Wait—"

Roxy didn't wait. She focused her power and turned it on the walls surrounding them.

Suddenly, there was a grinding and shrieking of metal, a hideous hiss and a deep straining cry that might have sounded forlorn if it had come from something human, or even alive. The walls shuddered and the box in which they had been trapped wrenched loose of its moorings, its ceiling drooping and collapsing under its own weight. There was a last spatter of energy beams fired from openings in the wall so tiny that nanite technology was probably involved, or so Caitlin guessed, and then the floor hauled itself up and to one side, dumping all five members of the team onto what had been the far right wall.

The man with them fell toward them and through them, disappearing.

One jarring impact followed another as their cage crashed through one floor after the next.

Caitlin had done some quick calculating, and had guessed that practically every floor of this building was deserted, and that this box would strike the ground floor in one of the untenanted sections. All they had to do was survive the ride!

The group was bumped, jostled, and tossed around, smashed and beaten at every turn, but finally their descent ended with a terrible crash. Roxy banged her head and lost her concentration just as the walls were beginning to fold inward because of their untenable mass.

Caitlin checked everyone over. "Nothing broken, thank God."

"We're a tough bunch," Grunge muttered. He looked like hell.

With a single punch, Caitlin was able to tear a hole through the walls trapping them. She grabbed at one end of the tear she had made and pulled hard. It moaned as it bent backward.

"But—we couldn't bust through this stuff before," Bobby said. "I don't get it."

"It wasn't the metal, it was all the fields that were working on it," Caitlin said.

Grunge nodded. "Yeah, I felt something going through me when I absorbed it. Didn't think about it so much 'cause I was like gettin' *shot* every two seconds, but I felt something weird."

They climbed out over a pile of rubble into a dark, unoccupied space. Banners proclaiming "Archabald's Fine Clothing for True Gentlemen—Coming Soon" were pasted on the unpainted walls.

Caitlin's gambit had paid off.

About thirty yards ahead, Caitlin saw a dim light. She led her friends to it and discovered a rounded corridor with track lighting. They followed it, and soon overhead lights appeared. The sounds of confused, frightened people drifted their way. Sharper voices rose above.

"Keep back, just keep back!" The growls of security guards. A hand radio squawked. "Listen, it's all we can do to keep these people in the restaurant and out of the tunnels. They want to know what happened. We want to

TIME AND CHANCE

know what happened. But we don't have anyone to spare. Just call 911, all right?"

Caitlin looked back into the darkness from which they had just emerged. "The first floor's set up as a circular plaza. Half of it's occupied, the other half isn't. If we go back that way, we're just going to run into civilians from the other shops."

She saw another unoccupied space. This one promised a chocolate factory. "There ought to be doors leading to the street from there. If not, we can bust our way out."

"Good plan," a familiar voice said. "Or it would be, if you weren't already as good as dead."

The voice had come from the darkened space that would one day be a chocolate factory. It was anything but sweet.

Caitlin and the others turned to face the man who had attacked them upstairs. He wasn't alone this time. A half-dozen soldiers in I.O. wear braced him. These guys held themselves differently from the decoys upstairs.

Caitlin tensed. Grunge and Roxy were able to walk, but that was about it. Neither would be any good in another fight.

Bobby and Sarah leaped forward. Her winds struck their opponents and sent them off-balance even as their weapons fired and streams of multi-colored energies tore at the ceiling and through the upper reaches of the building. Bobby moved in behind her, a wall of flame erupting from his hands, engulfing the mercs.

All but the tall muscular man who had spoken were down in seconds. He had stood still, arms folded over his chest, while Sarah and Bobby flew right through him.

Caitlin rushed at him while Sarah and Bobby circled back to pick up Grunge and Roxy. She knew that if he was going to make any contact with her, he would have to become corporeal. It was all a matter of timing...

She screamed, seemingly maddened with rage, and flung herself at the man. He grinned, allowing her to fall through him. Then, just as he was about to level a blow to her spine once more, Caitlin "regained" her balance, spun, and delivered a high kick to his jaw that connected with a satisfying *snap*.

He looked stunned. She pressed her advantage, kneeing, kicking, gouging, striking at him with all of her superhuman strength. Jabs were delivered to his solar plexus, smashing blows to his instep, an open-handed strike to the face that would have killed anything human by sending the cartilage from his nose into his brain— any move she could possibly make to keep him off balance while she studied him and tried to find a way to put him down.

His reactions surprised her. He wasn't a trained fighter. There may have been some soldiering in his past, but he wasn't used to wielding the kind of power he now possessed. His confidence was a pose. She could tell simply by sparring with him.

As she fought, Caitlin saw that two of the guards Sarah and Bobby had taken out were now back on their feet. They raised their weapons and Roxy, being hauled by Sarah, raised her shaky hand and snarled a curse.

Their weapons *exploded*. Twin novas of blinding energy rose up and became rolling fireballs of terrible force. Then—the fireballs twisted like balloons being filled with air, their shape changing until their energies struck out in a funnel upward!

The ceiling blew apart and a sound that might have been the howling cries of ancient gods echoed from above as the entire building shook and began to collapse around them.

Roxy dropped in Sarah's arms, spent.

The people, Caitlin thought. *The people!*

Suddenly, behind her, Grunge broke from Bobby and placed his hand on her opponent. Grunge became stone, like the floor, and allowed his power to flow into his victim. Caitlin watched as the man's molecular structure began to change, his cells transforming into a marble-like substance.

Then there was another explosion and Caitlin, Bobby, and Grunge were thrown back. They rose to see the building collapsing around them.

The man who had attacked them was on his knees, his body human once more, but intangible, ghostlike.

Bobby stared at him, then clutched the side of his head. "Mr. Joe?"

The man looked up sharply. A brief moment of recognition seemed to pass between them. The man mouthed Bobby's name, then looked away.

"I'm Cipher!" he spat, getting back to unsteady legs.

"His dampening field is gone," Caitlin said. "Grunge took it out. He's vulnerable if he becomes material again."

"No need," the man said with a cool smile. "Hear that?"

Screams pierced the sounds of falling debris.

"Go save them if you can." He looked to the others. "Wager says fall back. The press will blame these five for the entire disaster. They'll be as good as dead in the eyes of the world."

The mercs retreated.

Caitlin knew he was right. She couldn't turn her back on the people trapped in this crumbling building.

She signaled to the others. Bobby stayed the longest, watching with a blank expression as Cipher and his crew fled through a back door that led onto the street.

"Mr. Joe," he repeated.

Then he turned and followed Caitlin to help with the rescue.

CHAPTER 11

The fluid in the hypodermic that Lee held was so green it almost glowed. That was the stuff, Wager knew, that would make his every dream a reality. One shot . . .

"How much is there?" he asked.

Lee held it up to the light, measuring it against the faint markings on the cylinder's side. "Exactly the same amount we gave Monteleone," he said. "Your biochemical composition is similar enough to his that the chances of the same dose being equally effective are nearly one hundred percent."

Wager laughed. "You talk to me about percentages? About risk?" He looked down at himself, strapped into a chair just like the one that Cipher had broken free of when he had transformed. Everything Cipher had been through, he had also put himself through. Chemicals to strengthen his skeletal structure, so that the sudden increase in muscle mass wouldn't shatter his bones. Flushing his system of any impurities that might possibly interact with the Gen-Active solution. He was as ready as Cipher had been, and the results, in Cipher's case, had been all that he'd hoped for.

"Double it," he said.

"That's crazy," Lee burst out. "There's no way—you have no idea what'll happen."

"I know, within a range of three percent, what will happen," Wager said. "I observed the test subject carefully. I've seen all the reports. I know what happened to his body during and after the treatment."

"But he's not you," Lee argued. "He's close, as close as one unrelated human being is likely to get. But he's still a different man. You can't be sure enough."

"I'm sure enough. Do it."

"I won't," Lee said. "It isn't safe."

Wager strained against the restraints, sorry now that he had agreed to them. Lee had insisted that the subject had to be kept still while the fluid did its work, but Wager suspected that was more for the convenience of the doctor than real medical necessity.

"Suzanne!" he called.

She'd be watching, via the same video system on which he had seen Monteleone's transformation. He knew that. The delicate voyeuristic/exhibitionistic balance of their relationship demanded that she would, even though it was a reversal of their usual roles.

The door opened a moment later. Suzanne came striding in, powerful and elegant as a jungle cat. She smiled at him, awaiting instruction.

"Kill him," Wager ordered.

"W-what?" Lee stammered. "I'm only thinking of—"

Suzanne crossed the clean room before he finished his sentence. Her left arm swung in a swift chop that caught the doctor on the side of the throat. His larynx knocked off keel, his face reddened as he struggled for breath. He made ghastly croaking noises.

She wrapped an arm around his head, almost tenderly holding it to her breast, and then she twisted his neck and dropped him. He fell to the floor, a lifeless husk.

She held the hypodermic, which she had liberated from his grasp.

"Now, get the stuff," Wager said. "You know where it is, in the fridge."

"I know," Suzanne said. She had been present for Monteleone's treatment. She went to a stainless steel refrigerated cabinet up against a wall, opened the door. Inside was a vial of the Gen-Active formula—all that was left of it. There wouldn't be any more available. She bent over—farther than she had to, knowing that he was watching the swell of her behind against the fabric of her skirt—and retrieved it.

"Double what's in there now," he instructed.

"I heard." She inserted the needle into the top of the vial, and drew up the plunger. The green fluid filled the glass tube. When she had doubled the quantity, she walked toward Wager, still strapped into the chair. She held the needle before her cleavage, as if daring him to look at it instead of at her.

"Is this what you want?" she asked, her voice husky.

"You know it is," Wager said. "Give it to me."

"This is an interesting switch, isn't it?" she asked. "You're powerless, tied into that chair. I hold all the cards. What do you think of that?"

"I think you'd better give it to me now, or you won't live to see the morning," Wager rasped. "Now."

"My, we're anxious, aren't we?" she said. "You know I'm only playing with you. I have my role, and I know what it is. You're the boss. I do what you say."

"You'd better."

She bent over him, put her lips close to his ear. "This stuff will only make you stronger. More forceful than ever." Her breath was hot against his cheek. "I can't wait."

She jammed the needle into his forearm. Finding a vein, she drove the plunger down.

It felt like she had injected fire into his veins.

It burned.

He felt the heat race through him, carried by his circulatory system to every point in his body. When it reached his heart, he could feel that muscle hammering as if trying to break free of the prison bars that were his ribs.

He wondered, briefly, if he had made a mistake.

A sudden memory washed over him. His first day out of jail, after the prison term that had forever changed him.

TIME AND CHANCE

He was still Thomas Carlisle on this day. He had gone to a shopping mall, with a hundred dollars in his pocket, to buy some clothes that didn't look like the kind issued to ex-cons by the system. He hated criminals; he certainly didn't want to look like one.

It was the height of the Christmas shopping season. The place was packed. People everywhere, rushing around, huge shopping bags in their hands bumping into other people. Music blared from unseen speakers, holiday music, but no one listened to it; they were all caught up in the bustle of their own tiny lives.

He hated it.

A big space full of people—it was everything he despised, and everything he feared. He panicked. When a woman blinded by the three large boxes she carried slammed into him from behind, he whirled, knocking the boxes flying from her hands. Then he pushed her down, and, her screams ringing in his ears, began to run aimlessly.

Several hours later, the tone-deaf humming of a janitor penetrated both the walls of the men's room stall in which he had sought refuge, and the psychic walls he had thrown up against the wide world. He peered out through the crack between the door and the wall and saw a pimply-faced, skinny kid in a brown uniform refilling the paper towel dispenser. A cart with supplies and a big plastic trashcan filled the doorway.

Instantly, he knew three things. One, that the mall's stores had closed for business while he'd been holed up. Two, that he was something much different than ordinary men, much more than they. His power over probability confirmed that. He needed only an act, to begin to make his belief a reality. And three, he knew what that act would be.

The chance of being caught was slim enough. He flipped back the lock, emerged from the stall. The janitor barely spared him a glance.

"Mall's closed, dude," he said.

"I know," Thomas Carlisle said. He moved as if heading toward the door, then suddenly spun and lunged. His open hands caught the back of the janitor's head and drove him face-first into the mirror over the sinks. Glass cracked and the cracks filled with blood.

The janitor let out a gasp, and Carlisle turned him around, relishing the blood that streamed from his forehead, his nose, his pulped lips, a three-inch gash in his cheek.

"What—?" the janitor started to say. Carlisle grabbed a glass bottle of window cleaner from his cart and swung it into the kid's damaged face.

When he left the men's room, the mall was empty. It was almost pleasant, but the space still disturbed him. He hurried to his hotel room.

Now, with the serum flaming through his system, he thought he could almost smell a faint whiff of ammonia, the scent that he always associated with that day. But he knew it was an illusion.

The aroma of power.

That had been his first killing.

Not, by any means, his last.

His stomach heaved as his flesh swelled, shoved beyond its normal confines by ballooning muscle. Every part of him hurt, but the pain, he knew, was precursor to something else, and well worth it.

He looked at Suzanne through narrowed eyes. He could feel the skin of his forehead stretching, his brow enlarging. Her eyes were wide with wonder at his change.

And then it was over. The fire cooled. Wager's body was enormous, his muscles chiseled. He radiated strength. All his life he had lived in fear of the physically imposing, and now he was the ultimate specimen.

But he knew that was just the beginning of his power. The merest surface dressing.

Cipher, once the change had come over him, had been able to tear through his restraints.

Cipher, compared to him, was insignificant. He didn't need to break his bonds.

He thought his way through them.

One moment, they held his arms to the chair's, his legs to its base. But Wager's power over probability had changed, he understood. Where once he had been able to compute odds, he could now control them. He could make the impossible possible, the unreal real.

For his first demonstration, he turned the steel straps that held him down into gossamer ribbons, then the gossamer into butterfly wings.

His bindings flew into the air, circled around him twice, and vanished.

He rose.

Suzanne's usual self-assurance was shattered. She stared, open-mouthed at Wager. He loomed over her now.

"My God," she breathed.

"Yes," Wager said. "I am."

A few minutes later, Wager walked out of his lair, into the light of day. The street was wide but quiet, with a few cars and a bus passing by on a distant boulevard. The sun shone down through the chill air.

He was outside. He was in the world. And he was not afraid.

Everything he had worked for, since the day he left prison, was coming to a head. Plans set in motion long ago were playing out, just as he'd known they would. He would have everything that he deserved, would taste of every pleasure, would see the world's criminals bowing at his feet.

There was only one small loose end to deal with. And that would be no problem at all.

Roxy was jazzed. Mackey's sister, Belinda, had called just before dinner and told her that she should drop by the Blackout tonight. She and Mackey had first met at that club, and Roxy now knew that everything was going to be all right. She had worried about her relationship with the drummer for nothing.

She sat in the living room, listening to Caitlin and Sarah going at it, absently beating a rhythm on her leather stretch pants, her purple bangs falling into her eyes.

Her motions ceased when she saw the content, easy smile of Grunge. It was a look he only got two ways. If he had just gotten a nice buzz on, or if—

"I got a date, can we get over this, already?" Grunge asked.

Roxy sighed. She knew it shouldn't have bothered her, but it did. "What, are you paying by the hour?"

Grunge's face flushed. "I'm going out with Michele. The editor. She works at one of those big houses on Fifth Avenue."

Roxy waited.

"It was on her card."

"You learned how to read?"

Grunge rolled his eyes. "I'm in too good a mood, Roxy." He put his huge arms behind his head and angled his head from left to right, the bones making little cracking noises.

The card, Roxy thought. Then it all fell into place for her. The woman on the street. The one he had helped get her purse back.

She checked her watch. "Okay, so you've got a date with a New York book editor. The talking part of the evening should be over in about fifteen minutes. Then what?"

Grunge shook his head. "Yer jealous."

"Am not!" Roxy spat. She leaned forward on her stool and nearly tipped over. "I've got a date, too!"

Sarah raised her hands. "Quiet, both of you! We're discussing a major issue. Gen^{13} needs to—"

Grunge got up and belched. "I'll tell you what this little Gen-Active needs to do. One long glorious pee, then I'm out of here."

"Not on the carpet this time," Roxy said.

Grunge brushed past her. "Hope your little drum boy doesn't have any problem with his stick."

She kicked at his finely rounded backside, but he was out of range before she could connect. She considered using her gravity powers to make the bathroom door too heavy for him to push open, then decided against it. He probably *would* use the carpet.

The bathroom door slammed.

Caitlin shook her head. "What is it with you two? This is serious business."

Roxy sprang to her feet and snatched up her leather jacket. "Last time I checked, having a life was pretty serious business, too. Later!"

She left without looking back.

On the street, waiting for the doorman to flag down a taxi for her, Roxy felt a chill that had nothing to do with the cool night air.

She had acted like a ten-year-old up there. Grunge had that effect on her. And he was right, she was more than a little jealous.

But she had Mackey...

A yellow cab sped to the curb. The doorman moved to get the door for her, but she was too fast for him, getting it herself and sliding into the car before he could manage to do more than fade back to his post. She gave the driver the club's address, then settled back for the drive.

"Young love," the driver said. He was young, with curly black hair and a bad case of acne. "I can always tell."

"Yeah, whatever, you wanna put on the radio or something?" Roxy asked.

"Oh, *okay*," the driver said. "Young love on the skids. I get it..."

For the next eighteen minutes, he talked about relationships. Every woman he had ever dated, failed marriages his friends had suffered through, kinky encounters in the back of his cab, only one of which he had anything to do with . . .

Roxy tried to tune him out, but couldn't. He was about two sexist jokes away from having her fly out the rear window and stiff him for the fare when he pulled up outside the club.

Roxy tossed him a twenty and didn't look back. There was a line at the front of the club. The checker recognized her and let her through immediately, over the cries and complaints of the those who had been waiting for a chance to get in.

She found Belinda tending the smoke-filled bar. The pulsating techno-reggae was so loud they had to shout to be heard. The place was packed with the tattooed and pierced flesh of wall-to-wall pretty people. The lights strobed and occasionally flashed in Roxy's eyes.

"So where's Mackey?" Roxy asked.

"Seattle."

Roxy recoiled. *"What?"*

Belinda smiled. "Seattle. Some session work. He just packed his gear and took off. I only found out because he blew all his cash on the airfare and needed me to wire him more."

Roxy's chest was on fire. It felt hard to breathe.

"Hey, come on, don't take it like that," Belinda said. "He didn't tell you he loved you or anything, did he?"

Roxy shook her head.

"Good. I told him I'd kick his ass if he did that again when he was just having fun."

"Having fun," Roxy whispered. She was in shock. Was it because she was a Gen-Active? She had seen the way he had looked at her after the fight at the club.

He had seen. He *knew*. There probably was no gig in Seattle, he had just wanted to get away—

"Hey, I'm sorry," Belinda said. She set Roxy up with something to settle her nerves. "What's a Gen-Active?"

Roxy looked up. "How—"

"I can read lips. Occupational necessity," Belinda said.

"Oh, you didn't realize you were talking to yourself. Sorry."

Roxy ran her hands over her face, not caring if she ruined her make-up.

"Listen," Belinda said. "I asked you to come by because I didn't want Kim or Len or any of those guys to swing by and tell you about it, then try to get into your pants, working the sympathy angle. I've seen that one enough times when Mackey pulls this. I think they have it all worked out or something. Jerks."

Roxy looked up. "He's done this before?"

Belinda nodded. "It's kind of a standard dating hazard when you go with a boy in the band. And he always seems to zero in on the ones who wouldn't know that. No offense, but—"

"You're right," Roxy said. She picked up her drink. "Men are scum."

Belinda poured one for herself and toasted with her. "Yeah. To scum."

Their glasses clinked.

"Grunge?" Michele asked, drawing back her drink and taking a sip after their toast. It had been to justice. She'd asked if he was serious. He'd asked if a guy named Grunge would lie to her, which made her giggle, then repeat his name. "Grunge," she said again. *"Really?"*

He shrugged. They were in a nice restaurant, the kind of place he figured she'd enjoy. There was a piano player, a fountain, a pretty view, a pair of winding circular staircases, and a menu with prices that would have made him keel over if he had been paying for it.

Go get 'em, Mr. Lynch. The Platinum Visa parade salutes you.

"My full name is Percival Edmund Chang. I got the name Grunge when I was on the circuit. Surfin' and stuff."

"I'm afraid to ask why," Michele said. But he could tell she wasn't afraid at all. She was intrigued.

And she was gorgeous. She wore a simple, elegant

black dress, a sparkling necklace, and stiletto heels. He was the shortest member of Gen[13], and without the spikes, he and Michele would have been about the same height.

"I can't wait to dance with you," he said.

"Why wait for anything?"

They got up and danced a slow, wonderful dance. Then a fast number came on and Grunge started acting like John Travolta in *Pulp Fiction*. Michele loved it. She could only barely keep up and the whole time she didn't even try to stop herself from laughing.

They got back to the table, where their meal was waiting. Grunge pulled at the collar of his monkey suit. "Armani," he said. "Not me."

She looked down at her evening gown. "The last time I wore this was our company Christmas party. The last company I worked for. With all the down-sizing and mergers and stuff . . ." She shrugged. "I'm sure you don't want to hear about that."

"I want to hear anything you want to tell me," Grunge said.

She stared at him. "I think you mean it."

Actually, he did.

The evening went on magically. Dinner was sensational. There was more dancing.

Michele talked the whole evening. Grunge just let her take in his Californian surfer 'tude, while he genuinely listened to every word she had to say, taking more interest in her life and her work then he would have thought possible.

They walked back to her apartment. She shivered and he draped his jacket around her shoulders.

"Anyway, New York publishing isn't so bad. I was a D-girl in Hollywood for three years before I moved here. That was hell."

Grunge cocked his head to one side. "You mean—you were like in those movies with Brinke Stevens, those, y'know, Jim Wynorski and Fred Olen Ray flicks? *Beverly Hills Bordello, Bad Girls from Mars*, like that?"

TIME AND CHANCE

She elbowed him one for that. "Hah. Real funny."

He'd been serious, but he smiled and acted like he was in on the joke.

"Anyway, they talk about movies being in development hell. They don't know the meaning of that phrase. I'd spend my every evening, every weekend, reading these scripts, and my God, were they garbage. Of course, then there was that one time I had this little script called *Shakespeare in Love* in my hands, but the producer I worked for said costume dramas don't make any bucks, so we passed.... Smart, huh?"

Now he got it. D-girl. Development offices. Right...

She kept talking. Soon they were in her apartment. It was a cramped one bedroom, which cost her fourteen hundred a month.

"I just got promoted to full editor two months ago," Michele said. "Couldn't afford this place before then. I still do some part-time work to make it all come together."

The floors were bare wood, and the place hardly had any furnishings. Her TV had dials on it.

Damn.

"I know," she said, reading his expression. "New York book editor. Not what you'd expect."

"Lots of things aren't what you'd expect. Can I show you something?"

She nodded. He took off his shirt, revealing his chiseled, barrel-chested physique and his amazing eagle tattoo. A part of him worried that she might get all embarrassed or worried considering what he'd just done, but she took in the view with some undisguised interest and patiently waited for him to make his point.

"When you look like me, people think you'd only go to the library to use the bathroom."

"And to write socially conscious rhetoric there."

"Exactly. Hell, most people would have thought I wasn't that far off from that creep who took your bag."

She flushed at the mention of that.

"See?" he said. "Your cheeks are red. That is what you were thinking."

She shook her head. "No." She was smiling. "Just about how cool it was when you took that guy down for me. And how much fun it was kicking the son of a bitch."

He grinned. "Michele, I think I could fall in love with you."

And at that moment, he really thought he might.

Only . . .

What happened when she found out what he really was?

She turned and ran her hands over his bare chest, then leaned in and kissed him open-mouthed.

Grunge felt his skin nearly crackle with the fiery energies her kiss released within him. He shuddered as her tongue caressed his. His massive arms encircled her small form and he felt her shaking as she pulled away from the kiss.

"I've been hurt," she said.

He nodded.

"We can have fun, but I want to go slow. I don't want to rush things too much."

Grunge bit his lip lightly. "Yeah."

"You're good with that? Really?"

He remembered the look of horror and revulsion in his date's eyes last night. Then he took Michele in his arms. "As a matter of fact, I am . . ."

They kissed, and the horns blaring on the street and sirens from a few blocks off melted away and formed a moonlit sonata, accompanied by the trip-hammering of his heart.

CHAPTER 12

The morning sun slanted down the cross streets, shining into Cipher's eyes at every intersection as he trudged up Sixth Avenue. He could have taken a car—Wager had plenty to spare—or even a cab, but he preferred walking. He was used to Manhattan's streets; he thrived on the noise, the din of traffic and of the endless streams of people, their voices raised in anger, in passion, in fear—the staccato beat of his city's heart.

This morning he took delight in moving unseen up the stream, an invisible salmon heading for spawning grounds. Except what he was on his way to accomplish had nothing to do with spawning. Quite the opposite.

Wager believed he had a lead on where those annoying young people might be found. Gen[13], they called themselves. Cipher swallowed once, remembering Bobby. He was a good kid, but the past was past and there was nothing now but tomorrow and tomorrow and tomorrow, a different world from the one he'd known even a week before. Bobby had befriended Joe Monteleone, a man of the streets.

Joe didn't exist any more. He might as well be dead.

Which was what Bobby would be, as soon as Cipher found Gen[13]'s headquarters. Wager wouldn't make him do it himself. But Cipher knew that Wager wanted Gen[13] out of the way, and once he'd located them, Wager would send in his troops to take them out. It wasn't the way Cipher would have wanted Bobby and Sarah to end up.

But there was nothing he could do about it.

His mood was dark, in spite of the morning's brightness.

A salesman, late for a meeting, sample case slapping against his leg as he ran, was about to walk through Cipher. The man couldn't see him, of course. But he smelled like terror and desperation, flop sweat, and Cipher found himself offended by the man. So at the last instant he restored his physical body and the guy bumped into him.

"Sorry," the little man said, his head wagging apologetically. His tie was tied too tight and his jacket was too large; it looked like a suit bought when he'd been fat and successful, that no longer fit since he'd become scared and nervous.

Cipher grabbed the guy's necktie, yanked it even tighter. When he shook the man, his sample case flew up at the end of his rubbery arm and bounced off Cipher's shoulder. "Watch where you're going," he snarled. He touched his uniform—the guy's heavy case had collided with his comm unit.

"Urk," the salesman gasped.

Cipher pushed him against the hard stone wall of a building. The guy slammed into it and bounced away, his hooded eyes blinking shut and then open again on impact. Through it all, he held his sample case out to the side like it contained fragile treasures.

Cipher was half-tempted to kill the man, but even as he reached out, the impulse faded. *Some part of me is still Joe Monteleone,* he told himself. *I recognize myself in that man.* The salesman hurried away.

He crossed another street, another beam of bright sunshine that did nothing to warm the winter's day. He found himself surprised that Wager hadn't said anything about him materializing in the street, roughing up the salesman. Could the comm unit have been damaged by the clown's hard case?

"Wager," he said, as a test. "This is Cipher. You copy?"

There was no response. He was on his own.

Looking up at the next corner, he suddenly realized where he was. Part of him had known it all along, he now realized. It was almost surely why he'd chosen to walk in the first place. He was headed uptown, toward 57th and 5th, which is where Wager believed Gen[13] to be. But his course took him past 53rd and 6th, which was where the luxurious Regent Hotel stood.

And in the Regent, he knew, was his family. Well, Joe Monteleone's family. They'd never recognize him, he realized. But he could convince them. He remembered his life with them, in its every last detail. He knew things no one else on Earth could know. He'd be able to convince Margaret. Wager had sworn to keep them well cared for, as long as they lived. Living in a place like this, a place he never would have been able to afford—it looked like Wager was upholding his end of the bargain. Cipher's end—Joe's end—was that he would do Wager's bidding, and he wouldn't try to contact his family.

But he was right here. Right outside the hotel. Surely a brief visit wouldn't be a problem. Especially with the comm unit down.

He went blank, as he was beginning to think of it. Faded from view. He knew he couldn't get inside unobtrusively as Cipher. And he couldn't risk going inside invisible—what would happen if someone happened by while he was knocking on Margaret's door? He scanned both sides of the street and saw what he was looking for— Henry's, an upscale men's clothing shop. At this time of the morning it was open, but not yet crowded.

He went inside. A couple of sales clerks leaned against the counter, chatting, sipping from styrofoam coffee cups. One of them, tall and thin, almost birdlike, with a great big beak jutting from beneath dark round glasses, looked up at the sound of the door opening and closing. Seeing nothing, he shrugged.

"Wind," the other one said.

"All we need," the bird-man said.

Except for the sales clerks, the store seemed empty. Good. Cipher materialized.

"Huh?" the bird-man asked. He snatched his glasses off, wiped them on his white shirt.

"How'd you do that?" the other one said. "Mirrors?"

"I need a suit," Cipher said, ignoring their shock. His voice was steady but firm—don't mess with me, it said. They seemed to understand.

I don't know if we can fit you off the rack, pal," the bird-guy said. "You gotta be, what, a 48 long? But in slacks, maybe a 32, 34 waist?"

"I don't know," Cipher said, realizing that as Joe Monteleone, he hadn't bought a new suit in almost a decade. And since then, his sizes had changed considerably. "Just figure something out, and fast."

The two men scrambled for the racks, trying to piece together something that looked like it might work. While they did, Cipher thought about Margaret, about what she'd think when she saw him.

Sure, she'd be scared, at first. But once he convinced her it was him, in a whole new body—and he wasn't drinking, and he had put her into a fine hotel with clean sheets and room service and college money for the kids—she'd take him in her arms and squeeze him. She'd tell him how good he felt, how strong, how firm. She'd listen to his heart as she rested her head against his chest, and her hand would trail languidly up and down his forearm, the way she used to do when they were young and would stop anywhere, in the middle of a crowded intersection, or on the path outside the Pond in Central Park, or in the produce aisle of the corner grocery, to hug each other and hold each other close and profess their eternal love.

She'd whisper those words into his ear, and he'd do the same to her, tell her how much he missed her and loved her, how he would always love her. Then, after a while, he would go, because he had to kill those meddlesome Gen[13] kids. He knew he was who he was and where he was because of Wager, and he wouldn't forget that commitment. But still—a half hour with his family, holding his wife, talking to his kids, seeing how they'd grown—who could hold that against a man? Not even Wager. His employer was harsh, but he was human.

The suit almost fit, even over his uniform. It didn't really match—the jacket was from a blue pinstriped number, and the slacks were from a brown wool. But it covered most of his gear, and he thought it would be good enough to get him into the hotel without causing a stir. The sales clerks had tried to charge him four hundred dollars, but when he'd thrown the bird-guy across the room and dismantled the cash/wrap counter with one flex of his arms, they had become reasonable and let him leave. He hurried back across the street.

The Regent was more posh than any place he'd ever stayed. The lobby was all marble and glass—even the floor was marble. The counter was a big slab of some rich-looking dark wood, topped with another slab of marble. He knew all that marble had to be expensive, and he wondered for a moment just how much Wager was paying to keep his family in a place like this.

Then he had a moment of panic, because the truth came to him suddenly. He wasn't, of course. Wager had told him his family was staying here, but he had also warned him not to look for them. He was probably lying. They were probably in some dump, some tenement building somewhere, cursing the day they'd heard Joe Monteleone's name. Cipher stormed the front desk with a scowl on his face, expecting the worst.

"I'm looking for the Monteleones," he said. "Margaret Monteleone, two kids."

The clerk, barely out of his teens, looked at him like he was a moron. "Of course, sir," he said. "If you'll go to the house phone,"—he pointed across the lobby to a leather sofa with three white telephones on a little glass table in front of it—"I'll ring their room for you."

Cipher leaned closer to the kid, hands resting on the

edge of the marble. "I don't want to call them," he said. "I want to surprise them."

"I'm sorry, I can't tell you their room number," the kid said, his voice quaking a little. "That's against hotel policy. If you'd like I can ring them and tell them you're here."

"I said—" Cipher started.

"Five-seventeen," the kid interrupted. Cipher looked down and realized that he had crumbled the edge of the marble slab to powder.

"Thanks," he said. He went to the elevators.

The wait was short, and then he boarded, rode up five stories. A sign on the wall pointed to the left. Their door was four down from the elevator lobby.

517.

Brass numbers on polished wood. He didn't want to knock—he knew Margaret would look through the peephole, and see a stranger, and she'd be frightened. He wanted her to hear his voice before she saw him. His voice hadn't changed.

He took the doorknob in his hand. She could call down later for a new one. He turned it, feeling the lock mechanism resist, and then give under his superior strength. He pushed the door open. The room was dark, curtains drawn against the morning sun.

"Margaret," he called softly. "Elyse. Joey . . ."

There was no answer. Maybe they were out. If so, he'd wait for them, at least a little while. He had run the risk of angering Wager; he wasn't going to let it go for nothing.

"You here, Margaret?" he asked the room. "It's me, Joe."

He walked down the short hallway, past the door to the bathroom and the closet. Beyond, there was a sitting area, and two doors leading to two bedrooms. *At least Wager put them in a suite,* Joe thought. *Maybe they're still sleeping.* He picked the nearest bedroom door, tapped on it. "Margaret?"

Still no answer. He opened the door, found a light switch, clicked it on.

She was half on the bed, half dangling toward the floor. Blood had pooled beneath her, running out down her cheeks and temples from the slash in her throat. It was still wet and thick, hadn't yet had time to congeal. Less than an hour, he thought. Maybe much less.

He ran to the other door. The kids! He threw their door open.

The scene brought tears to his eyes.

Elyse had been fifteen, Joe Jr. nine. Elyse loved dancing and horses and pop music, while Joe Jr. kept himself amused with television and the Internet. At least, those had been the things they'd liked when they'd had a home. On the streets, you didn't have time for hobbies—part of why he'd sent them to live with Margaret's family after he'd lost their home. At least they'd still have access to schools and TV and the occasional book or toy.

But they'd never see another birthday, never log on to another web site, never hear another song.

Cipher—Joe Monteleone—stood in the middle of the room, fists clenched, blinking his eyes to hold back the tears. Who had done this? Why?

Someone would pay.

And it dawned on him that there was only one possible answer to his question.

Wager had done this.

Wager would die.

"You gotta admit, he always keeps his word," a voice said, behind him.

Cipher spun and saw Suzanne Sawyer, standing in the doorway to his wife's room. Behind her, three men he'd met briefly at Wager's brownstone headquarters. They were interchangeable muscle, as far as he could tell. He thought their names were Mike, Curtis, and Paco, but he wasn't even sure about that. They were all big, well-muscled—even Suzanne looked like she'd been enhanced in some way. They wore uniforms similar to his, the same

Ouroboros emblem on their chests, matching armbands encircling their biceps. They looked, to him, like something from a Flash Gordon movie, and it occurred to him that he must look even more ridiculous, wearing that outfit under an ill-fitting mismatched suit. He tore the clothes off and threw them to the floor.

"What are you talking about?" he demanded.

"Wager. He said he'd keep them in high style for the rest of their lives. He just didn't say how long that would be."

"That's my wife in there," Cipher said. "My kids. He shouldn't've."

"You fail to understand the most significant fact here," Suzanne argued. "Wager decides what he should and shouldn't do. You're nothing. A tool."

"Maybe that's what you think," Cipher replied. "Maybe that's even what he thinks. He'll learn different."

"Don't do anything stupid," Suzanne warned him.

"Too late for that," Cipher said. "I'm just gonna fix the mistakes I've already made."

Suzanne cocked her head toward him, speaking to her companions. "Stop him."

This was too much for him. His wife dead, his children slaughtered, and now this woman and her playmates thought they could stop him from exacting his revenge.

He'd never wanted to kill for Wager. Hoped to spend his whole life without taking anyone else's. But now, all bets were off.

"Try," Cipher said. He threw himself across the room at them.

The one he thought was Mike, with close-cropped brown hair and a beard, came forward to meet his charge. He raised his forearms and crossed them, and Cipher slammed into them. The impact was much like running headlong into a brick wall.

Staggered, he dropped to one knee. Wager had done something to these four. Even Suzanne looked different than he remembered her, bigger, maybe tougher.

But no matter what he'd done to them, they still weren't him. He charged again—this time, heading straight for Suzanne. When he smeared the walls with her brains, the others would be easy.

Paco met this advance with an upthrust boot, catching him in the stomach. He doubled around it, but managed to close his hands on Paco's leg. He yanked. The man flew backward, head slamming into the hotel room's carpet with a loud thud.

Cipher smiled at the sound.

But before he could capitalize on it, Curtis closed a fist over his collarbone and squeezed. The pain was excruciating, and Cipher fell to his knees again. He managed to clamp his hands over Curtis's forearm, and bent. Curtis's arm snapped like a dry twig, and he let out a scream.

Before he could regain his feet, Mike slammed the hotel room's desk into his neck and shoulders. Wood splintered around Cipher. He shook his head to clear it. These guys should know they couldn't hurt him with such primitive attacks. He was surprised that Curtis had been able to hurt him so badly. Something about whatever Wager had done to them—they'd been given some amount of the same stuff he had, Cipher guessed.

No other way they could do any damage to him.

But still, he'd take them. And then he'd visit Wager.

Thinking about the man filled him with rage. His vision clouded. He let out a guttural roar and flailed at Mike. His fists pounded flesh.

"This is ridiculous," he heard Suzanne say. Her voice sounded like it was coming from far away. He knew, vaguely, that his blood was pounding in his ears, deafening him. He looked away from Mike for a moment, trying to locate Suzanne.

When he found her, she was pointing at him. Not with a weapon, just with a single finger. And light seemed to emanate from that finger, blinding him.

Burning him.

He screamed. Threw his hands in front of his face.

Curled into a ball on the hotel floor.

"Finish him," he heard her say. Even farther away now, her voice traveling to him through the waves of pain that racked his body.

He knew he couldn't prevent them from killing him. But he also understood that, even if they had been the ones who pulled the triggers on his wife and children, they had done so at Wager's insistence.

If they killed him, he'd never have a chance to kill Wager. And he wanted, more than anything, to see Wager dead.

The realization gave him the strength to push himself to his feet. With a scream, he grabbed the corner leg of the room's sofa and raised it into the air, flinging it at them. Wouldn't hurt them, but he just wanted them distracted now.

He dove through the window.

This room overlooked an alley, so while there were people on the street beyond, there was no one immediately below. Where he hit the ground, the pavement buckled.

He went intangible before he reached the street. Behind him, he heard voices, but he knew they'd never be able to catch him. With the comm unit broken, he was untraceable, a free man. He ran.

The fact that Suzanne had been able to hurt him so badly worried him. It meant that there was power out there—power greater than his. Only one person on Earth could have given her such power, he thought. Wager.

One more reason to kill him.

An hour later, he stopped in a doorway a block from the Mary McCardle Shelter. He waited there, out of the wind, for another hour, until he saw someone he recognized walk past. He wore baggy brown pants, a moth-eaten sweater, and a long trench coat held closed with a length of rope.

"Ron!" he called.

The man stopped, looked around. Saw Cipher standing in the doorway.

"C'mere," Cipher said.

Ron looked uncertainly at him.

"It's me," Cipher said. "Joe. Mr. Joe."

Ron stepped closer. "You don't look like Mr. Joe."

"Close your eyes," Cipher instructed. "Listen to me."

Ron did as he was told. He shut his eyes.

"It is me," Cipher said. "My name is Joe Monteleone. You sat next to me at dinner, about a month ago. I let you have my biscuit, remember?"

"Yeah," Ron said. "Sure, I remember that." He opened his eyes and came closer.

"Listen," Cipher said. "I need you to do something for me."

"Sure, okay," Ron said. "Whatever."

"You know who Bobby is, right? Kid who works at the Shelter sometimes? Goatee?"

"Sure, Bobby, yeah."

"I need you to give him a message..."

Bobby Lane stood alone in Central Park near the base of Cleopatra's Needle. The obelisk stood near East Drive at East 82nd Street, a welcome sight to a collection of runners who pushed themselves over Cat Hill and completed their last leg. He watched the runners pass, noting a straggler, a big man, wearing gray sweats.

It was him. Mr. Joe.

Cipher.

Bobby tried not to look over at his teammates, who stood among the collection of tall trees behind him. Across the street, beyond another grove of trees, lay the Metropolitan Museum of Art.

Sliding his hands into the deep pockets of his trenchcoat, Bobby glanced at the surface of the obelisk. It looked at least forty feet high and it was tapered to a point at its crest. Egyptian symbols covered its walls. The sounds of a softball game taking place on the Great Lawn's diamond drifted to him.

The jogger came to Bobby, not the least bit out of

breath. Under other circumstances, Bobby might have made a joke about if it was safe or not, thinking about Marathon Man, that flick with Dustin Hoffman and Laurence Olivier that was shot not far from here. But he wasn't in a joking kind of mood.

And anyway, Mr. Joe was no dentist.

The man crushing the grass a dozen paces away had tried to kill him and his friends. He had changed—or been changed—by a madman.

Joe Monteleone stopped before Bobby and sighed. He seemed to listen to the sounds of people laughing and cheering, the high sharp crack of a bat hitting a softball.

"I used to bring my kids here," Joe said. "We played softball in that field."

"I remember." Bobby was still not looking at him. He couldn't. The man standing near him *sounded* like his friend. But one look in his direction and the illusion would be shattered. "You told me."

They didn't talk for a while. Instead, all that passed between them was a cool, whistling breeze. The earth smelled tired, ready for its season of sleep and renewal. The sun hung low on the horizon, a golden glowing orb that cast part of the needle in silhouette.

Finally, Joe said, "They're dead, Bobby. My wife. My son and daughter. Dead."

Bobby shuddered. He had been prepared for anything but this. He couldn't help himself, he turned to face Mr. Joe.

The man had changed—but his eyes were the same. Tired and wounded. Yet alive, burning with urgency. That had been one of the qualities that had arrested Bobby's attention about Mr. Joe in the beginning. Here was this homeless man who was bent, but not broken. He had the look of someone who was waiting for something, watching for an opportunity to begin again.

That opportunity had come, and God help him, Joe Monteleone had taken it.

"No, that's not right," Bobby said. "I saw them. Me

and Sarah, we went to the Regent looking for you—"

"Bobby," Joe said softly.

It stopped him. It was all he needed to hear. The pain in Joe Monteleone's voice left no room for mistakes. What the man said was true, whether Bobby wanted to believe it or not.

"I did it all for them," Joe said. He struggled to get the words out, his voice choked with emotion. "Then Wager decided..."

Bobby didn't have to hear the rest. He'd been through his share of double-crosses. He understood.

"There's blood on my hands," Joe said. "Some of it was almost yours. But you and your friends got away. Thank God."

Bobby knew that at least a part of him should be angry at this man. Mr. Joe had been weak. He had left his family when all they wanted was to be with him. He had decided without ever asking them what was most important to them. And he had done a thing that had ultimately led to the deaths of those he cared most about.

It was that last thing that staved off his anger. There was nothing he could say or do that could punish Mr. Joe worse than what he had done himself. What mattered was here and now.

"What do you want?" Bobby asked.

"Wager. Dead. But I can't do it alone."

Bobby shook his head. "We're not killers."

"I didn't say you were. Listen, I know where he is. I know how to get to him. What I need is help breaking through his defenses. You and your friends, you can take me there. I'll do the rest."

Bobby's mind was swimming. He felt a fury that nearly made him burst into flames. He wanted Joe's family avenged. He wanted Wager stopped.

But not like this.

He looked back to the obelisk, putting his hand onto its carved surface to steady himself. Then he saw something—odd. Several of the hieroglyphics had been chiseled to form words in English:

EAT AT JOE'S

Bobby almost laughed. He couldn't help it. Laugh or scream, his only options.

"You think this is funny?" Joe Monteleone asked. His shoulders tensed.

"No," Bobby said, looking away from the obelisk for an instant. "No, it's just—"

When he looked back, the hieroglyphics were Egyptian symbols once more. He stared at them in confusion.

"What is it?" Joe asked, his tone completely changed. "What did you see?"

"The—the letters changed," Bobby said. "For a second it said—"

Joe grabbed Bobby's arm and hauled him back. "He's here."

The obelisk shimmered. Caitlin and the others broke from cover. A door appeared in the face of the needle, a darkness deeper than any mystery, weightier than death.

Figures stepped out.

The first was a muscle-bound giant. *Wager.* Suzanne Sawyer and the men Joe had fought at his wife's townhouse followed.

Bobby looked to Joe, wondering for only a second if this had been another trap all along. But the man's startled expression told him all he needed to know.

"You bastard," Joe said, staring at the grinning man who led the procession. "You bastard!"

Joe launched himself at Wager—and fell through the man. He tumbled to the ground on the other side of his maker and struck the now solid obelisk once more.

"Don't flatter yourself to think that we're the same," Wager said. "The serum affected me far differently than it did you. My power is all power. To have my will done in all things. My dreams, your nightmares."

Bloody hands burst up from the ground, grasping at Joe Monteleone. A woman's hands. The hands of children. He screamed in terror and scrambled away.

The hands disappeared. Joe tried to strike at another of Wager's operatives, but his hand became intangible the moment before he could land a blow.

"You can't harm us," Wager said. "I told you that you were a thing of little or no importance. Now it's true. I willed it to be so and now it is."

Bobby understood what was happening, though he could only barely believe it. Wager was somehow controlling Mr. Joe's powers, making it impossible for the man to harm any of them.

Wager turned to Bobby and the others. "Come now, children, it's time to play."

Bobby shrugged off his trenchcoat and allowed the fires to consume him. His teammates flanked him.

"Oh, good," Wager said. "The traditional superhero battle. I've been reading about these since I was a child. And there were so many things I was wondering about . . ."

Caitlin tapped Roxy on the back. Bobby watched as she edged around to the far left, placing herself across from the muscular blonde woman.

"Right—this is the line of scrimmage part of things," Wager said. "Four of us, five of you, six if you count poor Cipher, everyone pairs off looking for a dance partner."

Caitlin stepped forward.

Wager giggled. "The fearless leader. I want you for my very own."

"Take them down," Caitlin said.

Bobby raised his hand but before he could make a move, he felt his flames leap out of him, unbidden. They made a wide sweep, torching the group. He gasped as he saw them all burst into fire, screaming and wailing as they twitched and fell upon the ground.

"Bobby!" Sarah screamed. She leaped into the air and frantically summoned winds and rain that doused the fiery, dying bodies.

Caitlin and the others stared at him. He looked down at the fires still in his hand.

"I didn't," he said. "I didn't!"

"I'll get help," Sarah said, watching Bobby with a look of stark disbelief. Sadness and anger played across her beautiful features. And sorrow.

The four figures on the ground had stopped moving. They were grotesque, charred husks.

They were dead.

"I didn't . . ." Bobby repeated.

"Dude, the fire came out of your hand," Grunge said.

"What are we gonna do?" Roxy said. "It's not supposed to be like this! It's never been like this!"

Bobby watched as Mr. Joe stood up slowly. He looked at the bodies with a desperate look of hope, disappointment, and fear.

"Withdraw your flames," Caitlin said.

Nodding, Bobby tried to pull them back.

Nothing happened.

Caitlin looked worried. "Bobby, I know you didn't mean to—"

"It just happened, I didn't do it!" Bobby yelled. This was a nightmare!

"Go get Sarah," Caitlin said. She was visibly shaken. "We'll phone 911. Something. I dunno. Mr. Lynch'll help us fix things. He'll know what to do."

"People will be coming soon," Grunge said. "They're gonna see!"

Bobby refused to believe this. He hadn't willed the flames upon his opponents. This was one of his greatest fears.

He was a murderer . . .

"Let 'em come," Bobby said, falling to the ground. "You guys go. Let 'em come . . ."

The others were silent. Were they considering his offer? Or simply too stunned to respond?

He didn't even look their way.

"This can't be right," Joe Monteleone said. "Wager's playing with us. This isn't real."

Roxy covered her mouth and looked away. "It sure smells real . . ."

Bobby felt hope rise up within him. Could this be an illusion? Was it possible that Wager was playing games with them?

He waited for the bodies to rise.

Waited.

Then all four of their opponents were standing in place once more, unscathed. Wager grinned.

Sarah suddenly winked into existence beside Bobby, her eyes wide with disorientation.

"That's one of the things I wondered about in these battles," he said. "You children have all this power. How can you know exactly how hard to strike, how much power to use, the amount of *heat* your opponents can take? It would be so easy to cross the line, to snap someone's neck or burn them to cinders. And how would that feel? Would some part of you like it? What would you do? The odds were 98 percent that in another 55 seconds at least one of you would have turned on the little fire-starter and suggested letting him take the blame. But—"

Caitlin surged forward, smashing her fist into Wager's face.

He kept grinning.

She pummeled him, beating on him until she was barely able to stand. No one else moved. Bobby tried, but he was frozen in place!

Finally, Caitlin stumbled back.

"Whatever you give will find countless ways back to you," Wager said.

Caitlin screamed as a volley of invisible blows landed on her, first on her jaw, then upon every area of the body in which she had struck Wager. Bruises and welts appeared. She fell back as blood spilled from her mouth and she collapsed.

Wager picked her up by the throat and examined her.

He stared deeply into her eyes and spoke to her. But his words were garbled. Bobby couldn't understand them.

Wager wished for this conversation to be *private*, Bobby realized.

How can we fight this guy? Bobby wondered. *What can we do?*

Whatever Wager was saying, his words were having an effect. Caitlin's eyes grew wide and moist. She swallowed hard, shuddering, desperately attempting to look away from the madman.

"Upsetting, isn't it?" Wager said, his words comprehensible again. "For one person to know another so well? And just by the evidence of the senses. Senses you should not deny, little one." He sighed. "You have one chance. Take it."

He dropped Caitlin. She snatched a weapon from the belt of the blonde-haired woman. A silver blade.

Caitlin, no! Bobby screamed in his mind. But he couldn't speak. Couldn't move. All he could do was watch as she rammed the blade into Wager's side with both hands—then fell over, the color draining from her face as a bloody wound appeared in her own side.

Wager frowned. "Hmmm. I still have questions and curiosities, but I also have something of a need to indulge myself with physicality. The rest of you, come, enjoy yourselves, I wish to experience that free-for-all battle scene that I've read about so many times!"

Bobby felt the paralysis that had gripped him suddenly disappear. He gritted his teeth and loosed a plasma bolt at the closest of Wager's soldiers, a man with long blond hair and hands that had elongated into talons.

The man took the blast and smiled.

Meanwhile, Roxy had loosed her powers upon Suzanne Sawyer, increasing the woman's gravity tenfold. She sweated as she trudged forward and struggled to raise her hand, but her eyes glowed with delight.

"A pretty one, aren't you?" Suzanne said. "I want to hear you scream . . ."

A dozen paces away from Roxy, Grunge had thrown himself against Mike, the human brick wall who had repelled Cipher. The man threw open his arms and caught Grunge in a powerful embrace.

Then he began to *squeeze*.

Bobby saw all of this, but could do little to help. The blond guy was on him, his raking talons slicing the air before him. Flames completely engulfed Bobby once more and he tried to fly, but the man grabbed his ankle and hurled him to the ground. Opening his mouth, he loosed a freezing cold that put out Bobby's flames and left him shuddering on the ground.

"Bobby!" someone yelled.

It was Sarah. Bobby saw her flying toward him to help, then suddenly her sailing form was jerked away.

Wager!

Bobby's field of vision was then consumed by the blond man and his flashing talons. He rolled to avoid them, and spun to deliver a kick to the man's face, driving him back.

He "flamed on" once more and leaped into the sky.

From above, he could see Sarah and Wager. The muscle-bound goon had his arms crossed over his massive chest. Sarah was before him on one bent knee, struggling against his will. An odd aura surrounded her, a gray, lifeless void that seemed to cut her off from the earth and the elements.

He was torturing her!

A scream came off to his left. He looked over and saw Roxy fall as Suzanne Sawyer loosed a steady stream of dark energies at her. Bobby made a strafing run, delivering a series of explosive plasma bursts at the tall platinum-haired woman. Sawyer's concentration was broken, and shards of a large stone shot up and struck her in the skull. She staggered back, giving Roxy time to go on the offensive.

Caitlin was still down. And Mr. Joe wandered through the battlefield, helpless, a screaming, impotent wraith.

Wager glanced up at Bobby. "This could become public quite easily, couldn't it? Then the fun would be over too soon."

He gestured and the ground shook. Four more stone obelisks, each the exact size and shape of Cleopatra's Needle, rose from the earth. They struck upward describing a five-pointed star, and lightning coupled with walls of shimmering energy reached out between them, creating a shining veil that hid their battle from the world. A dome reached over them, translucent, but hazy.

No one could see in or out of the field Wager had created.

And no one could escape.

Bobby saw strange symbols in the energy walls. Ancient ankhs. Hieroglyphs. And vistas of another time and place. Egypt itself.

Had Wager taken them out of their own space-time continuum simply to contain their battle? Would a legion of mummies and animal-headed men with god-like powers next appear to challenge them?

Someone tapped Bobby on the shoulder. He was two stories above the ground.

He turned to see Talon.

"You think you're the only one who can fly?" his enemy said. Then his claws struck out and all Bobby saw was a bloodred haze as pain lanced through him and he fell to the ground.

Rolling onto his back, Bobby lifted his arms and focused all the energy he had left on Talon. A single controlled plasma burst of the highest intensity struck his flying, incoming assailant square in the chest. It drove him up and flung him to the wall of the dome, where the strange energies and odd images curled beneath the sky.

Talon screamed—and disappeared.

"Roxy!" Bobby yelled. "Roxy, did you see?"

She had. Roxy gestured and Suzanne Sawyer suddenly flew upward, deprived of all gravity. She turned in midair and aimed her energies at the wall above, creating just enough force to keep her from vanishing into the matrix of energies Wager had willed into existence.

"Yo, Bob-man, could use some help over here," Grunge said.

Bobby looked over and saw that Grunge had turned a bright red, the vise-like grip of his assailant nearly crushing the life from him. Raising his hand, Bobby said, "Sorry, dude!"

A final plasma bolt left him, striking Grunge square in the chest. It flung him and the dark-haired man back to the ground. The moment Grunge was able to make contact with the grass, he took on its molecular composition, easily wriggling out of Mark's hands, then turning into vines that encircled and began to squeeze Wager's operative.

Bobby collapsed, spent.

Yet—Wager still had Sarah! The giant was draining her, ripping the life essence from her!

"Let the girl go," Joe Monteleone said.

Wager glanced up as the wraith approached. "Cipher. What will you do if I say no? Will you speak with me harshly?"

Cipher—and he was Cipher now, Bobby could see that, the running outfit was gone and his battle gear beneath was revealed—advanced on his maker.

Cipher pulled back his hand and *transformed* it into a sledgehammer. He struck Wager hard enough to send the giant flying backward.

Sarah fell back, the gray aura surrounding her instantly dissipating.

Bobby surveyed the scene. Caitlin and Sarah were down. Roxy and Grunge occupied. It was up to him and Mr. Joe now. Only—Bobby was drained. It didn't matter. He picked up a rock and stumbled forward.

As if sensing Bobby's thoughts, Cipher said, "Stay back!"

Wager sat up slowly. He stroked his chin.

"*This* is a satisfying feeling," Wager said. "Brute physical contact. Though I'm not sure how it's possible."

"Whatever you give will find countless ways back to you," Cipher said. "This is for my family."

Wager shuddered. "The percentages are not in favor of such a—"

"Shut up!" Cipher said, advancing again. As Wager stood, Cipher turned his hands into swords and ran his maker through. Wager gasped and Cipher withdrew his sword hands.

Then Wager straightened up and his wounds healed with a thought. He struck at Cipher, who fought back. The ground thundered and the shimmering walls of energy faltered as the titans battled. Their bodies shifted, mouths opening with jagged teeth, tendrils and tentacles erupting from their flesh, and they battered and bruised one another, but could do little more . . .

Roxy cried out with effort and sent Suzanne Sawyer a mile through the air. Grunge backed off as the unconscious body of Wager's other operative collapsed at his feet. Then she went to her sister, who lay curled up on the ground, clutching her side.

Bobby dropped the stone he carried and gathered Sarah up in his arms. Grunge stumbled over and helped Roxy with Caitlin.

"We gotta get out of here," Roxy said.

Bobby nodded. He knew this might be their only chance. But he couldn't leave Mr. Joe!

Bobby felt a sudden ache in his head. His power—his other power, which came sparingly these days—had engaged. He could feel Mr. Joe in his mind.

I'll hold him, Joe Monteleone whispered. *Go!*

Though it nearly broke him, Bobby turned his back on his friend and helped the others leave the shadow of Cleopatra's Needle.

They were at the very edge of the circle described by the five obelisks when a shadow rose up and fell upon them. Bobby looked back and saw Wager standing nearly as tall as the obelisk, Cipher crawling away in pain.

"Oh, yes," Wager said. "All the classic elements. Sacrifice. Duty. Honor. Vengeance. And it all amounts to nothing. I could kill any of you with a thought. I could wish you out of existence, or turn back time and make it that you were never sired. But I choose to let you live. As heralds. Messengers. Let others of your kind know that I exist, and I will not be denied. I cannot be undone. I am the alpha and omega. I am your god!"

With that, Wager laughed hysterically. Then, holding, his side, he giggled. "Sorry. Always wanted to say that." Then his expression became blank. "Though it *is* true."

He disappeared—leaving Bobby and the others to silently make their escape.

CHAPTER 13

Caitlin Fairchild was wounded. Her body would heal. She wasn't so sure about her mind—or her soul.

She had seen Wager do things, *become* things, that were impossible. Worse than that, he had seen inside her. He had known her every fear and desire. And he had laughed while he held her life in his hands.

The team had regrouped in their penthouse suite. No one had spoken since the battle. Their cuts had been cleaned and dressed, and most had showered and changed into street clothes. Only Caitlin remained in her shredded and bloody battle suit. Her ribs were taped, and an I.O. tissue regenerator was hard at work on the wound in her side. She had refused to go to the hospital. Too many questions. Too few answers.

She looked to the others. Grunge sat on the couch, flipping channels. Roxy and Sarah were in their rooms, sitting on their beds, their doors open. Bobby and Joe Monteleone stood near the window, looking out at the stars.

She brought her hands up to her face, staring at the flecks of blood dotting her flesh, the bits of skin beneath her nails.

It was over. They had faced Wager and had fallen before his power. He had let them live to act as heralds. To serve as living testaments of his authority.

Look at them. See how they are broken. This is what will happen to any who stand against me. . . .

Caitlin shuddered, hugging herself.

Grunge turned off the television. Without looking up, he said, "Maybe we should call in Mr. Majestic. Or someone."

Bobby lowered his head. "Good idea."

They're giving up, Caitlin thought. *They're gonna let Wager win!*

"Hold up," she said. "All right, we were blind-sided, we didn't understand what we were up against, but that doesn't mean we can't still take this scumbag down!"

The room was silent.

Again, it was Grunge who spoke first. "How?"

It was a simple question. Not a bullet from a gun, not a bolt of incredible energies fired from the hands of a power-mad god. Yet it struck her with almost as much deadly force.

Caitlin looked away, crushed by the weight of the silence that had risen up around her—and within her.

She had no answer.

Then a voice, long forgotten, rose up in her mind. *In science we find the answers. Through science, we can find the key to unlock any door....*

She almost smiled. Joquile Robeson. Her eighth grade science teacher. The first teacher to really take her interest in science seriously.

Why was she thinking of him now?

And why was the very idea of changing out of her bloody clothes and showering off the filth that had been left on her after the battle such a disturbing notion?

"I need time," Caitlin said. She strode off for the clean room. Her lab.

"Yeah," Bobby said. "Take all the time you need."

"Good luck," Joe Monteleone said.

Caitlin nearly hesitated at the older man's words. It wasn't his tone. She could appreciate the anger and bitterness in his voice.

Luck . . .

Another part of the puzzle. Yes, she was sure of it now.

A mystery lay before her. One she was certain she could solve.

She went into the clean room, locking the door behind her. She walked over the decontamination chamber and stripped off her clothing, piling the rags neatly on a metal cart nearby. Standing below the aluminum shower head, she hesitated before turning on the steaming water. The moment the waters struck the grid at her bare feet, a cleansing chemical mist would rise from below and every physical reminder of the battle—except her wounds, of course—would dissolve away.

She stared at her hands. Examined her nails.

The gasp that had escaped Wager when her clawed hand struck his face, leaving five nasty gashes came to her.

True, his skin had healed almost instantly, but . . .

His blood and flecks of his skin remained under her nails. She stepped out of the chamber and went to work, scraping off samples, and mounting them for one test after another.

When she was certain that she would have enough material to work with, Caitlin took her shower, her excitement rising with the steam that enveloped her perfect form.

She was in a white robe, sitting at her analysis console, when the knock came at the door. She tapped a few keys on a nearby panel and unlocked the door.

Sarah stood in the doorway. "Caitlin, what are you doing?"

"I am the key," she whispered, practically entranced by the images revealed on her many screens. "And he is the lock."

"Oh."

Caitlin was only dimly aware when Sarah left.

Half an hour later, she was back in the living room, the entire group assembled around her. Her eyes blazed with excitement. She sat cross-legged on the floor, a pile of papers in her lap. Lab read-outs.

"Mr. Monteleone, how long has it been since Wager took the serum?" Caitlin asked.

"He was normal when I left," Monteleone said. "I guess it's been about six hours."

"Then it all fits." She reached into the pocket of her robe and drew out a vial filled with shining golden fluid. "I needed time to think. And I needed a chance at getting my hands on some of the original Gen-Active solution. I got 'em both."

Grunge shook his head. "Huh? I thought Wager had the last of it."

"It's in his blood," Caitlin said. "And it's in ours, too."

"But you can't extract it," Sarah said. "You told me that. The serum is bonded to our DNA."

Caitlin dug through the papers in her lap then looked up, shaking the long red hair out of her face. "Right. But I've been doing research. Actually, it's been kind of a hobby of mine for a while now. I've been analyzing blood samples from each of us, collating data, and I've come up with a theory. A bunch of theories, actually. I'm blathering. Sorry. But this is exciting."

Sarah stepped forward. "Caitlin, *now*."

"Yeah," Roxy said. "You're making my head spin. What's the deal with all this, anyway?"

Caitlin grinned. "The deal is, we've come to accept that there's no going back. That we're stuck with these powers for the rest of our lives."

"Yeah, no kidding," Bobby said.

Caitlin shook the vial in her hand. "I think this is an antidote. I'm pretty sure it would work. That it would take us back. Any of us. All of us. Give us our lives *back*."

Joe Monteleone hung his head and looked away at those words. Caitlin immediately regretted them.

"It could make us human again," Caitlin said. "Get rid of our powers."

Sarah sat down next to Caitlin and took the vial from her hand. She held it up to the light and studied it. Within, strange energies appeared to swim about, like living things. "How is that possible?"

"Don't get our hopes up for nothing," Roxy said.

Caitlin shuffled the papers in her lap once more. "I keep checking and re-checking my data, and it always comes out the same. There seems to be a kind of incubation period when the solution is introduced into people who aren't born Gen-Active. Powers appear right away, but there's a twelve-hour window of opportunity during which the Gen-Active material can still be separated out from a subject's DNA. I took the blood and skin that I'd torn from Wager and worked it until I was able to pull the two apart. With the primary material, in combination with all the data and samples I had on hand, I've been able to synthesize an antidote."

"I don't believe it," Sarah whispered.

"I've run simulations on the computer and I've tried it on my own blood sample," Caitlin said. "It worked to neutralize the Gen-Active strands in the sample. In theory, it should work on any of us, with no harmful results."

Bobby came closer. "You really mean it. You honestly think it would work?"

Caitlin nodded. "I've *seen* it work."

The room fell silent. Roxy got up and looked out the window, at the magnificent view of the city. "We could be the same as everyone else."

Grunge nodded. "No more secrets. No more lies."

Sarah handed the solution back to Caitlin. "I don't know. Being one with nature, riding the air . . . That's a lot to give up."

Caitlin touched her perfect features. "Let me tell you something. Every morning, when I wake up, I go to the mirror, and I'm still expecting to see my old self. Small. Flat. Plain. Every day, I jump when I see this looking back at me. It's not me. It's not who and what I am. When I see people staring at me I feel like I'm some kind of freak, like I'm something that isn't even human."

"That's not why they stare," Sarah said. "You're beautiful."

Caitlin tapped the side of her head. "I know that. Up here, intellectually, I know that." She tapped her chest. "But in here, in my heart, it's wrong. It doesn't track. I don't think it ever will. I could be in *Penthouse*—"

"Please, God, yes, please, God," Grunge chanted until Roxy smacked him on the back of the head.

"You get my point."

"I do," Sarah said. "And I agree. It's . . . a burden. Yes, there are benefits to these powers. But there's a price, too. We could have died today. Wager could have killed us all. And we would have died for nothing. The crime continues. People still hate. What difference does it really make if Wager controls the underworld or if it's someone else? People don't change. Human beings don't—"

"Sarah," Bobby said.

She looked to him in surprise.

"Wager killed Joe's family. Joe's going after Wager." He turned to the behemoth. "Aren't you?"

Joe Monteleone nodded slowly. "I have to."

Bobby put his hand on Joe's shoulder. "Then you're not going alone." He looked to the others. "I don't know about anyone else. But I met these people. I saw the future in their eyes. Wager took that away. I don't give a god *damn* about anything else."

Caitlin had never seen Bobby like this. Never. For a moment, he reminded her of his father.

Sarah looked approvingly at Bobby. "You're right. I'm in."

Grunge turned to Caitlin. "You think you can come up with a plan for dealin' with this guy?"

"Yes," Caitlin said. The word surprised even her. A moment ago, she had felt so close, so ready to take the antidote.

Of course, she could have done that before returning from the clean room . . .

"I'll do it," Grunge said.

Roxy eyed the solution in Caitlin's hands. "We take this guy down, *then* we make a decision about that stuff. Deal?"

Caitlin slipped the vial back into her pocket. "Deal."

CHAPTER 14

The men met in the back room of a bar and grill. Through the door they could hear the faint sounds of business as usual—glassware clinking, silver rattling, voices raised in mealtime conversation. The scents of grilling steak and baking bread and simmering sauces permeated the room.

They paid attention to none of it. They were here for business, not a meal. There was money at stake, and lots of it.

"I want a piece of midtown," Big Tony said. "I've always had a piece of midtown, and I don't see why that would change now."

"Everything's changed now," Andreas the Greek told him, running a hand through his silver hair. "It's like Europe after the war. None of the old lines on the map mean anything with Wager in town."

"I'm tired of hearing about Wager," Big Tony said.

The other men scooted their chairs away from the table, as if expecting a bolt of lightning to strike it.

Chuck E. Bones interrupted the sudden silence. "You gonna tell him that?"

"I just might," Big Tony said.

"Right," English Neil said. "You don't mind if I take over your midtown interests when he's burned you alive then, do you? I've always rather fancied that neighborhood."

They all turned when the door opened, hands reaching under jackets and into waistbands. Seven guns were pointed at the door when a fragile-looking, dark-haired girl in a tank top, leather jacket, and spandex shorts walked in. Behind her was a broad-shouldered but short Asian-American boy, shirt open to reveal a bizarre tattoo emblazoned across his chest.

"Big Tony's right," the girl said, flipping her magenta bangs from her eyes. "You should listen to him."

"These friends of yours, Tony?" Andreas the Greek asked.

"I never seen 'em before," Tony replied. "But they talk sense."

"They ain't under anybody's protection, they're dead," Chuck E. Bones growled. He pulled the trigger of his automatic.

The other men began firing, too—except for Big Tony.

Roxy simply increased the gravity between her and the bullets, and they all dropped to the ground as if strings had yanked them down. After a minute, the firing stopped.

"Man, people are tryin' to eat dinner out there," Grunge said. "Even I can hear that racket, and my ears are like, way shot. Don't you guys have silencers?"

Roxy made an "ignore him" wave. "What my friend means is, that creep Wager is finished in this town," she said. "You don't owe him anything. He's yesterday's Go-Gurt. You go about your 'business' and, well, we might have some problems with you down the line, but oh well. For now, don't worry about Wager."

"She's nuts," Andreas the Greek said. "Or she's with him, and she's just testing us."

"Are you absolutely certain you know what you're talking about, young lady?" English Neil asked. "Are you even in the right room?"

"Unless there's some other New York crime boss meeting going on in the neighborhood," Roxy said. "I think we got the right bunch."

"Man, I'm getting' hungry just smellin' that chow, Rox," Grunge said. "Can we grab a bite or somethin' before we go?"

"I think maybe we'll eat somewhere else, Grunge," she said. "Let's let these gentlemen—and I use the term so loosely it's not even connected to anything—finish their little Cub Scout meeting."

She closed the door and they walked out through the now-empty restaurant.

"That was kinda fun, wasn't it?" she said. Grunge didn't answer. "Grunge?"

She turned around. He was busy forking a slab of rare beef from an abandoned plate and stuffing it into his mouth.

"Mwhuf," Grunge said.

Willy liked the fact that they trusted him. He was important to the operation, they always said that. Wasn't for him watching the back door, anything could happen. They'd be out of business.

Sure, it got cold and lonely. But he just tugged his cap down over his ears and put his hand inside his pocket, touched that big old strap he carried in there. Man carried, he always had a friend.

Anyway, bad as the alley smelled, piled high with trash and the sewage that flowed from a broken pipe, it didn't smell as bad as inside. People went inside were people who were hurting, people hadn't so much as looked at a shower in weeks, people in pain. Inside smelled like a hospital ward, the kind where Willy's grandma had been, where no one who was in one of the beds was ever expected to come out except in a box.

When they came out they were smiling. But they always looked worse on their next visit.

Another hour, and someone would come outside and pay Willy. He'd take his twenty bucks home and hide it in the sock with the rest of what he'd been able to save. He'd be sixteen in three years, and he planned to be able to buy a Mercedes by then.

"Hey, kid!"

He drew the .38 as he spun to see who had called him.

TIME AND CHANCE

It was a huge red-haired woman, tallest one he'd ever seen, with legs that reached almost skyscraper high, it seemed like. She wore a tight uniform that clung to every curve she had, and there were plenty.

"No, over here," another voice said. He turned to the other end of the alley, and there was a woman with a waterfall of straight black hair cascading down her shoulders, accompanied by a young man with a blonde goatee. Like the redhead, they were all dressed in skintight uniforms of some kind. He didn't recognize the colors as any gang's that he knew of.

"Put the gun down," the redhead said. "We're not here to hurt you or anyone else. We just want to inconvenience the operation a little bit."

"What, you think I'm just gonna let you in?" Willy said. "I fire this thing once, you'll have a dozen straps aimed at your butts."

"Then don't even think about it," the man said. He was holding one hand out in front of him, and a tendril of smoke snaked from that hand into the air, as if he were holding a chunk of burning wood.

But the hand was empty.

Willy started to worry. Maybe whoever these people were, popping a cap in them wasn't going to be good enough.

Twenty bucks was twenty bucks. He hesitated.

"Look, you'll be fine," the dark-haired one said. "I promise." They had all advanced on him, hemming him in from both sides. But she had a look on her face that he couldn't quite read. It almost looked like she cared about what happened to him. That was a sensation he wasn't used to.

"Just tell us which door it is," she said. "Just point to it."

"I ain't pointin' to nothin'," Willy said.

"Not good enough, bro," the man said. "I'm gonna burn him."

The dark-haired one threw a hand up to stop him. "No, Bobby."

"He serious?" Willy asked. "He could do that?"

"You can't imagine the things he can do," she said in reply. "Me, too." She gave him a quick smile and then raised her hands into the air. Suddenly, there was a cloud—a real cloud, like you saw up in the sky between the buildings, only it was floating in the alley ten feet over Willy's head.

A raindrop hit him on the cheek.

He pointed at a door.

Then he ran.

When he was gone, Caitlin kicked it in.

The place was a shooting gallery. Junkies turned over cash they'd borrowed, stolen, or otherwise absconded with, and in exchange were given enough drugs to keep the world at bay for another few hours, and a place to use them.

To Caitlin, it stank of desperation. The end of hope.

There were a dozen people inside, in a space meant for three or four. They sat on a worn-out couch, on the floor, in the corners. A couple of them barely looked up when Gen^{13} came in. One woman got up and tried to run, but tripped over her own feet.

The two healthiest-looking guys pulled shotguns. A quick burst from Bobby melted the barrels, and the guns were suddenly too hot to touch.

When they tried to sprint out the door, Caitlin caught them both by the collars, one in each hand.

"The money," she hissed. "Where is it?"

"What money?" one asked. She bounced him off the apartment wall and caught him on the rebound.

"No games," she said.

They reached into their shirts and drew out stacks of bills. Sarah opened a cloth bag with RECYCLE printed on it in soy ink, and they put the cash into her bag. When they were done, she asked, "That's it?"

"That's it for today," one said. "It's early, you know.

More of 'em come by later, but that's all so far."

"Okay," Caitlin said. "What you're doing here is wrong. I want you to stop it, and if I come back here and this is still happening here someone's going to be hurt, you understand me?"

They both nodded.

"The money we're taking from you will go to a good cause. We're not taking it because it's yours, I want you to be clear on that. We're taking it because you're going to give some of it to Wager. Anyone who deals with Wager will lose his or her money. Anyone who pays tribute to Wager is making a big mistake. Spread the word."

"Consider it spread, mama," one of them said.

"Now get out of here, all of you," Bobby said. As he spoke, he allowed low flames to dance about his body. "This place is going to get very hot in a minute if you don't clear out."

They cleared.

"Officer Golden, Officer Gonzales," Butch said when the two police officers walked into his bar. "Get you a drink?"

"We're on the job," Gonzales said, touching the bill of her cap. "How fresh is the coffee?"

"Just brewed it," Butch said. "Coming right up."

"Thanks," Golden said. He scraped a stool across the floor, lifted his bulk onto it. The bar was nearly empty; one serious drinker sat at the far end, striving for oblivion. There were three booths along one wall, nine stools at the bar. Butch's was little more than a hole in the wall, and Butch was its sole employee.

"You want these to go?" he asked.

"We've got a lot of stops to make today," Gonzales said. "Can't stay in one spot."

Butch poured coffee into tall stryofoam cups, wrapped napkins around them, and set them on the bar.

"Thanks," Golden said.

"Yup," Butch replied. He reached under the cash register, came out with a sealed brown envelope in his hand.

He put the envelope on the bar next to the steaming cups.

Golden slid it across the bar, tucked it inside his jacket. "See you next month," he said, climbing down off his stool. He picked up one coffee and handed it to Gonzales, then took his own.

They were heading for the door when the little bells hanging from the knob jingled.

Five young people dressed in outlandish spandex outfits walked in.

"You old enough to drink?" Gonzales asked.

"I'd show you my driver's license," Caitlin Fairchild said. "But I don't exactly have a lot of pockets in this outfit."

"Looks fine from here," Golden said, eyeing her voluptuous form.

"Keep your tongue in your head," Gonzales told him. "Excuse us, kids. We're off to keep the streets safe for fashion disasters."

"We'll take the envelope," Grunge said. "Then you can go."

"What envelope?" Golden asked. "We're in a hurry, people, so step aside."

"Let's not pretend anybody's stupid here," Grunge said.

Roxy punched his shoulder. "Though if we were going to, you'd be a good starting point," she said.

Grunge shot her a look, then reached out and touched the brick wall near the door. He felt the transformation come over him, an inch at a time, until he was a Grunge-shaped brick wall standing in front of the brick wall.

"The envelope," he said.

Golden and Gonzales both dropped their hands to their weapons.

"Don't," Sarah Rainmaker said. "There's no need for violence."

Roxy gestured toward the officers, floating them off the floor. As they lost contact with solid ground, their balance shifted and they forgot about their guns, throwing their arms out to maintain their equilibrium instead.

"Hey!" Gonzales said. "Put us down!"

"Freakin' superheroes," Golden muttered.

"The envelope," Fairchild insisted, holding a hand out.

Golden reached into his jacket, drew it out. He put it into her hand.

"That's better," she said.

Freefall lowered them to the floor.

"One more thing," Caitlin said. She tossed the envelope to Butch, who caught it with a broad smile. "You shouldn't be shaking down small businesses for insurance money. You're cops. You're supposed to be upholding the law."

"Yeah, that totally sucks," Grunge added as he allowed himself to revert to his fleshy state.

"I wouldn't want to see this happening again," Caitlin said. "But I'm not going to turn you in this time. I just want you to realize that I know Wager was going to get a cut of this. No more. Wager is done for, and anybody who's on his side is going to have to answer to us. Tell a friend."

"Let's scram," Bobby said. "Sight of crooked cops makes me sick." He pulled the door open, jingling the bell.

"Hey, I'm thirsty," Grunge said.

"When we finish," Roxy told him. "Come on, big guy. You're like a camel. You can wait."

As the sun dipped below the buildings, the wind off the East River picked up and day turned colder. Fairchild, Freefall, Burnout, Rainmaker, and Grunge, in full costume, stood on the sidewalk looking at a block of brownstone houses. They looked abandoned; windows were boarded up, doors had planks nailed over them. Everywhere was peeling paint, graffiti, dunes of drifting trash blown against the houses by the winds.

"Okay, rousting all those crooks made for a fun day,"

Grunge said. "But tell me again what good it's supposed to do. And what are we doing here?"

"This is Wager's headquarters, according to Mr. Joe," Bobby explained. "We're bringing the fight to him."

"His whole deal, Mr. Monteleone said, was bringing New York's underworld under his control," Caitlin added. As she spoke, she touched a zippered pocket in her uniform, reassuring herself that it was still there. The antidote, safely ensconced in a steel tube. And something else—a back-up weapon. She didn't want to think about "just in case," but better to prepare for the worst than not to. "He wants their respect, he wants their obedience, and he wants their money. What we were doing, I hope, was cutting into all three of those areas. Without them, his power structure is lessened. And by doing that, we'll be making him more and more angry. He's already a little nuts, it sounds like. If we get him mad enough, he won't be thinking straight."

"And then we can mess him up?" Roxy said.

"That's the plan," Bobby replied.

Caitlin looked at her teammates. The wind whipped her red hair around her lovely face, stung her eyes. She blinked, but held her gaze.

"We've faced a lot together," she said. "We've put our lives on the line a thousand times, and we've always come out ahead. But based on what Mr. Monteleone's told us, it's possible that we've never gone up against someone as powerful as Wager is."

"Even though we've been sniping at him all day?" Grunge asked.

"We've been going after his supporters, his troops," Caitlin answered. "It'd be nice to think we've hurt him. But he still has personal power, and we really don't know of what type, or how formidable. It's a gamble." She took a deep breath. "Anyone want out?"

There was silence for a moment. None of them had ever asked that question before, not out loud anyway.

"No way," Grunge finally said.

"I'm in," Bobby declared.

"Same here," Sarah echoed.

"Couldn't keep me away," Roxy said.

"Shouldn't we hold hands, like the Fantastic Four or something?" Grunge asked.

"I think that'd be taking things a little too far," Caitlin said. "Let's go in there and kick Wager's butt."

The team turned toward the brownstones.

"Uhh, one thing," Grunge said. "Which door?"

"From what Mr. Joe said," Bobby replied, "It doesn't sound like it really matters."

"Then let's drop in," Grunge said.

They climbed the nearest stairway. Grunge paused long enough to touch a rusting banister, taking on the molecular composition of wrought iron. "Allow me," he said. He raised both fists over his head and brought them down against the door, clubbing it in as if with a battering ram.

Sticking his black iron head through the cloud of dust he'd raised, he grinned a manic smile and announced, "Luuuucy! I'm hooome!"

The inside was a trash-filled mess, graffiti on every surface. There was no sign of the kinds of security they expected—it just looked like someone's house that they left years ago, which squatters had moved into since. Following the directions Joe Monteleone had given them, they worked their way back toward the center. The walls were no problem—Caitlin smashed holes through them, or Bobby burned through with controlled flames, or Sarah blew through them with powerful winds.

After they'd moved through several rooms this way, Roxy stopped before yet another wall, half-covered with strips of faded pink wallpaper.

"Okay," she said, "interior decoration disaster. But not scary, can I point out? Are we sure we've got the right place? This is almost too easy."

"You're right," Sarah said. "But I don't read it like you do."

"I'm with you, Sarah," Caitlin said. "We are in the

right place. Which means there should be some kind of security, cameras, booby traps, soldiers, something. Since there's not, it makes me think that maybe Wager isn't worried about us."

"But we're Gen[13]," Grunge said. "He better be worried."

"Unless he doesn't have anything to worry about," Bobby said. "Which means we didn't do him any damage today at all."

Almost as if Wager had heard them—exactly as if he had, in fact—the strips of wallpaper unrolled themselves, falling to the floor and revealing a flat video screen. It crackled for a moment, and then a picture spread across it. On the screen, the team saw a gang of punked-out kids robbing a small grocery in Koreatown. They ran out of the little store carrying a paper bag full of cash, which one of them held up toward the camera.

"This is for you, Wager!" the tattooed, pierced young man shouted.

"Whoa," Grunge said. "A TV built into the wall! Cool."

"There were no screens in those other walls," Caitlin pointed out. "Odd that there happened to be one here."

"What I was thinking," Roxy agreed.

Just as suddenly as it had appeared, the screen vanished and the wallpaper was just as it had been. But a noise from behind them alerted them, and they whirled to see another screen appearing against another wall—the wall they had just destroyed to come into this room.

"No flippin' way," Grunge said.

On this screen was an image of an uptown bank branch. The angle was like that of a bank's security camera, but the picture was in color, and high quality. Masked robbers with shotguns filled sacks with cash from the teller windows.

"Okay, I'm seriously freaked," Bobby announced.

As if in response, that screen blinked from existence and another one appeared, this one a flat panel floating in the center of the room. The image on this screen wasn't a moving one, but a still picture. Filling the screen was the head of Big Tony, resting in a pool of blood on a silver tray.

"I think we all are," Caitlin suggested. As the floating screen disappeared from sight, she looked around for the camera or viewing device that she was sure must be there. *He's watching us,* she thought. "Wager!" she shouted. "Gen^{13} is here! You might as well give up now and come on out!"

From nowhere—from everywhere—a chuckle sounded, growing into deep, ringing laughter that filled the room, the building.

Finally, the laughter ceased and Wager's voice echoed from all around. "Give up?" he asked. "Did it ever occur to you that you're right where I want you?"

The team members glanced at each other.

"That's not exactly surrendering, is it?" Grunge asked.

"If it's a fight he wants," Sarah said, "I'm happy to give it to him."

Caitlin turned, about to respond to Sarah's proclamation—and her teammates were gone. No, more than that. Her surroundings had changed completely.

The walls were steel, with strange, oversized lines of circuitry running along them, crisscrossing, their glowing color changing from aqua to orange, from blue to green, from violet to crimson. The floor and ceiling had become a steel grating with a dull white light radiating from above and a shimmering field of energy below. She was in a central chamber with a dozen branching corridors. The ceiling was high, at least thirty feet, and huge machines, some simple in design, others unfathomably complex, rose up all around her. She had no idea what purpose, if any, the machines fulfilled. One looked like it might have been a vast Victorian-styled steam-powered computation device; another some type of air processor or purifier, with its many tubes and vents.

She started as two of the machines sprouted legs and casually walked across the chamber right past her, sauntering down opposite corridors. One hissed mildly while the other clunked and clattered.

"Rox?" she called. "Grunge? Sarah? Anyone?"

No response.

It's all in my head, she thought. *Wager's playing head games with me, that's all.*

She closed her eyes and *willed* the illusion away.

When she opened them again, a machine with huge mechanical claws stood in front of her.

It struck with enough force to send her hurtling across the chamber, and flying down one of the many corridors.

Bobby stood with Sarah on a small hill. The sky was red, the earth beneath them a blighted amber. Streaks of gold and silver drifted over the bleak, barren landscape, along with dark, cancerous clouds. There was no life, no hint of civilization, in any direction.

"Where are we?" Sarah asked.

"Wager's place," Bobby said. He hoped the uncertainty didn't tell in his voice. "Has to be."

Sarah tilted her head. "Try to use your powers."

Bobby didn't question. He held out his hand and allowed a small orb of flame to come into existence.

In seconds, it flickered and died.

Sarah raised her hands and attempted to summon a wind. A breeze lifted her hair and quickly fell away into nothingness.

"This land is dead," Sarah said. "And the elements, the forces we command, are out of balance."

In the distance, a doorway appeared. A single black opening.

"It's a trap," Bobby said. "Has to be."

Sarah nodded. "So let's go."

They walked down from the hill. The earth at its base was more like gently shifting sands. It clung to their boots and sank beneath their weight.

"We're strong enough to make it out of here," Bobby said. "We just have to stay focused."

Sarah was about to reply when a shape burst from the sands at her feet, grabbed her, and pulled her under. Bobby leaped at the slight indentation that marked her passing, digging frantically until something grabbed him from behind and pulled him into the hungry, burning soil.

Grunge and Roxy knelt behind a row of metal carts bearing medical apparatus. They watched as armored guards led a small group of teenagers to a round table fitted with steel chairs that jutted outward. Cuffs and restraining straps waited near the arms and legs of the chairs. A man and a woman wearing long white lab coats followed the teens. They carried needles filled with the Gen-Active serum.

Grunge didn't wonder exactly what this place was or how he got here. He took in the situation before him, felt his flesh burn with anger, and grasped a titanium scalpel laying on a nearby tray. The change came quickly, heady and intoxicating, then he was on his feet, smashing at the chestplates of the guards, cracking gauntlets before weapons could be pulled, punching faceplates and feeling the satisfying snap as shattered helmets broke open and the sweating, frightened faces of little men appeared. His opponents fell beneath his attack while the teenagers stared at Grunge in shock.

He turned, his titanium covered body shining in the harsh fluorescent glow from above, expecting to see the technicians radioing for help or running like hell.

Instead, they floated near the ceiling, whimpering helplessly.

"Good job, Rox," Grunge said. He turned back to the teenagers. "Listen, we're gonna get you out of here. All of you. No one's experimenting on you. No one's gonna do to you what was done to us."

Roxy called his name. He turned quickly, worried that some new threat had appeared. But there was none. He relaxed—until he saw the armor-piercing handgun in Roxy's hand.

"What—?" he began.

It was all he could say before she fired and the pain became his world.

Sarah struggled as inhumanly long fingers closed on her, wrapping themselves in her hair, clawing at her body, dragging her down while the fine earth threatened to suffocate as well as blind her. She heard the chattering of sharp teeth and felt wet, huge, sluglike bodies pressing up against her.

All her life, she had been one with nature. One with the earth, the sky, and the wind. This nightmare was almost too much for her. She had been taken into the body of a corrupted world. She couldn't breathe—and didn't dare open her mouth for fear of the hot, poisoned soil entering her body, and somehow changing her, taking her life by giving her a new one, one that would bind her to this place for all eternity.

She had been wrong about this place. It wasn't lifeless. Far from it. But whoever, *whatever* had resided her had been changed. Mutated. She could feel it.

And that's what would happen to her, if she couldn't find a way to fight back.

Sarah marshaled her power. She called to a place deep within her, feeling the rush of her blood through her veins as if it were the flowing tides upon an ocean from her world; she drew upon the air trapped in her lungs as if it were ancient winds raging through valleys in some far-off land; she felt the thunderous beat of her heart and told herself it was the sound of a gale smashing against windows in Manhattan.

The elements were within her.

She *would* command them.

With a silent cry Sarah felt her power surround her like a cocoon, pushing away the corruption of this terrible place. She willed herself upward, driving herself against the hands and the earth and the teeth-filled slug-like *things* that sought to make her one of them—and burst from the sands!

She rose into the sky, coughing, shaking, spiraling dizzily. A fiery shape appeared before her.

"Bobby?"

Yet even as she spoke her friend's name, she knew it wasn't him.

The burning man turned nightmare black, becoming a terrible void. For an instant, his form flickered and took the shape of the doorway she had seen in the distance.

"I am the gateway," he said. "But I am not for you."

The man changed shape once more, becoming a thing that might have been human, or perhaps a scorpion, and reached for her.

Caitlin ran.

Hundreds of tiny devices scuttled after her. Walls expanded outward and withdrew, as if they were breathing. Steel arms with grasping claws materialized from their reaches.

A figure appeared before her and Caitlin struck at it.

Her fist went straight through the figure and she nearly stumbled. Turning, she heard a familiar voice behind her.

"Caitlin, it's me. Cipher."

She saw him materialize. "I thought you were staying behind, you said—"

Cipher reached for a pair of the mechanical arms that clawed at him and yanked them out of the walls. He used them to beat at the collection of hungry, snapping little machines that sped their way, on wheels, tracks, and mechanical feet.

"What's going on here?" Caitlin asked, joining the fray.

"Wager having a little fun, what else?" Cipher said. "You have a love of science. Technology. You think of yourself as a brain while others view you as little more than a body. Wager looked into your soul when we fought. He's seen into all of us. It gets him off, killing us with what we love. Corrupting it."

Before them, the machines backed away and began to leap at one another. They formed three distinct figures, one larger than the other two.

With hissing mechanical voices that were otherwise perfect replications, Joe Monteleone's wife and children held out their arms and called for him to join them...

Roxy wandered through the halls of a vast, deserted lab. The place looked eerily familiar, reminding her of the facility where she had been *changed* into something more than human.

She hated being here alone. One moment, she had been with her friends, ready to take on the monster that had nearly killed them all once before. Then—she was here.

Nothing had happened to her. No bogeymen had leaped out and attacked her. There was nothing here but dust, the smell of old, spilled chemicals, and a palpable feeling of dread.

She wanted to be anywhere but here.

Footsteps came from a corridor directly ahead. She stopped, wondering if she should take cover.

No.

Whatever the threat, she would face it full on.

A shadow crept forward, and a figure became clear. Short. Hulking.

"Grunge!" Roxy yelled, her arms open wide.

He leveled a gun at her. His chest was torn open. Bleeding. She saw now that he was on the verge of staggering.

"Sorry, babe," Grunge said. "You don't get me twice the same way."

His finger tightened on the trigger of the weapon he held.

He fired.

• • •

Bobby was on the ground, fighting a handful of creatures that were part-human, part-slug, and part-piranha, when Sarah had burst from the earth. He had called to her as she spun high into the air and confronted the mysterious figure that had appeared. Was it Wager? Another of his agents? Or simply another monstrosity pulled forth from his twisted mind?

Bobby felt the heat of the blighted earth. He drew on it, and felt his body burst into flames. The monsters he fought drew back, and he sailed into the air to help the woman he cared most about in the world.

Sarah was grappling with the dark, shifting form. It was an amorphous thing, a void whose borders remained constant for no more than a few seconds at a time. Always it looked something like a man, but with other aspects blurring its form.

It was darkness.

Bobby was the light. He flew through it and the creature wailed as its body was dispersed. Sarah fell back and away, spinning and countering her fall before she struck the ground or came near the mutated creatures below.

"He said he was the doorway, but not for us," Sarah said. "How are we going to get out of here?"

Bobby wished he had an answer. He had been the one to lead them to this place. To insist that they come.

In so many ways, it really was up to him.

He reached out with his slowly evolving psychic powers and felt a *presence* that informed this entire region.

And suddenly, he knew the answer. "It's not about getting out, Sarah. It's about getting further in . . ."

Grunge wasn't sure why he flinched at the last second and let his shot go wide. This wasn't Roxy. It was another drone. Or illusion. Or whatever the hell Wager was sending against him.

Yet—he just couldn't do it. Even after she had nearly killed him, even knowing what he did, he couldn't bring himself to hurt her.

The young woman before him quaked and nearly burst into tears. She looked at the seared wall beside her. Then she looked over his shoulder, at the teenagers he had rescued after he had disarmed the fake Roxy and drove her off.

She raised her hands. "Look out! Grunge, look—"

They struck him down from behind. He was in his human form, his body rapidly healing, but still weakened from the trauma of being shot. The sheer number of his attackers and the ferocity of their attack was too much for him. He struck the floor hard and heard inhuman wails and high shrieks of laughter. The second he felt their skin he knew they weren't human any longer. They had already been *turned*.

Then—the biting, stabbing mass lifted from him. He rolled onto his back and saw creatures that were now only partially human striking the walls and ceiling.

"They're kids, just kids, like us!" Grunge said. But he wondered—was that true? Was there even a chance of it?

He turned back to Roxy, the weapon still in his hand. He aimed it at her as he got to his feet.

"How do I know it's you?" he asked. "How am I supposed to trust you or anything here?"

Roxy's hands lowered. Her shoulders slumped. "Grunge, I..."

Two words escaped her lips. He only barely heard them, as they were little more than a whisper. For a very long time, he would question if she had really spoken those words at all.

But he sensed in his heart that the young woman before him was Roxy, and that the love she felt for him, however she meant it, was real.

He felt it, too.

Grunge lowered the weapon and held out his hand. Roxy raced ahead and took his hand, stopping short of hugging him when she saw his still healing wound.

"If none of this is real," she said, her lips reaching

toward his. "If that's true, then we can do anything here. Anything."

He nodded, and an instant before their lips met, they were—elsewhere.

Caitlin watched as Cipher's resolve faltered and nearly collapsed. He stared at the mechanical amalgam that had taken the shape of his wife and children and spoke to him with their voices.

"Daddy's a secret agent. A superhero," Joe Jr. said. "He won't let anything happen to us. Not again."

"I love you, sweetheart," the woman said. "More than anything in the world. You know that."

The girl looked away. "Daddy, you won't hurt us. You won't, will you?"

Caitlin considered what Cipher had told her. "It's the past. You can let it trap you or you can make it a part of you and move ahead. The choice is up to you."

Cipher looked over his shoulder at her. "See?" he said. "You're not all brain or body. It's your heart that knows ..."

He stepped forward and the robotic creatures broke apart and swarmed him. At the last instant he became intangible, then, when he and the mechanical killers shared the same space, he took on flesh and form.

Cipher screamed as his body and blood merged with the technology, drawing it deep inside, swallowing it whole.

Then it was over.

"Time to end this," Cipher said. He took Caitlin's hand, and the mechanical, sterile setting vanished.

Bobby saw the shadow being slowly reforming as he floated near Sarah. "Wager's a part of all of this. It's reality. It's illusion."

"It's whatever we allow it to be," Sarah said, beginning to understand.

"Whatever we want it to be. His will—or ours."

The shadow creature leaped for them. This time, they did not fight it. They let it overwhelm them. It seemed surprised, then tried to pull away. But it was too late.

"You are the doorway," Sarah said. "And you are for us."

The barren landscape faded. Bobby and Sarah found themselves in a small room with Caitlin, Cipher, Grunge, and Roxy.

Wager stood before them. "Welcome to my private place," he said. "My most holy of holies. Enjoy what you see."

The madman grinned. "It's the last sight any of you will ever have..."

CHAPTER 15

"I'd like to say this'll be a piece of cake," Bobby said. "But I'd be full of it."

"You are anyway," Grunge said. "But in this case, I have to agree with you."

"Doesn't matter," Caitlin countered. "We need to take him down."

"I'm ready," Cipher added.

At those words, Wager laughed. Bobby had heard his laugh on the way in, echoing through the empty rooms of the brownstones that surrounded his inner sanctum. But seeing him, immense arms at his sides, fists the size of New Jersey on his hips, head thrown back—that was different. Terrifying. He was reminded of how easily he'd defeated them before. Wager's laugh sounded more like furious thunder than anything resembling mirth or joy.

Bobby stared at him for a moment, concentrating, trying to get a mental lock on the man. Or what used to be a man. He was still developing his mental powers, and could never quite tell what was going to work.

Nothing. It was as if the guy was either not human, or Wager's own mental abilities so far exceeded Bobby's that he was able to block Bobby's attempts.

Bobby hurled a plasma blast directly at him.

"What are we waiting for?" he asked as he threw it.

Wager raised a hand, almost casually. The ball of flaming glanced off his fingertips.

TIME AND CHANCE

The wall it flew into exploded. Behind it, some of Wager's troops stood, open-mouthed.

"Right result, wrong target," Roxy pointed out helpfully.

Bobby tossed her a scowl. "Like I don't know."

"I'm only saying."

"Impressive display," Wager said. "Got anything else, or is that the best of it? I had calculated at least a seventy-three percent chance that you'd come up with some new tactics to use against me this time."

"Oh, that's just a beginning," Sarah replied. She raised her hands over her head. A fierce wind whipped up around her, blowing her long black hair forward. In her hands she gathered a massive lightning bolt, which she threw, Zeus-like, at Wager's chest.

Again, Wager flapped his hands dismissively at the bolt. It whipped past him, smashing into the bank of video and computer monitors at his desk. Sparks shot to the room's low ceiling, and a small flame began to flicker inside the ruined electronics.

"A little better," Wager said. "My turn now."

With that, he glanced at the flaming pile of video wreckage. Almost at once, it began to change. Almost like a spilled liquid, the bits and pieces of it flowed together. The mass of the whole equipment bank expanded, pushing against another wall, punching through it. The team watched as it took on a definite shape.

In less than a minute, a dragon stood before them. Its head, twenty feet high, tore through the ceiling above, raining plaster down into the small room Wager had occupied. Its tail was in yet another room. Scales of shiny black plastic covered its length. It stood on powerful hind legs that ended in reptilian feet and claws made of shards of glass that had once been monitor screens. With its front legs, it pawed at the air as if anxious to be loosed on them. Its eyes were unbroken monitors, glowing with phosphoresence.

"Okay," Roxy said. "Superfreaky, but we can deal."

"We can?" Grunge asked. "I mean, sure we can." He reached down, touching the stone floor, and let his molecules take on its hardness. "Ready now."

Amazing, Caitlin thought, watching the dragon form. She'd seen him do this before, but that didn't help defray the sense of awe. *It's almost as if he has the power to reshape reality,* she thought.

No, never mind the "almost."

Cipher pushed his way to the front of the team. "I'll take this one," he insisted.

"Be my guest," Grunge said.

"Careful, Mr. Joe," Bobby warned.

But Cipher wasn't listening to them. He had taken three steps toward the dragon. His entire will was focused on the beast, and the dragon eyed him through squared-off eyes, glass teeth gnashing together. Cipher held out his right hand, and a long sword appeared in it. He extended his left and a shield was there.

"He's not the only one who can play like that," Cipher said. *To a vastly lesser extent,* he thought. *But here goes.* He raised the sword to swing at the dragon.

But the great beast reared back its head, then thrust its neck forward. Its mouth fell open and a great jet of—well, something—blasted out like a fountain of flame. Cipher raised his shield instinctively, and the stuff bounced from its surface, flowing around him. As it hit the ground, it sizzled and melted like snow on a hot plate, but Caitlin could see what it was—random letters and numbers.

"It's breathing *information* at him," she whispered, awestruck. "Pure data. Incredible."

"Yes," Sarah breathed in her ear. "It's phenomenal. But don't let it distract you from what needs to be done."

"Right," Caitlin agreed.

Cipher pressed his counterattack, moving in under cover of his shield. He swung the great sword. Its broad blade bit into the beast's plastic scales, just above the front left leg. The thing let out a staticky wail. Encouraged, he yanked the sword away, and drove it forward again, point first this time. The tip buried itself in the dragon's chest. But before Cipher could take advantage of the wound, the thing's heavy tail whipped around and slammed into him, sending him flying into the room's only remaining wall.

Caitlin chose that moment to make her move, while Wager was distracted by his dragon's battle. She slipped the hypodermic containing the Gen Factor antidote from its metal case and lunged at him.

He held up a hand toward her, and she stopped as if running into an invisible wall. The hypodermic flew out of her hand, rolling into the corner behind the dragon.

Cipher sat up, somewhat dazed by the impact with the dragon's tail. The thing's snout was lunging toward him, teeth snapping. He still clutched the shield, which he held out before him. The dragon's head rammed into it. The shock traveled up Cipher's arm, and he dropped the shield, but the dragon's attack was stopped.

"We gotta help him, Bob-man," Grunge said. "Flame on."

"Right," Bobby agreed. He'd been almost in a trance, watching the miraculous battle take place. But now he allowed his entire body to be covered in flames. Grunge reached a stone hand out to touch his friend's shoulder, and then let himself become flame too, matching Bobby's molecular structure.

"Cool," Bobby said. "Let's go."

Together, they charged the beast.

Caitlin shook Roxy's arm. "Rox, the antidote," Caitlin said.

At first, Roxy didn't know what her sister meant. She'd been too caught up in watching the dragon. But she followed Caitlin's pointing arm, and saw the hypodermic, still lodged in the corner behind where the dragon held its ground.

"Gotcha," she said. She focused on it, lifting it from the ground and levitating it well over the dragon's head. She moved it slowly, not wanting to attract Wager's attention to it.

Or the dragon's, she thought. *That thing swallows the needle, I'm sure not climbing into its guts to retrieve it.*

Bobby took to the air, and hit first, high up on the dragon's already-wounded chest. He flamed his way through the thing's hard plastic shell. The dragon screamed, its tail whipping this way and that as it tried to shake the burning invader loose.

But Grunge caught the tail in his fiery grip. He was lifted off his feet by its writhing, then managed to find his footing. As Bobby cooked the dragon from within, Grunge twisted its tail, knocking it off-balance. Once it had fallen to the floor, Grunge worked his way up its body, hands and feet melting through its scales every time they touched. The monster bucked and curled from the pain, its deafening screams filling the building.

Cipher joined them then, sword held tightly in both hands, shield forgotten. Grunge and Bobby had the thing down on its side. Its head, thrashing on its stalk-like neck, was just a couple of feet off the ground. He raised the sword over his head and brought it down. The steel flashed in Bobby's firelight before slicing cleanly into the neck. Plastic shattered; shards flew every which way. On the other side, the sword hit the stone floor.

The dragon's head clattered to the floor right after.

Its corpse gave one final shudder, and then it was still, bleeding wires and tubes and circuit boards out its stump.

Cipher let the sword vanish, turning back to the ladies. Sarah and Roxy were watching, and Caitlin was hiding something in her hands.

She had retrieved the hypodermic. There was still a chance to end this thing.

He turned to Wager, expecting to see the man downhearted by the defeat of his dragon.

Instead, Wager was smiling, rubbing his hands together.

"Much better," he said. "There's my seventy percent in action. It's such a pleasure to see real teamwork. I was almost worried that when I achieved this level of being,

TIME AND CHANCE

there would be no one capable of testing me. You certainly weren't much of a danger last time we met. I'm glad to see you making some strides. Ultimately pointless, of course."

"We'll do more than test you," Grunge announced, extricating himself from the melting goo that had been a dragon. "We'll give you a mother of a final exam."

"Emphasis on final," Bobby added. He had flown out of the dragon and hovered above Wager now.

Cipher, Caitlin, Sarah, and Roxy also faced the man. They had him surrounded. It would only take Caitlin a single leap, with her long legs, to bury the needle in the exposed flesh of his neck.

She poised herself.

"Sarah, Bobby, cover!" she called. As one, they loosed a barrage of flame and electricity in the man's direction. When they did, Caitlin moved.

Wager blinked.

And the room fell away.

They stood, suddenly, on a vast plain, miles across. The ground was hard and dry and bare of vegetation, just mile after mile of reddish rock. It might have been the surface of Mars, for all they could tell.

Mountains ringed the plain. It was impossible to tell how tall they might be, or how far away.

Wager stood, laughing, a thousand yards from them.

When he spoke, though, it was as if he hadn't moved an inch away.

"You can't still hope to defeat me," he gloated. "At best, you can pray that I let you survive."

"Sheee," Grunge said. "How'd he do that?"

"He controls reality. He can warp it to his will," Sarah said. "Haven't you been paying attention?"

"Figured it was somethin' like that."

"Like when we went up against Max Faraday?" Bobby asked.

"Very much like that," Caitlin replied.

"How'd we beat him, again?" Grunge wanted to know.

249

"We didn't, Einstein," Roxy told him. "He killed himself, remember?"

"Right," Grunge said. "You don't suppose Wager will"

"It seems very unlikely," Sarah said. "He's kind of got the upper hand."

"He'd never do that," Cipher agreed. "This is what he's lived for."

"Swell," Grunge said. "Why do the fruitcakes get what they want, and I can't even find a decent skate ramp in Manhattan?"

"We're wasting time," Caitlin said. "We've got ground to cover."

She tucked her head and began to run, her long legs eating up the space quickly. Above her, she saw Bobby, Roxy, and Sarah flying toward Roxy. Grunge and Cipher brought up the rear, running as fast as they could.

When she figured she had gone halfway, she raised her head, looked toward Wager.

He was still just as far away.

The plain seemed to expand as they ran. No matter how far they went, there was no getting closer to him.

She stopped, breathing hard.

"Okay," she called. "Pull up!"

The others gathered around her.

"We're just knocking ourselves out, doing that. It's not working. We need another plan."

"I don't know what the elements are like here," Sarah said. I can try to call up a big momma of a storm, but there's no guarantee that my powers will work in whatever reality this is."

"Worth a shot," Caitlin suggested. She stood with her hands on her thighs, still winded from the pointless dash.

But Roxy tapped her shoulder.

"I think we have something else to worry about," she said. "Look."

The others turned.

The plain between them and Wager was no longer empty.

It came alive. Popping up from the ground were hundreds of warriors, seemingly composed of the same reddish earth. They were seven feet tall, heavily muscled. There was no fine detail—they looked like the beginning stages of a sculptor's project, quickly chiseled from stone.

"Looks like we gotta go through these guys," Bobby pointed out.

"No time like the present," Sarah replied. She lifted her arms toward the sky, materializing thick black clouds overhead. The clouds crackled with energy. Lightning flashed inside the darkness.

Grunge approached Caitlin with one hand outstretched toward her chest. "Kat," he said. "Let me touch."

"Are you crazy, Grunge?" she shot back. "This is not the time—"

"I mean the ring, on your zipper," he protested. Her uniform zipped up near her collarbone, and the zipper pull was a metal ring. "I just want something harder than these guys are gonna be."

Caitlin blushed. "Sorry, Grunge. Be my guest. Just be, you know, careful."

He touched the ring and felt the metal wash over him. "Don't worry," he said. "I'm not gonna try anything."

Sarah began the assault with a dozen bolts of lightning. Warriors of earth crumbled under the onslaught. Bobby followed suit, unleashing a furious barrage of plasma blasts at the stone soldiers. Roxy altered the gravity beneath them, slamming them into one another.

Caitlin, Grunge, and Cipher took a more basic approach, wading into the thick of the warriors and pounding them with powerful fists and fast kicks. Some went down, but there were always more where they came from.

After what seemed like a long time, Caitlin looked between and around the earthen soldiers. Wager was just as far away as he had been, and there were just as many warriors between them. She sucked at a bleeding knuckle.

"This isn't working," she said. "We're not making any progress."

Cipher hammered a soldier with a heavy fist and the thing burst into dust. "You're right," he agreed. "We aren't getting any closer to Wager."

Grunge overheard. "What else can we do?" he asked. "There's so many of these overgrown garden trolls."

"You know what we have to do, Caitlin," Cipher said.

"But we really don't know what it might—"

"We don't know how it'll affect me," Cipher finished. "But we don't have any choice. We don't stop Wager now, who's to say he won't turn his power loose on the whole world?"

"You're right," Caitlin sighed. She unzipped her pocket, removed the second steel cylinder. She unscrewed the cap and slid another hypodermic needle into her hand. "But this is Wager's own DNA. Who's to say you won't become just like him?"

"That's a chance we have to take," Cipher said. "But I didn't start out like him. So we can hope . . ."

"Hope's all we have," Caitlin said. She jammed the needle into his neck, pushed down the plunger.

Roxy, Sarah, and Bobby joined them. They formed themselves into a circle to hold off the slowly-advancing rock-men. Working together, as a team, seemed more efficient than blasting away at them one by one.

As Caitlin withdrew the now-empty hypo, Cipher clapped a hand to his neck. With a grimace of pain, he dropped to his knees.

"Mr. Joe!" Bobby called. "What'd you do to him, Kat?"

"What he wanted," Caitlin said. "Our last option. I gave him a shot of Wager's DNA."

"But how can you tell what effect that'll have on him?"

"I can't. I just have to hope that, because their body chemistries are so similar, it'll be safe."

Cipher rolled on the hard ground, knees drawn up to his chest. His skin had turned red and blotchy and rippled like a pond someone had tossed a pebble into.

"Doesn't look safe from here."

Sarah touched his arm. "She had to try it, Bob."

"I know, I know. But . . ."

Cipher cut him off with a long scream. He rolled over to his hands and knees, back in the air. He pushed himself off the ground, stood up. His face was a mask of agony.

He was at least a foot taller than he had been. And wider, deeper-chested.

"Dude," Grunge said. "Remember those ads in the old comics, where the bully kicks sand in a geek's face and then the geek goes all Arnold on him? They coulda used some of what you got goin' on."

"Cipher?" Caitlin asked tentatively. "Are you?"

"I'm fine, Caitlin," he answered. "Better than fine."

"But you're still Cipher, right?" Roxy asked. "I mean, on the side of the angels and all that?"

"Yes."

"No," Bobby cut in. "You're not. You're Joe Monteleone. Whatever happens, don't lose sight of that. You're a decent man, a kind man who got into a bad spot."

Cipher put a huge hand on Bobby's shoulder, dwarfing it. He squeezed once, and let go.

"I have something to do," he said simply.

He turned to face Wager. The stone soldiers had paused in their advance. Caitlin figured Wager had stopped them while he waited to see what was going on.

Finally, something the creep hadn't counted on.

"Interesting metamorphosis," Wager called out. "I hadn't thought you could take that much more of the serum."

"This isn't more of it," Cipher said. "It's something else."

"Meaning?"

"You didn't compute the odds right," Cipher said. "You let us get a sample of your DNA."

"Impossible."

"Nothing's impossible, Wager. Only highly unlikely. Isn't that your philosophy?"

"No matter," Wager said. "I still—"

Cipher waved a hand before him and the soldiers vanished.

"Still nothing," he said.

He snapped his fingers, and the plain was gone. They were back in Wager's claustrophobically small lair. The walls were still knocked out, ceiling gone, computer and video equipment a smoldering mess.

Wager backed toward the corner, fear beginning to show on his face. Beads of sweat lined his brow.

"You can't . . ."

"I can."

Wager gestured to the space between them and there was suddenly a massive energy-man there, crackling and sparking like pure electricity.

Cipher blinked, and he was gone.

Wager's mouth fell open.

Cipher lunged.

He caught Wager around the neck, slamming him back into the wall. "Nooo!" Wager shouted. Cipher let go with his right hand, curled it into a fist, and drove it repeatedly into Wager's gut.

The man doubled over.

Caitlin yanked the syringe from her pocket, rushed to Cipher's side. "Hold him still!" she called.

Cipher did, putting Wager into a hammerlock. Caitlin thrust the needle into him, found a vein. She pressed the plunger.

"Nooo!" Wager called as the needle impaled him. "You can't."

With Cipher holding him, he began to transform. Pounds fell away, muscles vanished. In a few moments, Wager was the diminutive man he had once been.

Powerless and scared.

His lip trembled and his eyes blinked furiously, holding back tears.

Cipher released the man who had been Wager.

"You killed my family," he said. "You made me into

... into this. You are evil and you need to die." He cocked a fist.

"P-please," Thomas Carlisle begged.

"Joe!" Bobby called. "He's nothing, now! Leave him for the cops. They can deal with his kind!"

Cipher shook his head. "If there was any justice in this world, my children would be alive."

"You can't believe that," Bobby argued. "Cipher might, but Mr. Joe is smarter than that."

"Shut up, Bobby," Cipher warned. "Even if the police take him, what's the worst they'll do? Lock him away in prison? That's not good enough. He needs to die. And it needs to hurt."

"I won't! Not until I know you're listening. Not until Mr. Joe is listening. You're still inside there, somewhere. And I know you understand mercy and compassion. I know that Mr. Joe respects the law."

Cipher hoisted the squirming Carlisle, ready to deliver the killing blow.

Bobby went on. "I know that Joe Monteleone is no killer!"

Cipher stopped. "Let the authorities deal with him," he said. "My family is gone. I won't bring shame to their memory by killing this piece of human filth." With an expression of deep disgust, he threw Wager to the floor.

EPILOGUE

By the time the police had taken Carlisle and his few remaining thugs into custody and asked their questions of the team, another evening was slipping over the city. They had gone to a coffee shop, and sipped steaming mochas and lattes against the chill. Now they stood on a quiet dusky street. Manhattan was going through one of its daily changes, around them, as lights flicked on and the city metamorphosed from its daytime face to its nighttime one.

"You got the stuff, Kat?" Bobby asked.

"What stuff?" Roxy wanted to know.

Caitlin, still holding a cup of coffee, fumbled two vials from her purse. "Here they are," she said.

"What's that?" Roxy asked again.

"More of the antidote," Bobby explained. "The stuff that counteracts the Gen Factor. And the Gen Factor serum itself. Kat says she can make an antidote for us all. The time doesn't matter, like it did for Wager, because we were born this way." He looked at his teammates. "Any takers? Normality is in our grasp."

They all looked at the vials in Bobby's hands.

Rainmaker had never asked for power over storms and weather, had never dreamed of being able to call lightning from the skies. She abhorred violence, and yet, since becoming part of the team, it seemed that all she did was fight.

She started to reach for the vials, then pulled her hand

back. "I guess not," she said. Sarah, after all, had not—would not have been able to—help stop Wager. Or any of the other threats they'd encountered over the last few years. *No one person can save the world,* she thought. *But for a team of superheroes—all in a day's work.*

Grunge remembered taking out that purse-snatcher without using his powers. That had been sweet. And he'd seriously freaked out Therese, back at the club, when he'd done the change.

But it had never bothered Roxy. He knew she had it kind of bad for him, even though they were both seeing other people right now. If his power disturbed her any, she'd never have stayed interested in him this long.

He figured there would always be some people in the world who didn't like anything that was different than what they were used to. But those weren't the kind of people—clearly—who could put up with him for long, or who he wanted to spend time with.

His powers didn't take anything away from him, they just added another layer.

Who knew, maybe Michele would be more open-minded.

"I'll pass," he said.

For her part, Freefall had already made up her mind, during the battle with the stone soldiers. She would, she guessed, always be into the party thing. But she had realized that she was also into the family thing. Sure, maybe Caitlin was only her half-sister, but that was more sister than she'd had before. And the others, hot-headed Bobby, self-righteous Sarah, even Grunge, who was just, insufferably . . . Grunge—were as much a family as the people who had given birth to her. She shook her head.

Fairchild had been mulling this over ever since she had started making the stuff. To be normal again. To be appreciated for her mind, for her intellect, for what she really had to offer. Not to be the body, the center of unwanted attention. It was all so very attractive.

But at the same time, she thought, *you really can't go*

home again. History is a one-way street. No one wakes up in the morning the same person they were the night before.

Any more platitudes? she asked herself. *Because you have a decision to make here. And it's a big one. The biggest.*

She looked at the tube Bobby held. She had done that. No one else had. The Gen Factor hadn't made her any smarter—but it hadn't subtracted anything, either. She was as intelligent as she was, and the rest of it was just casing. Surface stuff. What did it matter if she was tall and strong and had giant boobs, really?

Maybe she just needed to exercise her mind a bit more. The body would take care of itself.

"Not for me, thanks," she said.

There was a time—not so long ago, in fact—that Burnout would have just gone along with the others to be going along with the others. He was no leader, and he'd come to accept that about himself. He followed Caitlin into battle, followed Sarah into causes, followed Grunge into trouble.

But that had changed, hadn't it? He'd been the one who pushed to find Mr. Joe. He'd been the one, really, who'd been behind this whole adventure, the one who was responsible for bringing down Wager.

And he'd done that by making his own decisions. Maybe it had taken him a long time to start growing up—after all, he was the only one in the team whose dad was the team's mentor, right? How could that help him mature? But he felt like he'd at least started the process, now. And it felt good. He liked it.

He turned to Cipher.

"You got to take this, man," he said. "You're still changing, look at you. Caitlin said that extra dose is going to kill you if you don't do this."

"I don't know," Cipher said. "All this power."

"What good's it gonna do you, you fall over and die?" Grunge asked.

"So you'll be Joe Monteleone again," Bobby said. "So what? Joe's a good man."

"But he's a useless one," Cipher countered. "He's a loser. He means nothing—to anyone, now that his family's gone."

"He means something to us."

"I appreciate that, Sarah. Really. But you guys told me my son died thinking his old man was some kind of secret agent, right. Some kind of hero."

"You were always his hero," Bobby pointed out.

"Not like I was then. Not like I am."

"But Joe . . ."

"No, Robert," he said. "We don't know how long I have. A year? An hour? There's no telling. But in this form, with these powers, maybe I'll be able to do some good for somebody in the time I've got. I think you've all made a very similar decision in the past few minutes."

"But it isn't going to kill us," Bobby said.

"Better to die doing something worthwhile than live without hope," Cipher said. "You think I have anything to offer, Bobby Lane, let it be that." He shook hands all around, double-checked to make sure the street was clear, and then flew off into the sky to begin the newest phase of his life.

Bobby shrugged. "Guess that's it, then," he said. "No takers."

"You know what to do, Bobby," Caitlin said.

"That I do." He closed his fist around the vials, and concentrated.

The others had to back away from him, while maintaining a ring around him there on the frosty morning sidewalk. His fist began to glow, to radiate incredible heat. But that was nothing compared to what was happening inside his closed hand.

When he opened it again, it was empty. The unimaginable heat he had generated had vaporized both the vials.

"Guess we don't have to worry about that stuff anymore," Grunge said. "Anybody know what time it is?"

"Why, Grunge?" Roxy asked. "Got a hot date?"

"As a matter of fact," Grunge said, a broad smile creeping across his face. "Michele's taking me to some off-off-Broadway play she wants to see. Supposed to be nudity in it, so I'm down."

"Glad I asked," Roxy said. "What about you, Kat? Want to rent some chick flicks and polish off a gallon of Fudge Ripple with me?"

"I've got somewhere to be, too," Caitlin said. "Now that Sam's turned in all his I.O. weaponry, he wants to get started working on a new software program he came up with. No military applications whatsoever, he says. I told him I'd give him a hand."

"Sarah? Bobby?" Roxy asked.

"Sure, Rox," Sarah said. "Give me an hour to go talk to the organizers of a rally next week, and I'm there. One carton, three spoons. I'm for it."

"I've got to stop by the shelter for a shift, but I'll join you later, as long as the videos aren't too weepy," Bobby said. "It's embarrassing to cry in front of chicks."

As Manhattan's lights blinked on and the nighttime city overruled the day, the five friends went their separate ways. And each of them, in his or her own way, was comforted by the knowledge that, no matter where the others were or what they were doing, they were a team.

They were Gen[13].

There was no taking that away from them.

Ever.

LUCASFILM'S ALIEN CHRONICLES™

A New Saga. A New Universe. A New Destiny.

Here is an epic set in a far distant universe—a saga of faraway planets and of races strange and more fantastic than any ever seen on our world.

Yet their struggles are universal: for justice, for freedom, for peace. Lucasfilm's Alien Chronicles is a sweeping trilogy that will transport you to another time, and another place where a legend is about to be born.

An Unforgettable Trilogy

__Book I: The Golden One   0-441-00561-6/$6.99

__Book II: The Crimson Claw   0-441-00565-9/$5.99

__Book III: The Crystal Eye   0-441-00635-3/$6.99

®, ™, & © 1999 Lucasfilm Ltd. All rights reserved.

Prices slightly higher in Canada

Payable by Visa, MC or AMEX only ($10.00 min.), No cash, checks or COD. Shipping & handling: US/Can. $2.75 for one book, $1.00 for each add'l book; Int'l $5.00 for one book, $1.00 for each add'l. Call (800) 788-6262 or (201) 933-9292, fax (201) 896-8569 or mail your orders to:

Penguin Putnam Inc.
P.O. Box 12289, Dept. B
Newark, NJ 07101-5289
Please allow 4-6 weeks for delivery.
Foreign and Canadian delivery 6-8 weeks.

Bill my: ❑ Visa ❑ MasterCard ❑ Amex _____(expires)
Card# _____
Signature _____

Bill to:
Name _____
Address _____ City _____
State/ZIP _____ Daytime Phone # _____

Ship to:
Name _____ Book Total $ _____
Address _____ Applicable Sales Tax $ _____
City _____ Postage & Handling $ _____
State/ZIP _____ Total Amount Due $ _____

This offer subject to change without notice.   Ad # 752 (3/01)

NEW YORK TIMES BESTSELLING AUTHOR
PETER DAVID's PSI-MAN

☐ **PSI-MAN: MIND-FORCE WARRIOR**
                                0-441-00705-8/$5.99

Chuck Simon is an ordinary man with extraordinary mental powers. A top secret government agency is aware of his existence—and now Simon has become the most hunted man on Earth.

☐ **PSI-MAN #2: DEATHSCAPE**
                                0-441-00710-4/$5.99

On the run, Simon hides out in a toxic wilderness populated by mutant predatory animals—and eco-terrorists whose psi-powers rival his own.

☐ **PSI-MAN #3: MAIN STREET D.O.A.**
                                0-441-00717-1/$5.99

☐ **PSI-MAN #4: THE CHAOS KID**
                                0-441-00745-7/$5.99

☐ **PSI-MAN #5: STALKER**
                                0-441-00758-9/$5.99

☐ **PSI-MAN #6: HAVEN**
                                0-441-00764-3/$5.99

Prices slightly higher in Canada

Payable by Visa, MC or AMEX only ($10.00 min.), No cash, checks or COD. Shipping & handling: US/Can. $2.75 for one book, $1.00 for each add'l book; Int'l $5.00 for one book, $1.00 for each add'l. Call (800) 788-6262 or (201) 933-9292, fax (201) 896-8569 or mail your orders to:

Penguin Putnam Inc.
P.O. Box 12289, Dept. B
Newark, NJ 07101-5289
Please allow 4-6 weeks for delivery.
Foreign and Canadian delivery 6-8 weeks.

Bill my: ☐ Visa ☐ MasterCard ☐ Amex _____(expires)
Card# _____
Signature _____

Bill to:
Name _____
Address _____ City _____
State/ZIP _____ Daytime Phone # _____

Ship to:
Name _____ Book Total $ _____
Address _____ Applicable Sales Tax $ _____
City _____ Postage & Handling $ _____
State/ZIP _____ Total Amount Due $ _____

This offer subject to change without notice.   Ad # 900 (6/00)

The battle for the future of humanity begins here...

EVERGENCE
THE PRODIGAL SUN
by SEAN WILLIAMS & SHANE DIX

Commander Morgan Roche of the Commonwealth of Empires is charged with escorting an artificial intelligence unit to her superiors, with the aid of a genetically engineered warrior whose past is a mystery even to him...
__0-441-00672-8/$6.99

"A personal story told on a galaxy-sized canvas. Filled with action as well as intriguing ideas."
—Kevin J. Anderson

Don't miss the second book in the national bestselling series:
EVERGENCE: THE DYING LIGHT
__0-441-00742-2/$6.99

Prices slightly higher in Canada

Payable by Visa, MC or AMEX only ($10.00 min.), No cash, checks or COD. Shipping & handling: US/Can. $2.75 for one book, $1.00 for each add'l book; Int'l $5.00 for one book, $1.00 for each add'l. Call (800) 788-6262 or (201) 933-9292, fax (201) 896-8569 or mail your orders to:

Penguin Putnam Inc. P.O. Box 12289, Dept. B Newark, NJ 07101-5289 Please allow 4-6 weeks for delivery. Foreign and Canadian delivery 6-8 weeks.	Bill my: ❑ Visa ❑ MasterCard ❑ Amex _____ (expires) Card# _____ Signature _____

Bill to:
Name _____
Address _____ City _____
State/ZIP _____ Daytime Phone # _____

Ship to:
Name _____ Book Total $ _____
Address _____ Applicable Sales Tax $ _____
City _____ Postage & Handling $ _____
State/ZIP _____ Total Amount Due $ _____

This offer subject to change without notice.   Ad # 898 (4/00)